RUNNING TARGET

There was danger in the air. McBride felt it. He was exposed out there in the flat, and the hidden rifleman had come close twice. But if he'd tried to cut and run, his back would have been to the bushwhacker, giving the man time for a clean shot.

He was still bucking the odds, he knew, but he had a weapon in his hands and his face was to the enemy . . . if the man was on the ridge.

Fate is only a name for the result of a man's own efforts, and now it rewarded McBride for his cold, scared walk across open ground into the gun of a waiting marksman.

He was ten yards from the base of the ridge, his eyes scanning the rocks, when he stepped into a shallow hole scraped away by some animal. The depression wasn't deep, but it was unexpected. McBride's ankle turned and he stumbled awkwardly to his left. At the same instant a rifle shot snapped from the ridge. . . .

Ralph Compton

Shadow of the Gun

A Ralph Compton Novel
by Joseph A. West

A SIGNET BOOK

SIGNET
Published by New American Library, a division of
Penguin Group (USA) Inc., 375 Hudson Street,
New York, New York 10014, USA
Penguin Group (Canada), 90 Eglinton Avenue East, Suite 700, Toronto,
Ontario M4P 2Y3, Canada (a division of Pearson Penguin Canada Inc.)
Penguin Books Ltd., 80 Strand, London WC2R 0RL, England
Penguin Ireland, 25 St. Stephen's Green, Dublin 2,
Ireland (a division of Penguin Books Ltd.)
Penguin Group (Australia), 250 Camberwell Road, Camberwell, Victoria 3124,
Australia (a division of Pearson Australia Group Pty. Ltd.)
Penguin Books India Pvt. Ltd., 11 Community Centre, Panchsheel Park,
New Delhi - 110 017, India
Penguin Group (NZ), 67 Apollo Drive, Rosedale, North Shore 0632,
New Zealand (a division of Pearson New Zealand Ltd.)
Penguin Books (South Africa) (Pty.) Ltd., 24 Sturdee Avenue,
Rosebank, Johannesburg 2196, South Africa

Penguin Books Ltd., Registered Offices:
80 Strand, London WC2R 0RL, England

First published by Signet, an imprint of New American Library,
a division of Penguin Group (USA) Inc.

First Printing, February 2008
10 9 8 7 6 5 4 3 2 1

THE IMMORTAL COWBOY

This is respectfully dedicated to the "American Cowboy." His was the saga sparked by the turmoil that followed the Civil War, and the passing of more than a century has by no means diminished the flame.

True, the old days and the old ways are but treasured memories, and the old trails have grown dim with the ravages of time, but the spirit of the cowboy lives on.

In my travels—to Texas, Oklahoma, Kansas, Nebraska, Colorado, Wyoming, New Mexico, and Arizona—I always find something that reminds me of the Old West. While I am walking these plains and mountains for the first time, there is this feeling that a part of me is eternal, that I have known these old trails before. I believe it is the undying spirit of the frontier calling, allowing me, through the mind's eye, to step back into time. What is the appeal of the Old West of the American frontier?

It has been epitomized by some as the dark and bloody period in American history. Its heroes—Crockett, Bowie, Hickok, Earp—have been reviled and criticized. Yet the Old West lives on, larger than life.

It has become a symbol of freedom, when there was always another mountain to climb and another river to cross; when a dispute between two men was settled not with expensive lawyers, but with fists, knives, or guns. Barbaric? Maybe. But some things never change. When the cowboy rode into the pages of American history, he left behind a legacy that lives within the hearts of us all.

—*Ralph Compton*

Chapter 1

Sergeant John McBride, formerly of the New York Police Department's Bureau of Detectives, was a long way from home. To be exact, he was in grass and scrub country a few miles south of New Mexico's Zuni Plateau. A two-hour ride to the west lay the Arizona border, to the east the vast bulk of Santa Rita Mesa.

Ahead of him . . . danger.

But the man who now rode beside McBride had assured him that Deer Creek Tom Rivers, his Chiricahua Apache wife and his three half-breed sons would meekly pack up and leave the range without a fight.

"That nester riffraff won't draw on the man who killed Hack Burns," Cliff Brennan had told McBride when he hired him for the job. "Easiest five hundred you'll ever make, gunfighter. Just run them filthy squatters off my grass and the money is yours. In gold coin, mind you."

Brennan was a hard, uncompromising man who had hanged both rustlers and Apaches with a ruthless disregard for the law. He rode a big American stud that dwarfed McBride's mouse-colored mustang, and from his lofty perch he kept his eyes fixed on the trail ahead. The rancher clutched the Winchester across his saddle horn until his knuckles grew white and he fingered the trigger almost nervously. But the man's weather-scarred face looked like it had been chipped from granite and the belligerent jut of his chin suggested a man whose constitution requires that he kill or be killed.

Watching Brennan's intent, tight-lipped face from under the brim of his plug hat, McBride decided that the big rancher was lying about Rivers and his clan. He did not expect the squatters to saddle up and spinelessly ride away. What he did expect was gunplay and the violent deaths of men.

McBride felt a tightness rise in him. Brennan had contacted him in Albuquerque as a named man looking for investigative work. Impressed by his reputation as an up-and-coming gunfighter, notoriety McBride knew he did not deserve, the rancher had told him he needed a range detective to evict nesters from his property.

"The law will be on your side, McBride," the man had said. "Just show your gun and tell the trash to go." A smile had touched his lips. "They'll go, all right."

McBride had needed the money and took Brennan's offer. Now he wasn't so sure he'd made the right decision.

Back along their trail, he'd talked to men who knew Rivers, or of him, and the consensus of opinion was that the old man had sand and there was no backup in him.

Now McBride realized that Cliff Brennan's grim face confirmed that estimation. The rancher knew, or at least feared, that Rivers and his sons would reach for the gun.

All McBride could do now was to go through with the job and hope to talk his way out of a revolver fight. His plan was thin, mighty thin, but there was no going back from it. He needed the five hundred real bad and he had it to do.

McBride glanced up at the faded blue of the sky, weighing what his chances would be if there was to be a fight. He was a fair hand with the .38 Smith & Wesson in the shoulder holster under his left arm, hit-and-miss with the Winchester in the saddle scabbard. If worse came to worst, as it invariably did in the West, it would be four against two. And if the Rivers boys had as much sand as their old man, the outcome of today's work could be an uncertain thing.

His mouth dry, McBride scanned the sun-scorched land ahead of him and tried not to build houses on a bridge he hadn't yet crossed. There would be time enough for that when he reached the Riverses' place and the war talk began.

He and Brennan let their horses drink at a narrow creek, its waters shallow and still, then rode into greener country made difficult to cross by stands of prickly pear, stabbing chaparral and steep tumbles of volcanic rock. Here and there clumps of dust-covered mesquite stood like motionless ghosts, barring their way. The sun was right overhead and the air smelled of hot sand, horse and man sweat and the fleeting suggestion of distant pines. Only the surrounding mountains looked cool, their peaks a darker blue than the blue of the sky.

Brennan nodded once toward some cottonwoods growing around a pond that was little more than a shallow rock tank. "Yonder are a few of my cattle," he said.

McBride glanced at a dozen or so white-faced cows grazing in dappled tree shade but took no joy in what he saw. Somehow seeing Herefords out there in the wilderness served only to make the land appear more hostile and a man to feel even more alone.

For thirty minutes he and Brennan rode in silence, the only sound the creak of saddle leather and the dusty plod of hooves.

Finally the rancher pointed to a craggy height ahead of him. "That's Eagle Peak and to the northwest of that Tejana Mesa. We're getting close."

The day was stifling, with sultry air crowding thick and close, the alkali stretches around them burning white in the merciless sun.

McBride drew rein and reached for his canteen. He took a pull, swirled it around his mouth and spat out a mix of dust and water, then drank again. He hung the canteen back on the saddle horn and said to Brennan, "How come none of your hands are with us?"

Brennan had also drunk. He wiped drops of water off his mustache with the back of his hand and answered, "I got three men working for me. But one is so stove up with the rheumatisms, all he can do is cook. The other two are younger, but they're not gunfighters. Sure, they'll ride for the brand, but I decided to leave them behind. All them two boys would do is get in the damned way."

"And you, Brennan—how are you with the iron?"

The eyes the rancher turned to McBride were suddenly cold. "I'm fifty-one years old, and I killed my first man down in the Nations when I was fourteen. I've killed another three since, and every man jack of them took my bullets in the front."

McBride nodded. "All of them named men?"

Brennan shook his head. "Hell no, not a one of them. Two were rustlers and the last was a bull-headed city marshal down Texas way who wouldn't allow me to drive my herd through his town. 'Too much crap to pick up afterward,' he said. Well, when I told my trail boss to go ahead and push those cows along Main Street, the lawman drawed down on me." A wry smile flirted with the rancher's lips. "It was the worst an' last mistake he ever made."

McBride nodded. "I guess you'll do."

"Maybe, but I gunned that lawman twenty years ago. I've slowed down considerable since then and I've been thinking that maybe I don't have the stomach for gunfighting no more."

"Then you'd better put some fire in your belly," McBride said. "This might not be as easy as you think."

"I know that. That's why I'm paying you gun wages." Brennan's eyes were suddenly shrewd, thoughtful. "Ever since I met you, McBride, I've been trying to figure you out. There's something about you that don't fit the gunfighter mold. You don't have"—the rancher thought for a moment—"style. And I have a feeling you've worn a tin star yourself in some hick town along your back trail."

McBride grinned. "You know, Brennan, you're right. I did wear a star in a hick town once."

The rancher was pleased. "Knew that! Dang me, but I had you pegged right off, huh?"

"You sure did. But one thing that hick town taught me was that a police officer must always present a fine appearance to the public." McBride climbed awkwardly out of the saddle, the mustang so small the stirrup was only six inches off the ground. "As for style," he said, still smiling, his hands on the small of his back as he arched against the stiffness, "maybe I can change your mind."

As Brennan watched in fascinated amusement, McBride took a new gray coat from his blanket roll, dusted it off and placed it carefully over the saddle. He found a high celluloid collar in his saddlebags and a red and black striped tie. He studded the collar in place and knotted the tie at his throat. Then he shrugged into the coat, wiped his boots free of dust on the back of his pants and settled the frayed brown derby squarer on his head. A forefinger and thumb smoothing of his dragoon mustache and he was done.

"See, Brennan?" he said. "Style."

"You could call it that," the rancher said, interested but unimpressed.

"Now let's go talk to Mr. Rivers," McBride said.

Born and raised in the teeming slums of New

York's Hell's Kitchen, McBride was no hand with horses, and mounting was always an uncertain undertaking for him. But for once the mustang stood still, its ugly head hanging, and he managed an ungainly mount.

Brennan raised an eyebrow. "You must have paid all of five dollars for that hoss."

"If I remember correctly, it was five plus another twenty."

"Then you were robbed," Brennan said.

They rode across a stretch of brush flat; then the ground rose gradually toward a rise where a scattering of juniper and piñon grew among high rocks. When they crested the hill, Brennan drew rein and McBride saw the land drop away from them toward a narrow creek. Here the air breathed cool and thick. It was like drinking water from a deep well.

"See the cabin?" Brennan said. "There, among the cottonwoods."

McBride's gaze reached out into the distance and he saw a tumbledown log cabin standing near the creek, shaded by the tree canopy. Smoke, straight as a string, rose from a crooked wattle chimney before dying into a smear of gray against the sky. A rickety pole corral stood near the cabin, a few horses inside, and a covered wagon, its tongue raised, was parked nearby. The whole tumbledown spread looked like it was held together with baling wire and spit, and McBride decided that the Rivers clan appeared to be a lazy, shiftless bunch.

Cliff Brennan was talking to him. Formal and distant. "Gunfighter, before we ride down there, let me tell you something: Deer Creek Tom Rivers is hell on wheels with a gun, but his eldest son, Mordecai, is a devil. He's half Apache, half English and all son of a bitch. He's lightning fast on the draw and shoot and he's killed more than his share."

McBride nodded, the tightness in him again. "How will I know this Mordecai?"

Brennan's voice was flat, taut. "You'll know him when you see him. Anyhow, he's the one who will do all the talking, if there's talking to be done."

"Let's go find out," McBride said, heeling his horse forward off the crest of the rise. He'd seen uncertainty, maybe fear, in Brennan's face and it troubled him. The man had talked big enough on the trail, but now that they were about to choose partners for a revolver fandango, his guts seemed to be turning to water.

"Hello, the cabin!" McBride yelled when they were still a ways off. He called out, not to alert Tom Rivers, but to draw scant comfort from the confident tone of his own voice.

The cabin door swung open and three young men stepped into the yard, watching him and Brennan come.

McBride calculated distance and drew rein when he was twenty feet from the Rivers boys. At that range he could score with the .38 self-cocker if he were pushed to it. He opened his mouth to speak, but the oldest of the three men roughly headed him off.

"What the hell do you want?"

"Ah," McBride said, smiling. "You must be Mordecai."

"And what's it to you?"

Mordecai wore a belted Colt as did his brothers. His high-cheekboned face was very dark, blackened by sun, but his eyes were pale green, and he had the slitted, cold stare of a snake. His lank black hair fell over his shoulders and McBride noticed that the walnut handle of his gun had been notched several times, one of the notches raw and fresh. The man looked small, thin and dangerous and he'd be almighty sudden.

"Your name means nothing to me," McBride said pleasantly. "I'm a range detective and I'm here to talk to your father." Then, carefully taking the sting out of it before he spoke, he added, "I'm afraid you're squatting on my employer Mr. Brennan's property and you must pack up and move on." He hesitated a heartbeat. "Now."

"This here is open range," Mordecai said, taking an aggressive step toward McBride. "And we've claimed it. Now, turn around that poor excuse for a horse and get the hell out of here."

The other brothers had spread out, ready to back their brother's play. McBride saw the move and his spiking belly told him he didn't like any part of it.

He managed to keep his voice level and reasonable. "I think we should let your father decide. I'm sure he doesn't want any trouble with the law."

"Law!" Mordecai spat in McBride's direction. "You ain't the law."

His eyes wary, his voice surprisingly weak, Brennan said, "Mordecai, we'll talk to Tom. If he gets off my range, no law need be involved."

If it came down to it, would Brennan stand? The man looked scared.

McBride had no time to answer his own question. He was listening to Mordecai again.

"Pa's going nowhere." He was tense and ready, the Apache in him rapidly coming to the fore. "He fell off his horse a month back and he's a dead man"—with the flat of his hand the man made a downward, sweeping gesture from his waist—"from there to his toes."

"He's paralyzed?" McBride asked.

"His back's broke," Mordecai said.

Brennan shook his head and found his voice and his courage again now that the invincible myth he'd built around Mordecai in his mind had solidified into a skinny half-breed no taller than the top rail of a corral fence. "The state of your pa's health is no concern of mine," he said, making his mistake. "Now, load him into the wagon over yonder and get off my land."

McBride saw it then—a hundred different kinds of hell in Mordecai Rivers' eyes.

The man was all through talking.

He was going to draw.

Chapter 2

The combination of an ornery mount and John McBride's poor horsemanship saved his life.

As Mordecai's hand streaked for his gun, the mustang became alarmed and reared, throwing McBride over the back of the saddle. He hit the ground hard, raising dust, and rolled, aware of the angry statement of Brennan's rifle. The mustang bolted and Mordecai took a step out of the animal's way. His Colt came up to shoulder height, his eyes seeking McBride.

Brennan fired again. McBride heard a scream followed by the rancher's triumphant yell. But Mordecai had McBride spotted. He grinned as his gun leveled.

"Hell, I'm throwing this away!" The panicked thought flashed through McBride's brain.

He drew the Smith & Wesson, got on one knee and held the revolver at arm's length, sighting, as his police instructors had taught him. Mordecai fired, his bullet throwing up a startled exclamation point of danger an inch in front of McBride's bent leg. The breed fired again, and McBride felt the slug clip an arc from his left ear.

Cursing, McBride squeezed the trigger and a sudden scarlet flower blossomed on Mordecai's chest. The man roared his rage, took a step back, his gun lowering as if all at once it had become too heavy for him.

McBride shot again, the self-cocker bucking in his hand. Hit a second time, Mordecai dropped to his knees. But he was half Apache, game as they come and hard to kill. He gritted his teeth and his Colt came up fast, his green eyes on McBride, filled with pain, shock and an insane hatred.

Brennan's Winchester bellowed. Mordecai's head erupted into a crimson fan of blood and brain and he fell backward, the look of rabid venom frozen forever in his dead eyes.

"Got the son of a bitch!" Brennan swung out of the saddle, grinning from ear to ear. "An' I drilled the other two. Head shots, McBride, both of them."

McBride rose to his feet. Through a sullen mist of shifting gray gun smoke he watched the rancher lever his rifle.

Brennan's cold eyes slanted to the cabin. "Now I'm going to kill Deer Creek Tom, make a clean sweep. That thieving, white trash squaw-man has already lived too long."

A sickness in him, McBride's gaze swept the three dead men. All were young, too young to have died in the dust for a worthless patch of scrawny range in the middle of nowhere.

"Let it be, Brennan," he said wearily. "The old

man's paralyzed and he'll probably die soon enough."

"The hell with that, McBride. He's nesting on my ground and he has to take his medicine. I'm paying you to do a job—now let's finish it."

The futility of arguing showed in McBride's face. The blood madness was riding Brennan and he wouldn't let it go. His eyes moved to the cabin, its single window staring blankly at the carnage outside. Brennan moved into his line of sight, striding purposefully toward the door, the Winchester slanted across his chest.

McBride saw the burlap curtain in the window twitch a warning and he screamed, "Brennan! No!"

The rancher was just outside the door. Inside the cabin a shotgun blasted and buckshot tore through the thin wood, ripping the door off its rawhide hinges. Hit hard, Brennan shrieked and fell, the front of his shirt splashed with blood.

"Damn you! Damn you all to hell!" McBride yelled.

He ran to the door and took a single step inside. Tom Rivers, gray-haired and wild-eyed, was sitting up in his bunk, snapping shut a 10-gauge Greener on a pair of fresh shells.

The old man's glance met McBride's and he swung the scattergun in his direction. Quickly McBride fired, fired again. Hit twice, Rivers slammed back on the bunk, his toothless mouth an O of surprise at the manner and time of his dying.

McBride heard rapidly shuffling feet to his right. He turned and saw a raised axe poised above his head. Away from the doorway, the cabin was dark and he saw only the shadowy outline of a figure. Instinctively he took a step back, triggering the Smith at the same time. In the gun flash he caught a momentary glimpse of a fat woman falling away from him. The axe thudded to the dirt floor, followed immediately by the heavier thump of a body.

His ears ringing, the acrid smell of smoke in his nostrils, McBride felt around the cabin and found an oil lamp. He thumbed a match into flame, lit the lamp and in its eerie orange glow saw what he feared he would see.

A plump woman lay on her back on the floor, her dead, open eyes staring fixedly at McBride. Her black, braided hair showed strands of gray and her greasy buckskin dress had ridden up over her naked hips. McBride's bullet had struck her in the throat and the Apache woman had been dead when she hit the ground.

Bending, McBride pulled down the woman's dress, guiltily ashamed at seeing her nakedness.

Deer Creek Tom was dead and so was Cliff Brennan, and their feud was already forgotten. Dead men need no range, just six feet of ground.

In less than a couple of minutes six people had met violent deaths and he was responsible for three of them, one a woman. He rounded up his mustang and led it back to the cabin, his conscience nagging at him. Right then and there he decided that the profession of range detective was not for him.

There had been too much killing, too much blood throwing a dark, ominous shadow over his short time in the West. Already he was a named man, carrying the status of gunfighter, and such a title was a heavy burden. He had the five hundred dollars Brennan had paid him and it came to McBride then that it could be enough to buy a store in some small town. He fancied that he might prosper in the hardware business.

Or he could take Inspector Thomas Byrnes up on his offer to return to New York and be reinstated as a detective sergeant of police.

But as soon as he considered that option, he dismissed it. Despite the violence, despite the killing, the western land had a hold on him. She was a beautiful enchantress, wooing him with tall, pine-covered mountains, blue lakes and vast plains where a man could ride from sun to sun forever, and each morning the air smelled clean and new.

There could be no going back to the city with its stone canyons, teeming, filthy alleys and their warrens of slums overlaid by the stench of crowded, desperate humanity.

McBride was now part of the West and he told himself that he would never leave. To think otherwise was both foolish and futile.

He stopped outside the cabin, the warm sun on his shoulders. The stiff celluloid collar and strangling tie had not done what he'd hoped, and now he removed them. Then he took off his coat, slung it behind the saddle and rolled up his sleeves.

There was burying to be done.

Chapter 3

John McBride rode through the foothills of the Guadalupe Mountains at the point where the peaks plunge like an arrowhead from New Mexico into north Texas. To the west lay the massive stone rampart of Martine Ridge and beyond soared the fractured backbone of the Brokeoff Mountains.

McBride sat his mustang at the crest of a shallow rise and studied the bleak landscape around him. At first glance the mesquite and piñon-covered hills offered nothing by way of shelter from a keening fall wind and the coming of night. White clouds spread like coral branches across a denim blue sea of sky, but to the north other, more ominous thunderheads were gathering above the mountains, building high like thick black smoke.

McBride had come from that direction, and he had no desire to go back. For the most part he'd ridden well shy of the forbidding Guadalupe range. He'd followed the southward course of Piñon Creek before he'd lost his way and swung east into Big Dog

Canyon—only to find his path blocked by a massive barrier of rock that he'd later learn was the Guadalupe Ridge.

Now McBride studied the ridge, estimating that it rose seven or eight thousand feet above the flat. He was looking for a switchback trail that might take him across the steep side and down into Texas. He saw nothing but outcroppings of bare rock, brush and swaths of red and yellow aspen. Above the aspen line the ridge grew steeper still, and toward its crest grew stands of spruce and fir, casting long shadows on the broken ground.

McBride swore softly as frustration ate at him. There was no way over the ridge, so he'd have to retrace his steps back along the canyon, turn south again and ride across the brush flats to the Texas border.

He sighed deep and long and the mustang tossed its head in sympathy, its bit chiming in the silence. The air smelled of pine and the raw iron tang of the approaching winter. He shivered inside the thin cloth of his new suit coat. He turned in the saddle, worked a blanket out of his bedroll and wrapped it around his shoulders. The rough wool brought him some warmth but did little to improve his foul mood.

McBride swung his horse off the rise and rode closer to the foothills. He had to find a place to camp before the threatening clouds were right overhead dropping rain or snow—he could not guess which.

A fire, hot coffee, some fried salt pork and then sleep—if he could find shelter for the night.

McBride gloomily began to scout the hard, unfor-

giving land around him, a tall man astride a small
horse; a man who had not the slightest inkling that
at that moment he was lucky to be alive. Not three
miles away a raiding party of seven Mescalero Apaches
had cut his trail just east of the northern slope of the
Martine Ridge.

Unlike McBride, the Apaches knew with certainty
the gathering clouds heralded rain and they decided
to hole up for the night. After all, there was no hurry.
They knew the man on the shod horse was trapped.
Tomorrow they would kill him at their leisure.

After an hour, McBride's search was rewarded. He
rode into a narrow, grass-covered arroyo that ended
at a slab of solid gray rock. A few stunted junipers
and piñon grew around the base of the wall, enough
to offer some slender protection from rain or snow.
A thin stream of water cascaded from a cleft in the
rock and splashed into a hollowed-out basin of sandstone, forming a shallow pool several yards across.
The runoff seeped over the rim of the basin and lost
itself in the surrounding muddy ground.

McBride decided, given the circumstances, it was
as good a place as any. As he unsaddled the mustang, he realized he'd found the arroyo not a minute
too soon. Already he could hear the rumble of thunder in the distance and the sky was turning black.

As the horse drank from the rock tank, McBride
found a spot at the bottom of the stone wall protected from wind and rain by a wide overhang. There
he would build his fire.

Wood was plentiful around the base of the trees

and McBride gathered an armful and carried it to the wall. Then he found some dry tinder, pulled his blanket closer around him against the increasing cold and set about starting a blaze.

Having been born and bred in the slums of New York, McBride had little expertise when it came to making campfires. On his long ride down from the Zuni Plateau country he'd more often than not eaten cold rations, wishful for hot coffee, staring morose and defeated at a few charred twigs marking yet another failed fire at his feet.

He was determined not to fail this time.

Carefully, McBride thumbed a match into flame and poked it into the small pile of dead leaves and sticks against the rock wall. For an instant, a feeble flare of flame fluttered like an orange moth in the guttering wind, then promptly died. He swore softly but vehemently and tried again. This time the match was snuffed out by the wind before he even got it close to the kindling.

Irritated, he muttered angrily to himself as he pushed his scuffed plug hat back on his head and bent over the twigs. The match burned away in his fingers, scorching him painfully, but failed to ignite even a feeble blaze. Squatting back on his heels, McBride took a couple of deep breaths, trying to calm himself. All right, John, if at first you don't succeed . . .

He thumbed another match alight. . . .

And met with no more success than he'd done in his earlier attempts.

Angry with himself, with the glowering clouds, with the spiteful wind, with the contrary notions of

matches, leaves and twigs, McBride bent low, opened
his arms wide and spread his blanket around the
kindling, shielding it from the icy wind.

His face only inches from the kindling, he fumbled
for another lucifer and brought it into the tent he'd
made around the base of the rock wall. He bent
lower, the match in front of him, and carefully
thumbed it into life. The match flared. Too close! He
smelled burning as his mustache caught fire. McBride
howled and sprang to his feet, throwing off the blanket. He swatted at his smoking top lip, cursing a blue
streak, his elastic-sided boots dancing a demented jig.

That's when he turned and saw a man sitting on
his horse, staring at him, his eyes puzzled.

Satisfied that his mustache was no longer on fire,
McBride turned to the rider, moving his hand to the
Smith & Wesson .38 in the shoulder holster under
his left arm.

The man had a brass-framed Henry rifle across his
saddle horn, but he made no move to raise the gun.
Instead he said, his voice edged with what could
have been genuine wonder, "Pilgrim, what in hell
are you doing?"

Stung, McBride snapped, "Lighting a fire, if it's
any business of yours."

"In your mustache?"

"That was an accident. The match was too close to
my face and . . ." McBride stopped. "Why the hell
am I explaining myself to you?"

"Beats me," the man said, smiling. "But I reckon
it's just as well you never got your fire lit, sonny. The

Apaches are out, playing hob from the Rio Grande to the Mogollon Rim and points east and west. I heard tell over to the San Carlos in the Arizona territory there's only old men and women left an' that two regiments of black cavalry out of Fort Grant and Fort Thomas are already in the field with rations for sixty days." The man leaned forward in the saddle. "Hell, boy, when your smoke climbed that rock wall yonder and drifted in the wind, you'd have had every renegade buck within a ten-mile after your hair."

Despite his run-in with the Rivers brothers, all McBride knew about Apaches he'd learned from the dime magazines he'd read back in New York. Apparently the feathered fiends swooped down on defenseless wagon trains, brandishing their dreaded tomahawks, sparing neither man, woman, child nor clergy. McBride had read that the painted savages had undone many a blushing maiden and scores of stalwart frontiersmen had met a dreadful end at their bloodstained hands.

"I haven't seen any Apaches," he said, remembering. "Well, I met a half one a while back."

"I reckon if you'd met a whole one, you'd already be dead." The old man looked at McBride for a long time. He said finally, "This is your camp, pilgrim. Mind if I light an' set?"

"Name's John McBride and I'm not on pilgrimage to anywhere." He hesitated a moment, breathed out wearily and said, "Sure, light and set if you want. That is if cold coffee and raw salt pork suits your appetite."

The man nodded and swung out of the saddle with an easy elegance that belied his age, an ability McBride, a poor horseman, found himself envying.

"Name's Clarence Miller," the man said, sticking out his hand. McBride took it. "But most folks call me Bear on account of how one winter up in the Tetons I hibernated in a holler log alongside an old she bear. Worst winter I ever spent. That old grizz growled and fretted the whole time, all riled up at me being there. I didn't get a wink o' sleep for a three-month an' when I crawled out of the log come spring, I was just as tired as I was when I crawled in." There was a silence before Bear said, "Boy, if'n you ever want to hibernate away the snow months, find yourself a cougar cave. Most times a female big cat will let you catch some shut-eye, even if she don't like you much. So will a wolf, but she's more unpredictable, like."

"A thing to remember," McBride said. He had some doubts about the old man's story but didn't let it show. Now he studied him. Bear was about the same height as himself, four inches above six feet, but where McBride was heavily muscled in the arms and shoulders, the old man was wiry, skinny as a whip. His gray hair, arranged into two Cheyenne braids, hung to his shoulders and the fringes adorning the chest and sleeves of his beaded buckskin shirt were a yard long. He wore yellow-striped cavalry pants tucked into knee-high boots and a holstered, well-used Colt hung from the cartridge belt around his waist. Like McBride, he wore a full dragoon mustache but no beard. His black eyes were as bright as a bird's, lively and intelligent.

Bear Miller, McBride considered, was tough as they come and in a fight, close up or far off, he probably shaped up to be a wildcat.

"Rain's coming," the old man said, glancing at the threatening sky as he unsaddled his black. "Best we cook our chuck and bile up some coffee."

"I thought you said I couldn't have a fire?"

"I didn't say that. I said you couldn't have a fire where you were fixing to build it." Bear grinned. "But after I seen you set your mustache on fire, I figured you wasn't about to get one lit anyhow."

The matter of his scorched mustache still rankled, but McBride let it go.

"We'll make our fire among the trees where the leaves will spread the smoke," Bear said. "And not the bonfire you was planning. All the fire we need can be covered with that fancy plug hat of your'n."

The old mountain man watched his horse wander off to graze beside the mustang; then he said, "Anyhoo, I don't reckon we have anything to fear from Apaches tonight. They don't like to be out in the rain any more than we do."

To McBride's considerable chagrin, Bear quickly got a fire going among the trees and within a few minutes their coffee was heating. They rigged up a shelter of sorts from fallen tree branches and Bear's slicker, and by the time the light died around them they were sharing broiled salt pork and bacon and drinking hot coffee.

Bear gave McBride a sidelong glance. "What brings you this way, John?"

"I could ask you the same thing."

"I was a mountain man, then an army scout until I retired a month ago," Bear said. "Now I'm just an old coot looking for a shady porch and a rocking chair."

McBride laughed. "You won't find them out here."

Bear shrugged. "A man never knows. I reckoned maybe I'd meet up with a propertied widder woman along the trail, if one was to be found."

The old man's face still held a question and McBride answered it. "I'm passing through, looking for a store to buy. I thought I might prosper in the hardware business."

The rain started, slowly, making a sound like a loudly ticking clock. Bear took a sip of coffee. "There's a settlement to the east of where we're sitting, about a two-hour ride from the Delaware Mountains and the salt flats. They call the place Suicide and there's two accounts of how it got the name. One is that a man named Elliot founded the town, then for some reason shot himself. The other is that only folks bent on suicide would settle there in the first place." The old man gazed intently at McBride. "Seems to me somebody might be willing to sell a store down there."

"Does it have a hardware store?" McBride asked, his interest quickening.

"I don't rightly know. As I recollect, there's a saloon, another Mex place where they sell mescal and a livery. There might be a store or two. I don't rightly remember. One other thing—a big white-painted house on a hill overlooks the whole place."

"Who lives there?"

Bear's eyes had a guarded look. "You'll find out when you get there."

"Sounds fair. I'll ride down that way and take a look," McBride said.

Suddenly Bear's glance was searching as he turned to McBride in the gathering darkness, firelight staining the bronze planes of his face with shifting scarlet. "Now why would the man who gunned Hack Burns and is reckoned to be better with the iron than Hickok ever was want to sell pots and pans?"

McBride was taken aback. "How did you know?"

"I knew it right off," Bear answered. "You're a famous man, John, and as soon as you gave me your name, I figured you for the Tenderfoot Kid. Who else has shoulders an axe handle wide, dudes up like a city gent and carries a stinger gun under his armpit?"

Earlier McBride had been taken aback; now he was appalled.

"That's what they're calling me, the Tenderfoot Kid?"

"Around these parts they do, and maybe in other places." Seeing the tangled emotions on McBride's face, Bear said, "The gun casts a long shadow, John."

"Then I want no part of it. I'll be more than content to sell pots and pans and never have to wear a gun again."

"Good plan, I guess. If you can use them pots as a running iron to alter your gunfighter brand."

As the rain started in earnest, drops falling, hiss-

ing, into the fire, McBride's eyes sought Bear's in the
gloom. "There's another reason I'm here. I have three
wards being cared for by friends up in the Colorado
Picketwire country. They're young Chinese girls and
I'd like to send them to a finishing school back east
for a couple of years. I'll need a steady source of
income for that, and a thriving hardware store fits
the bill."

Thunder rolled across the sky and silver lightning
flickered around them. The rain was driving harder,
hissing like a dragon, rivulets of icy water streaming
into their rickety shelter.

Bear Miller didn't seem to notice. "Knew some Ce-
lestials once, over to Deadwood. They did laundry
and sold opium."

Like most Westerners, the old mountain man's
opinion of the Chinese was low and, disinterested in
the fate of McBride's wards, he did not press him for
details. He waited for an explosion of thunder to
pass, then said, "Best we get some shut-eye, Kid. It's
going to be a long night."

"Enough with the Kid stuff already," McBride
said. "The name's John."

Bear nodded. "Suit yourself. Then John it is."

The old scout curled up on his side and was asleep
instantly. McBride, wet, chilled and miserable, envied
him, then rationalized that a man who once hibernated all winter long in a hollow log with an ill-
tempered grizzly could sleep through a thunderstorm.

McBride had never seen a grizzly bear. But back
in New York he'd read in dime novels that the creatures stood twenty feet tall, had horrible fanged jaws

and had torn to pieces many a blushing maiden and stalwart frontiersman. Only brave outlaws like Billy the Kid and heroic scouts like Buffalo Bill Cody dare face the ravening beasts, using their six-guns to deadly effect ere the terrible animals rend them asunder with their sharp claws.

McBride smiled into the night. Now he was sleeping alongside a bear, but this one was just a skinny old man who snored.

He lay on his back and closed his eyes. Rain showered through the roof of the frail shelter, and the fire had long since died in a feeble wisp of smoke. All night long the thunderstorm raged, lightning cracking the sky apart. Once McBride heard Bear's horse whinny in fear as a bolt struck a cottonwood farther along the creek. He rose and gazed into the rain-lashed darkness. The tree was split in half and on fire, scarlet tongues of flame fluttering on its trunk and branches. But one by one the fires blinked out in the downpour, leaving the night darker than it had been before.

McBride wiped raindrops off his mustache with the knuckles of his index finger, then crawled into his meager shelter. At some point he managed to fall asleep and he woke to a gray, watery dawn.

He put on his hat, stepped outside and, looking around him, worked a kink out of his back. Bear Miller was gone, probably chasing his horse. The skeleton of the lightning-struck cottonwood stood black against the surly sky and the air smelled of wet earth and rain. A wind, driving chill off the snow peaks of the Brokeoff Mountains, made McBride shiver. He considered trying his hand again at a fire to warm up the coffee but immediately dismissed the idea. Everything was wet and all he'd achieve would be a strand of flimsy smoke that came and went and a bellyful of disappointment.

He reached into the shelter, lifted the pot from the muddy coals and drank from it. The coffee was cold, gritty and bitter . . . but it was coffee.

Pot in hand, McBride strolled to his mustang. He was looking at the ugly little horse and it was looking at him. The animal seemed to have fared all right and even allowed McBride to pat its neck a time or two before it lashed out with a flinty rear hoof, missing his knee by inches.

"Never at your best in the mornings, are you, horse?" he said.

The mustang regarded him with a mean eye, then moodily lowered its head to its grazing.

McBride drank from the pot again and nodded. "Not too bad once you get used to it," he said aloud, licking his lips. "A man could get to liking a drink of cold mud."

A couple of minutes later Bear Miller rode into camp . . . and the old man looked scared to death.

Chapter 4

McBride's raised eyebrows asked a question and Bear answered it. "Apaches! Coming this way!"

"How many?"

"Enough."

"Can we go around them?" McBride asked, the coffeepot forgotten in his hand.

Bear leaned forward in the saddle and shook his head. "No. We could try to go through them, but our hair would be decorating some buck's lance by noon."

"How much time do we have?"

"Time enough to start over that." Bear nodded toward the grim peaks of the Guadalupe Ridge. "And hope we're out of rifle range afore the 'Paches get here."

"Bear, will they come after us?"

"Boy, you can bet the farm on it. Now saddle that thing you call a hoss and let's get the hell out of here."

McBride picked up his saddle. "Do you know a trail across those mountains?"

"Nope. Never tried to find one."

"I looked, but didn't see any kind of trail."

"There will be one. All we have to do is find it." A frown gathered between the old man's eyes. "Now saddle that damned hoss. You ain't sitting on your porch on a Sunday morning with all the time in the world."

A few minutes later McBride was moving the mustang at a slow walk along smooth rock that seemed to rise straight up. Ahead of him rode Bear on his rangy black and ahead of Bear . . . a nightmare landscape of steep slope, gravel and brush. Higher, the slope met up with a band of thick pines, interrupted here and there by massive outcroppings of rock and small grassy areas.

The air was thinning as they rode higher. Clinging to the wind, rain and snow-polished slant like moss on a rock, McBride looked beyond his right stirrup. The mountain fell almost vertically away from him, past a boulder jam and then . . . dizzying nothingness. He swallowed hard, realizing that if his pony slipped, he would fall for a mile before hitting ground.

It was a thought that did little to comfort a man.

The clouds were dropping lower, towering gray banks of them that looked like the ramparts of an ancient fortress. It was as yet only early morning but McBride had the feeling that the sun was dead and that darkness was about to take over the entire world. Ahead of him Bear Miller kept looking over his shoulder, his troubled eyes searching their back trail, a sight that did little to soothe McBride's jangled nerves.

Bear dropped lower onto a narrow ledge that rose again gradually and disappeared around a jutting rock face shaped like the prow of a ship. He turned in the saddle and yelled, "Game trail! I reckon she'll switchback up into the pines."

McBride grimaced. And what if it doesn't, old man? If the trail peters out around the rock face there will be no going back. Did you think of that?

He estimated they were maybe seven thousand feet above the flat and climbing. It was a long way to fall. A long time to think about dying.

Then two dire events happened one right after the other, stabbing equal spikes of fear into McBride's belly.

The first was a rising wind that slapped pitilessly at his face . . . and carried icy drops of rain.

The second was the bullet that spaaaanged! off the rock a few inches above his head.

Startled, Bear swung around in the saddle. "They're after us! Unlimber that rifle, boy, an' have at it."

Easier said than done!

The ledge was so narrow McBride had no room to turn and bring the rifle to his shoulder. In any case he was not much of a hand with a long gun and all he'd do is make noise.

A second bullet hit the rock, another right after it. The mustang tossed its head, made jumpy by the gunfire and the sudden unease of its rider. The pony's hoof slipped, raining down a shattering shower of shingle and gravel, and McBride's heart stood still.

He drew rein. Ahead of him Bear disappeared around the prow-shaped rock. The old man hadn't once looked back, intent on saving his own hide, and McBride cursed him loudly and passionately.

He drew his Smith & Wesson and turned his head as much as he dared. A small, wiry man with long black hair bound by a red calico headband was walking along the ledge toward him. The Apache wore a faded, Mexican shirt, white breechcloth and moccasins to his knees. He carried a Spencer rifle and a holstered Colt.

So that's what a whole Apache looked like!

McBride raised his revolver, fired over his shoulder—and missed. The Apache pressed himself against the rock slope, then threw his rifle to an aiming position. The man fired and McBride felt the bullet burn across the thick muscle of his right bicep.

Another Apache inched along the ledge, saw McBride and took a kneeling position. He threw up his rifle and McBride fired, this time with better effect. His bullet ricocheted off the rock, close to the Indian's face, throwing splinters of rock into his cheek. The Apache yelped and his finger closed on the trigger. The shot went high and wide.

A third Apache appeared and then a fourth. McBride knew his time was short. He kicked at the mustang's sides, but the horse refused to budge. Cursing a blue streak, at any second expecting a bullet in the back, he lashed at the horse with the reins.

Nothing. The mustang tossed its head, snorted and refused to budge.

The rain started in earnest, hammering into McBride's face, making the narrow trail slick and even more dangerous. The Apache fire was hitting around him as they began to find the range and they were edging closer. Then it dawned on McBride why they hadn't already killed him—they wanted him alive! As though he'd set out to learn them by heart, the words of a dime novel he'd read came back to haunt him:

Joachim van Sloot, that stalwart frontiersman, bore well the torture of the feathered fiends for the first few hours or so, not a sound escaping his bearded lips. But after three days of torment, his skin flayed from his body, his eyes and ears gone, he begged his callous captors for death. The savage reply of the buckskinned beasts was to cut out his tongue. Being a strong man, Joachim lingered in mortal agony for two more long days ere our merciful Lord finally put an end to his suffering and he cast off his mortal coil.

McBride had no intention of being tortured to death. If worse came to worst, he'd empty his service revolver into the Apaches, then jump the mustang off the ledge. His death would be just as certain, but much quicker.

Behind him he heard an Apache yell at him in

English, ordering him to stay where he was. He turned in the saddle, ready to make his fight. The Apache fired a warning shot. The bullet bounced off the rock just behind the mustang, then burned across the top of its hindquarters. The little horse shrieked in fear and took off along the ledge at a gallop.

McBride heard disappointed yells behind him as the mustang rounded the bend at breakneck speed. All he could do was hold the saddle horn in a death grip and pray as the mountains cartwheeled crazily around him.

To his relief the ledge opened up to a width of several feet, climbing steeply upward toward a stand of pine surrounding a pile of huge boulders that had tumbled down the mountain during some ancient earthquake.

McBride had almost reached the pines when a rifle fired, a puff of gray smoke rising from the top of the boulders. Behind him he heard an Apache scream as he pitched over the ledge into the abyss below.

The frightened mustang reached the pines and skidded to a stop, throwing McBride over its head. He hit the ground with a thud and lay there, all the air knocked out of him.

Suddenly Bear Miller took a knee at his side. "Are you hit, John?"

McBride tried to answer, gasped a few times and gave up. He pointed to the wound on his arm.

Bear studied the bullet burn and nodded. "Uh-huh, just a scratch. You were lucky, boy. When I saw you fall off your pony, I thought for sure you'd been hit bad." The old man's face took on a shrewd look.

"Don't have a very secure seat in the saddle, do you?"

McBride let that go and rose to a sitting position. He was able to breathe again, barely, but managed, "The Apaches?"

"Gone, I reckon. After losing one man, an Apache is too savvy to climb a narrow ledge into the fire of two waiting rifles. He'll bide his time and lift your hair another day when the odds are more in his favor."

A few moments later Bear's analysis of the situation proved accurate. A lone Apache appeared at the bend of the trail and, his hands cupped around his mouth, started hollering.

"What's he saying?" McBride gasped.

"Well, he's cussing us out in a mixture of Apache, Spanish and English, but mostly Apache. He says we're a couple of old women who are too scared to leave the trees and come out and fight." Bear listened for a while, then grinned. "He's got a special word for you, John."

"What's that?"

"He says you can't ride, can't shoot and from now on should stay home with the white squaws."

"Well, he knows I can't understand a damn thing he's saying, so more fool him."

The Apache turned his back, raised his breechcloth and bared his rump in McBride's direction.

"Understand that?" Bear asked, his eyes twinkling.

"I think," McBride said, "he just made his opinion of me pretty clear."

Chapter 5

The settlement of Suicide lay about five miles due south of Gunsight Canyon and the Black River country. An hour after crossing the Texas border, McBride and Bear Miller topped a shallow rise and looked down on the town, a sprawling annex of hell huddled along the bank of a shallow creek that showed dry in places.

McBride's gaze took in the sun-hammered, gray adobe and wood buildings, rickety corrals and scattered, tar-paper shacks, and his heart sank. Not a single shade tree or tall building redeemed the squat, squalid ugliness of the place.

Suicide did not look like a town where a man might prosper.

"Well," Bear said, "what do you think?"

"You call this a town?"

"Nearest thing to a town you'll find within a hundred-mile, John. A man can ride on down there and get grub, a drink and a bed. What else does a town need?"

"People, for one thing."

"Folks are all indoors, warming at the fire. Maybe you hadn't noticed, but it's turned right chilly since we cleared the ridge."

McBride eased himself in the saddle. Bear was right about that. The earlier rain had turned to a slanting, wet sleet driven by a keening wind that cut him to the bone. The old scout said it was early in the season for sleet, but in this neck of the woods a man never knew. The Texas weather was just as contrary as Texans themselves.

Stunted by a lack of water, the cottonwoods along the creek were smaller than usual and crowded close together, but prickly pear and mesquite grew thick everywhere. McBride's eyes followed the course of the creek. Beyond the settlement it took a sharp dogleg to the north, then cut across a quarter mile of sandy brush flat before disappearing into the base of a steep, hog-backed hill.

"Bear, is that the white-painted house you were talking about?"

"Uh-huh, halfway up the hill."

Unlike the other buildings in Suicide, the sprawling, three-story house was built of timber. It had a couple of high, tower rooms above the first two floors and was adorned with much elaborate gingerbread decoration. Behind and above a shady porch that ran the length of the house, eight wide windows showed to the front. No smoke rose from brick chimneys at each gable end and behind the house, cut into the hillside, were a barn, corral and other outbuildings. The place had a seedy, run-down look, like an ancient and impoverished dowager trying to cling to her last shreds of dignity.

McBride turned in the saddle. "Strange location to find a big house like that."

"Kind of takes a man by surprise, huh?"

"Who lives there?"

Bear frowned. "Hell, John, you want to keep talking up here, freezing to death, or should we find us a warm berth in the saloon? We can talk all you want then."

McBride grinned, the devil in him. "Bear, I'm making you suffer for leaving me up on the mountain with the Apaches."

The old man opened his mouth to speak, seemed to realize that he could well dig himself into a deeper hole and shut it again. After a few moments he said, sighing in resigned exasperation, "The house belongs to a gal called Allison Elliot, and by all accounts she's a mighty pretty young filly, a beauty they say."

McBride's chin pointed the way. "What's a young woman doing up there in the middle of nowhere?"

"The story is that her pa was a gold miner who struck it rich. He figured everybody in God's creation would be after his money, so he moved here to get away from folks. He built the house and then sent for Allison. That was ten years ago, when she was only fifteen years old. Well, Allison's pa died a few years back, shot himself I'm told, and the little gal has lived there ever since."

Bear irritably wiped sleet from his mustache. "They say there's half-a-million dollars in gold bars hidden somewhere in the house, and there have been them as wanted it." The old man pointed. "You've got young eyes, John. Look to the right of the place, near where the manzanita grows out of a split rock."

McBride scanned the hillside, then nodded. "I see it."

"Now look at the base of the rock. What do you see?"

It took a few moments, but McBride said finally, "I can make out five mounds of dirt."

"Graves," Bear said. "At one time or another, five men have tried to take from Allison Elliot what's rightfully hers. The last of them was Happy Jake Mitchell, an outlaw who ran with Billy Bonney and them over to Lincoln County way. That was just a four-month ago."

"What happened to those men?"

"Allison keeps a Sharps .50 ranged at a hundred yards. Does that answer your question?"

"She killed them?"

"Her or the old black man who does for her. His name is Moses and he don't take a step back from nobody." Bear leaned from his saddle, spat, then knuckled his mustache. "If you ask me, I reckon Allison herself does the shooting and Moses does the burying." He gave McBride a sidelong glance. "Now, can we get off this rise and into somewhere warm afore my rheumatisms stiffen me like a board?"

McBride nodded. "Sure." But he stayed where he was, thinking. Finally he said, "Allison Elliot is a woman to avoid, huh?"

"Only if'n you want to keep on living. She don't cotton to strangers, especially menfolk."

"Something to remember," McBride said as he kicked his mustang into motion.

But he knew he badly wanted to meet Allison Elliot, a woman who was as beautiful as she was mysterious.

Chapter 6

John McBride led the way off the rise and into the town of Suicide.

He and Bear rode past some outlying shacks, black smoke lifting from their crooked tin chimneys, then past a blacksmith's shop and a general store.

McBride paid close attention to the store as he passed. The place had a solid wood door and one small display window and did not seem to be well stocked. A few dusty high-button shoes for women were arranged in front with a hand-lettered sign propped against them that read: SOLD AT COST. Behind those was a zinc bathtub lying on its side, an old McClellan saddle and a rusty pyramid of canned peaches.

The ramshackle store had a forlorn, down-at-heel look and McBride decided his five hundred dollars would remain in his money belt.

A patch of open, weed-grown ground followed, then a yellow adobe building with a narrow, blanket-covered door. Next to that, on the wall, hung a painting of a howling, blue coyote, and around it in passable script were the words: EL COYOTE AZUL.

"That's the Mex cantina," Bear said. "The food is passable good but if you're not used to it, steer clear of the mescal. Blow a man's head clean off his shoulders."

The spicy odors from the cantina were tempting and McBride's stomach grumbled. He rode past a livery stable with a pole corral out back, another adobe building with the hopeful sign HOTEL tacked above the door, and then drew rein when Bear stopped outside the saloon. It was a windowless adobe structure with a sagging pine door and no name. Here and there what looked to be bullet holes pocked the front wall and a skinny, yellow dog lay outside, his muzzle on his outstretched paws, his eyes bleak.

The sleet had stopped, but an icy wind reached out from the Guadalupes and from horizon to horizon the sky looked like a sheet of curled lead. The air held the raw smell of snows to come and though it was still early afternoon, the day was already dark. Gloomy, cold shadows pooled everywhere and the saloon's rickety door rattled restlessly in the relentless wind.

Bear swung from the saddle and glanced up at McBride. "This here shapes up to be a warm berth." He looked up and down the muddy street. "Hell, I may winter here."

"Even Suicide beats a hollow log, anytime." McBride smiled. He waved a hand. "Well, take care of yourself, Bear Miller."

"Where you off to, John?"

"I'm not one for saloons, so I guess I'll head back to the cantina for a meal. After that, I don't know. Maybe I'll ride on."

"Maybe you will, but I doubt it. I saw the light in your eyes when I was talking about that little Elliot gal."

"You may have a point there," McBride conceded, grinning.

Bear stepped to the door of the saloon and turned. "You be careful now, John. A Sharps big .50 don't much care who it shoots."

McBride swung the mustang away from the saloon and raised his hand again. "So long, Bear. I'll keep in mind what you said."

The old man called out after him, "You do that, John, and watch your back. Remember what I told you about the shadow of the gun."

When McBride reached the cantina he glanced toward the saloon. But Bear had already disappeared inside.

The El Coyote Azul was snug and warm. A rough pine bar propped up on a pair of sawhorses ran down the left side of the room, with a barrel of mescal set on a wooden stand at one end. On shelves behind the bar was a variety of bottles and glasses. A few scattered tables and chairs, like the bar made of unplaned timber, completed the furniture. The cantina was lit by smoking oil lamps, and the orange light cast blue shadows in the corners of the room. Opposite McBride another blanket-covered doorway presumably led to the kitchen, judging by the smell of frying beef and onions wafting toward him.

There were no other customers. He took a seat at a table and laid his plug hat on the chair beside him. From behind the curtain he heard women talking in Spanish, then a startled female yelp followed by a burst of laughter.

Someone back there was bottom pinching, McBride guessed.

The kitchen curtain pulled back and a small, plump man stepped into the room, grinning. His glance fell on McBride. "So sorry, senor, I did not hear you come in."

"I just got here," McBride said.

The little man bowed. He wore a pencil-thin mustache and his hair was parted in the middle and slicked down on each side of his head, black and shining like patent leather. "My name is Manuel Cortez and I am the keeper of this fine establishment. Can I bring you something? A glass of mescal, perhaps?"

"Just food. I'm some hungry."

"Ah, then the hungry man has come to the right place. I will bring your meal right away."

Cortez turned toward the kitchen, but McBride's voice stopped him. "Shouldn't you ask what I want first?"

The little man shook his head, smiling. "For you, senor, the specialty of the house. Beef, onions, frijoles and tortillas." Cortez gave another bobbing bow. "How does that sound?"

"Sounds good," McBride allowed. "And cold buttermilk if you have any."

A small disappointment chased its way across the man's face. "That I do not have, senor." He brightened. "But I can bring you a bottle of beer."

McBride nodded. "That will do."

The food was good and McBride ate with an appetite. He was aware of Cortez standing behind the bar, polishing the same glass over and over again with a red and white checkered cloth, watching him, a benign smile on his face.

After McBride sighed and pushed back from the table, the little Mexican came around the bar and hovered over him. "The food was to your liking?"

"Very good." He took a swig of beer and swirled it around his mouth. "It had some fire to it, though."

Cortez shrugged and spread his hands. "It is the hot peppers, senor. We Mexicans believe that without pain there can be no pleasure."

McBride smiled. "I just experienced both of them all right."

A silence stretched between the two men; then Cortez asked, "What brings you to Suicide, senor? If you are on the dodge, be assured, there is no law here."

"I'm not on the dodge, just passing through."

"With the Apaches out?" The Mexican was shocked, his black eyes rounding in disbelief.

"I didn't know they were on the warpath until very recently."

"You were lucky, senor, to make it this far."

The food and the beer had mellowed McBride and he was prepared to be sociable. "I was helped by a man named Bear Miller. Know him?"

"Si, I know Bear. He is ver' wise in the ways of the Apache." Female laughter drifted from the kitchen as the Mexican said, "Where will you go?"

McBride shook his head. He was feeling warm and drowsy. "South I suppose. I'm looking for a store to buy. I thought I might prosper in the hardware business."

"Ah," was all Cortez said, but McBride read something unspoken in his eyes.

"Do you know of a hardware store for sale?" he asked quickly, rousing himself.

"Prosperity is good," the Mexican said, stepping around the question. "A man does not know what stuff he is made of until prosperity and ease try him." He sighed. "That is what I believe, but soon I must leave all this"—he waved a hand around the cantina—"prosperity and life of ease behind and remain as yet untested."

McBride slipped back into relaxed lethargy. "Selling the place, huh?"

Cortez nodded. "I have to return to Sonora. My mother, she is very sick and prays that her oldest son will soon be sitting at her bedside."

Suddenly the Mexican's face lit up and his teeth flashed in a dazzling white smile. "Providence has brought you here, senor!" he said, his voice pitched higher by excitement. He dropped into the chair opposite McBride. "You want to buy a business and I have one to sell. We meet in the wilderness like long-lost brothers!"

It was McBride's turn to smile. "Maybe you haven't noticed, but the El Coyote Azul isn't a hardware store."

"Pah, there are no fortunes to be made in tin pots and nails. Look here, this is the business for you. I have two fat ladies in the kitchen and all you'll have to do is sit back and"—Cortez laid his arms on the table and made a grand, sweeping gesture—"rake in the money."

Intrigued despite himself, McBride shook off his apathy and leaned forward in his chair, stroking his chin. "You interest me. The two fat ladies do all the work and I rake in the money, huh?"

"Si, senor, you rake in the money and live a life of ease."

McBride detected a fly in the ointment. "But, except for me, you have no customers."

"Tuesday is always a slow day," Cortez said. "Is sad."

"This is Monday."

"Another slow day." The Mexican added quickly, "Three times a week the McAllen Brothers stage stops here to feed its passengers. Six, sometimes eight people eat here and they pay plenty for mescal and frijoles. Then there are the citizens of Suicide. On Saturday nights you can't get a seat in here." Cortez warmed his enthusiasm to boiling point. "And during spring roundup all the surrounding ranchers bring their punchers here." He raised his hands and made in and out motions. "The walls go like that, there are so many hungry and thirsty men in here."

"And you just sit back and rake in the money, huh?"

"Si, senor, I lie back at my ease and count, count, count."

"Lie back at your ease . . . ," McBride repeated, considering, stubbly chin rasping under his rubbing fingers. Suddenly he threw his hands in the air. "Hell, what am I thinking? I can't afford a place like this."

"How much do you have, senor?" the Mexican whispered archly, moving closer. His eyes were bland and guileless.

"Five hundred dollars."

"In gold?"

"In gold."

Cortez bounced with excitement. He slapped the table with the flat of his hand. "That is the very amount I am asking for the El Coyote Azul! Truly the fates have brought us together this day."

McBride was surprised. "You'll let all this go for five hundred?"

"A sacrifice, yes. But with a sick old mother who needs me I must sell cheap."

A full minute ticked by as McBride considered his good fortune and its effect on his young Chinese wards. The last he'd heard, the girls were thriving, and looking forward to attending school.

His mind made up, he stood and stuck out his hand. "Mr. Cortez, you have a deal."

The Mexican shook hands vigorously, grinning

from ear to ear. He took off his stained white apron and looped it over McBride's head. "Behold, the new keeper of El Coyote Azul."

If anything, McBride's grin was even wider. He had his store at last and would surely prosper in the food and drink business. Everybody had to eat.

Cortez coughed, smiled and rubbed his thumb and forefinger together. McBride said, "Oh yes, I got so excited I forgot." He unbuttoned his shirt, unbuckled his money belt and passed it to the Mexican. "No need to count it. It's all there."

Cortez's smile thinned and his eyes grew harder, like chunks of polished obsidian. He carefully counted the twenty-five double eagles onto the table, then raked up the coins and shoved them into his pocket.

"As you say, senor, all there. Now I must say a quick good-bye to Maria and Conchita, then saddle my mule and ride fast for Sonora." He made a little bow. "Now I bid the fortunate new proprietor of this cantina farewell." He waved a hand. "*Vaya con Dios.*"

He disappeared into the kitchen. A few moments later the women started wailing; then their caterwauling slowly faded into snuffling sobs.

McBride would console them later. Right now he was too excited. He took off the apron and suit coat, removed the holstered Smith & Wesson and folded the coat around it. Now that he was a businessman he'd later oil the revolver and put it away for good. The days of the gunfighting Tenderfoot Kid were over.

He tied the apron around himself again, stepped behind the bar, found an empty shelf and placed the coat and gun there. Then he checked the levels of the whiskey and rye bottles.

John McBride, late of the New York Police Department's Bureau of Detectives, now proud owner of the cantina El Coyote Azul, placed both hands on the rough pine counter . . . and, smiling in anticipation, waited for his customers to arrive.

Chapter 7

The dismal, sunless day gave way to a murky, moonless evening.

McBride lit all the oil lamps and stepped to the door. He pushed the blanket aside and looked up and down the street. Several horses were standing three-legged at the hitching rail outside the saloon, and rectangles of pale yellow light spilled into the mud from the windows of the shacks and cabins behind the commercial buildings. Icy, stinging sleet slanted like steel needles in the wind and McBride's breath smoked in the cold air. Lamps had been lit in the Elliot house on the hill, glittering like fireflies in the darkness. McBride imagined Allison in there, perhaps sitting at a fire with a book, tall, elegant and beautiful, lonely for company. Soon he'd take a ride up there and pay his respects. . . .

His horse!

Only then, with a pang of conscience, did he realize he'd left the mustang ground-tied outside the cantina. The little horse had moved to the lee of the building, out of the wind, and stood head-down and miserable, its reins trailing.

Feeling like a man who had just kicked a kitten, McBride caught up the animal and led it toward the livery stable. He had left his coat behind and he shivered as he squelched across the muddy ground, the mustang plodding behind him, taking an interest in nothing.

McBride screeched open the sagging door of the stable and led the horse inside. A single lamp lit the interior, casting the barred shadows of pinewood stalls onto the dirt floor. Somewhere in the gloom a horse snorted, stamped an irritable hoof and a rat squealed and scurried for safety. The barn smelled of manure, straw and neglect, but because of its tight timber walls it felt marginally warmer than outside.

McBride stood just inside the doorway with his horse, uncertain of what to do next. Feed the mustang, he supposed. But where was the hay?

Straw rustled back in the shadows at the rear of the buildings and McBride heard a man groan as he got to his feet.

"Can I do something for you?"

The voice from out of the darkness was rough and lacked even a hint of friendliness.

"I need food for my horse," McBride said, his eyes searching the gloom. "And a stall."

"A stall and hay and oats twice a day for two bits. Grooming, shoeing and anything else is extry."

"Sounds fair."

"Mister, I don't give a damn if it's fair or no. Take it or leave it."

The darkness parted as a man emerged into the lamplight. He was no taller than four feet and he had short stubby arms and legs, the latter badly bowed. His head was huge and wisps of straw were sticking to his black, unruly hair. He wore cut-off pants made for a much taller man and suspenders over a dirty red undershirt. His feet were bare.

"I guess you're the hostler." McBride smiled, prepared to be friendly despite his chilly reception. After all, he had to do business in this town.

"If you mean do I look after the livery stable, the answer is yes." He lifted humorless, almost hostile, black eyes to McBride's. "Well, is it a go?"

"It's a go. Hay and oats and a stall, and I'll need the stall for quite some time." McBride hesitated a moment, choosing his words to make certain the importance of his next statement would not be lost on the little man. "I'm the new proprietor of the El Coyote Azul."

"Uh-huh."

Despite his small size, the man easily stripped the saddle from the mustang and led it to a stall somewhere in the darkness. McBride heard hay forked, then the hiss of oats falling from a scoop.

The little man returned and held out his hand. "Pay by the week—in advance."

Now that his five hundred dollars was gone, McBride's money supply was dwindling fast. He gloomily started counting coins into the hostler's palm, but after the last half-dollar clinked beside its fellows he had cheered considerably. When the profits started to pour in from the cantina, a dollar-seventy-five would only be loose change.

After the little man's stubby fingers closed on the money and he turned to walk away, McBride's voice stopped him.

"My name's John McBride and I hope you'll patronize my restaurant."

"The El Coyote Azul ain't your restaurant," the man said, facing McBride again. "It ain't your restaurant any more than this is my stable."

"You're mistaken. I paid Manuel Cortez for the place fair and square."

"I know. He saddled his mule and took off out of here like the devil himself was after him, heading west. It don't much matter what direction he took since he's dead by this time anyhow."

McBride frowned. Maybe this man's mind was as malformed as his body. "I don't understand," he said.

The little man stood in silence for a few moments, sizing up McBride. When he spoke his voice was edged with sarcasm. "Mister, when you walked in here I pegged you for a pilgrim, maybe from back east somewheres. Now I'm sure of it. You don't know a damn thing, do you?"

Anger flared in McBride at the insult. "I do know if you talk to me like that again I'll kick your—"

Swiftly, the small man's right hand moved behind him and when it appeared again it was holding a short-barreled revolver aimed right at McBride's head.

"You're like every other giant, thinking you can pound on little people anytime you feel like it." He was scowling, his eyes hard. "Well, mister, Sammy Colt made all men equal and I'm holding the proof right here in my hand."

He was a respectable businessman, all through with guns and gunfighting, and McBride backed off. "Sorry, you're right, I shouldn't have said that." He made an effort to sound reasonably contrite. "Now please put the iron away and tell me why I don't own my cantina."

It took the small man a while. His eyes bored into McBride's and his gun didn't waver as he figured that the giant had learned his lesson now that he'd been read to from the book. In the end, he lowered the Colt and shoved it back in his pants.

"She owns it," he said. "Just like she owns this livery and everything else in Suicide. You're renting the cantina, McBride. You don't own it. Get my drift?"

"Who is she, for God's sake?"

"Miss Elliot. Up there in the big house on the bluff."

McBride was stricken. "You mean I have to pay Allison, I mean, Miss Elliot, rent?"

The little man shook his head. "Not a penny. She allows Angel Guerrero to do the collecting and Miss Elliot allows him to hold on to what he takes."

"And who the hell is he?"

"If you don't know, you'll find out soon enough."

"Miss Elliot holds paper on the El Coyote Azul?"

"Yup, and every other business in town, including the store and saloon."

"How much rent . . ."

"You'll know that soon enough as well. Angel will tell you."

McBride suddenly had the urge to sit down. His head was reeling. He'd paid Manuel Cortez five hundred dollars for nothing.

As though he were reading his mind, the little man said, "Maybe you'll get your money back after it's taken from Manuel's body. But don't count on it."

"Who—who will take the money?"

"A person who has killed him already, a person you don't know now and don't want to know."

McBride shook his head, trying to clear his spinning brain. "But why would anyone kill Cortez? He seemed harmless enough."

The little man shrugged, his half smile malicious. "Because, Mr. High-and-Mighty McBride, no one is allowed to leave Suicide. And now you're here, that includes you."

Chapter 8

John McBride walked, head bent against the sleet and wind, in the direction of the cantina. The dwarf had refused to tell him more than that his name was Jim Drago and that he'd lived in Suicide since the town's founding by Allison Elliot's father.

What did Drago mean that no one was allowed to leave Suicide? And had Manuel Cortez been murdered because he'd tried to leave? Who was behind it all? Surely not Allison, a woman both rich and beautiful.

But McBride realized he knew nothing about the woman, only the gorgeous fantasy creature he'd created in his mind. By Bear's account Allison had killed five men, robbers certainly, but shooting down hard men with a .50-caliber rifle was hardly the act of a blushing young innocent.

"Damn it, McBride," he told himself. "You're a trained detective. Now act like one and get to the bottom of all this. If Cortez was indeed murdered, find out why and see that the guilty are punished."

Four orphaned Chinese girls were depending on him to make a success of the cantina. Rent or no rent, he had to make it pay. Solving the mystery of Allison Elliot and making Suicide a safe town to live in must be his first priorities. He didn't want any potential customers murdered.

Out in the dark, sleet-lashed plains the real coyotes were yelping their misery as McBride stepped into the El Coyote Azul.

So far he had avoided Maria and Conchita, leaving them alone to grieve for their former employer. Now he decided to do his best to console them. But he heard giggles from the kitchen, not sobs. He pushed back the curtain and stepped inside.

An adobe stove ran the length of the opposite wall, covered in pots and fry pans, all of them dirty. There was a shelf to McBride's left, holding half-empty sacks of flour, beans and salt, and a side of bacon hung from a rafter. A barrel leaked molasses onto the dirt floor, to the obvious delight of a tiny calico cat, its pink tongue busily lapping up the stuff. There was no cooking being done, but wood blazed in the stove, its iron door wide-open, and the place was stifling hot. A table and two chairs completed the furnishings. To McBride's dismay the table groaned under the weight of stacks of tortillas, rounds of corn bread, bowls of fried beef and onions and mounds of frijoles.

The fat ladies didn't get that size by accident. Just keeping them fed would literally eat up a high percentage of his profits.

Maria and Conchita had risen to their feet when

McBride stepped inside. Now they stood close together, looking at him and at each other, giddy giggles making their huge bodies jiggle.

"Good evening, ladies." McBride smiled. He figured each woman would dress out at about 350 pounds. Their coal black hair was pulled into buns and their low-cut, embroidered peasant blouses revealed generous Vs of cleavage.

The women giggled some more behind their cupped hands; then they pulled out their calico skirts and dropped McBride a little curtsy. One of them, Maria or Conchita—McBride never knew who it was, since he was forever unable to tell them apart—grinned and said, "Welcome, boss."

"Thank you," McBride said. "And you are?"

"Welcome, boss," the woman said again.

He understood then. After those two words, obviously rehearsed, the fat ladies' English was all used up. This was starting to become a chore and McBride regretted coming into the kitchen in the first place.

"Well, I'll leave you to it," he said, backing out. "We'll probably"—his eyes slid to the huge spread on the table—"have hungry customers later."

"Welcome, boss."

McBride retreated into the dining room, a fresh burst of giggles showing him the way out.

Thirty minutes later, during which time McBride had checked his watch six times, his anxious eyes on the door, the blanket swung back and a man stepped inside.

It was Bear Miller, the shoulders of his buckskins black from wetness, the Henry hanging in his right hand. His eyes slid around the room and stopped at McBride standing behind the bar. He laughed. "What the hell, did they put you to work?"

"I bought the place," McBride said, as though he had just been voted president. "It isn't a hardware store, but it will do for now." He grinned. "You're my first customer."

"Only I ain't buying, unless you've got something behind the bar other than mescal."

McBride's face fell. "You're not hungry?"

"Nah, I ate at the saloon." Bear stepped to the bar and propped his rifle against a sawhorse. "It's owned by an Irishman by the name of Clyde Kaleen. He keeps a good spread down there, cheese, crackers, salted sardines, stuff like that."

"How much does he charge?" McBride asked glumly. The last thing in the world he needed right now was competition.

"Nothing. The grub's free. It's the drinks that come expensive." Bear's eyes wandered over McBride's chest. "Hey, where's your gun?"

"Behind the bar. Later I'll pack it away. A businessman has no need for a gun."

Bear's glance was skeptical. "Seems to me everybody in Suicide needs a gun with the Apaches out and the town setting astride an outlaw trail into New Mexico." He shrugged. "But you know best, John. Now, how about that drink?"

McBride searched around the bar and after a couple of minutes found a bottle of bourbon with about two inches remaining in the bottom. He wiped dust from a glass with his apron and poured Bear his drink.

"How much does Kaleen charge for this?" he asked.

"Fifty cents, but that's for the barrel whiskey he makes himself. I don't know about the bottled stuff."

"Well, that one's on the house," McBride said.

Bear tried the whiskey and declared it good. Then his eyes lifted to McBride's face. "So, you bought the place."

"Uh-huh. I've got two fat ladies in the kitchen and all I have to do is sit back and rake in the money."

The old man's glance swept around the empty room. "I can see you're already prospering."

"This is a slow night. Come Saturday the El Coyote Azul will be jumping." Feeling the need to justify his business smarts, McBride puffed a little and added, "Besides, the McAllen Brothers stage stops here three times a week to feed passengers and during spring roundup the cowboys eat here. I'm told the cantina is jammed to the walls with thirsty, hungry men."

Bear Miller raised a shaggy eyebrow. "Is that a fact?"

"Sure as I'm standing here."

"Well, John, here's a couple of natural facts: The McAllen stage line went out of business a year ago. They couldn't make it pay, not enough folks wanting to visit these parts. As for the spring roundup, the punchers eat their bacon and beans on the range. They don't have time to go gallivanting when there's work to be done. Sure, a rider will stop by now and then for mescal, but not often. Three, four times a year if you're lucky."

There was a silence before McBride said, "But Cortez told me—"

"Manuel Cortez would cut his grandmother's throat for fifty dollars. He saw you coming, John. He sized you up as a pilgrim and unloaded this place on you. How much did you pay him?"

"Five hundred dollars."

Bear almost choked on his drink. He gulped down a breath and said, "He robbed you. He might as well have stuck a gun in your face and taken your money."

McBride stood perfectly still, in shock. When he finally spoke it sounded like the words were strangling him. "You're telling me it doesn't look good?"

"I'm telling you to unload the place on the first sap you can find."

"There's worse, Bear. I don't even own the cantina. The man who runs the livery told me Allison Elliot owns every building in town. I have to pay her rent for the place. The money is collected by a man called Angel Guerrero."

"The Poison Dwarf told you that?"

"His name is Jim Drago."

"Yeah, I know, but around these parts he's the Poison Dwarf. He's killed more men than you have fingers on your right hand. He's a back-shooter and bushwhacker who notches his guns. A man can't sink much lower than that."

Piling misery on misery, McBride said, "Drago told me something else. He says Cortez rode out scared and is already dead. He says no one is allowed to leave Suicide. You ever hear that?"

Bear shook his head. "Never have. Mind you, I've only passed through here a few times. Last time I camped by the creek for a week and then moved on without trouble." The old scout hesitated, thinking. "Of course, I had a colonel, three companies of blue coat infantry and a mountain howitzer with me. There wasn't anybody about to tell us we couldn't leave."

Bear laid his glass on the counter and McBride refilled it. "Hell, John," he said, his eyes searching the tall man's face, "look at you, you're standing on your nerves. I just can't figure you out. The Tenderfoot Kid, the named gunfighter who outdrew and killed Hack Burns shouldn't be worried about serving frijoles and washing dishes in a cantina."

"I didn't outdraw anybody. Burns had a gun in his hand and so did I. He fired and missed and I didn't. I was lucky, that's all."

"Luck and pluck bookend a gunfighter. You got both, boy, so don't throw them away. Ride out of here with me tomorrow and cut your losses. Maybe we'll rob a nice fat bank along the way and get us a road stake."

"No, Bear, I'll stick. I plan on making the El Coyote Azul prosper. I've got four young—"

"Yeah, I know, four Celestial gals depending on you. You've proved your point. Don't wear it out." Bear sipped his drink, considering. He said finally, "Well, I guess that's your decision. Tell you what,

John. One of your ladies can look after the cantina tomorrow while we ride out at first light and look for Cortez. If we don't find him dead, that will take one worry off your mind." He smiled. "At least you'll know that you can leave Suicide without getting gunned."

McBride thought for a while and decided there was logic in what Bear was suggesting. Suddenly he found himself looking forward to having words with Cortez. He'd demand at least half his money back.

"The fat ladies don't speak English," he said. "How am I going to tell them I'm riding out tomorrow?"

"I'll tell them." Bear's eyes shifted to the curtain. "Back there?"

McBride nodded and the old man walked across the room and stepped into the kitchen, letting the curtain drop behind him.

Immediately McBride heard giggles, followed by Bear speaking in Spanish. More giggles. Then one of the women said something and the old man laughed. He was still laughing, giggles following him, as he parted the curtain and walked to the bar.

"Dang me, John, but I like them big gals. If I could find me a rocker somewheres and put them two in my bed, I'd be a happy man. They'd keep me warm in winter and give me plenty of shade in summer." His eyes slanted wistfully to the door. "An' that's a natural fact."

"You couldn't handle those fat ladies, Bear, a skinny old coot like you." McBride grinned. "They'd put you in the ground within three months."

"Maybe so . . . but what a way to go."

Bear drained his glass. "Ah well, it's about time I found a bunk at the hotel. I'll meet you at the livery come sunup."

He stepped to the door but McBride's voice stopped him. "Aren't you forgetting something?"

"What's that?"

"Fifty cents for the second drink," McBride said.

Chapter 9

The sleet and gloom of the night had gone as McBride walked to the livery stable under a blazing scarlet sky streaked with ribbons of gold and jade. The wind had dropped to a whisper and the air was warmer, the scent of the pines and aspen growing on the slopes of the Guadalupe Ridge reaching far.

He stepped into the barn and heard Drago snoring, lost in the darkness of a stall. He had already saddled the mustang when Bear Miller stepped inside. The old man muttered a gruff good morning, then led out his black. He threw his saddle on the horse and as he tightened the girth he said conversationally, "Drago, you hear me?"

The snoring stopped abruptly.

"Figured you was faking it," Bear said. He was smiling. "Drago, I see you coming out of that pigsty you sleep in with a gun in your hand, I'll up my Henry and blow you clean through the wall of the barn." His smile stretched into a grin. "You understand me?"

Drago's voice drifted from the shadows. "Bear Miller, you got no call to talk to me like that."

The old scout caught up the reins of the black. "Just you remember what I said. I reckon folks don't call you the Poison Dwarf for nothin'."

A taut silence stretched thin across the distance, then snapped. "One day, Miller, I plan on killing you."

Early-morning irritability riding him, Bear faced the stall, his hand on the butt of his belt gun. "No time like the present. You want to open the ball?"

"In my own time, at a place of my own choosing. That's how it will be."

"I'll be waiting."

Bear led his horse outside and stepped into the saddle. He looked at McBride as he clambered onto the mustang's back. "That," he declared, "is the sorriest-looking hoss I've ever seen, an' I've seen plenty."

McBride nodded, his right foot searching for the stirrup. "Maybe, but he gets me to where I want to go."

"Eventually, I guess," Bear said. He kneed the big stud into a walk and threw over his shoulder: "A man would be a fool to ride a hoss that was too much for him."

"That he would," McBride said, refusing to be baited.

"But then again, most horses are too much for you, huh, John?"

McBride said nothing. Even though the truth hurt. He caught up with Bear and rode beside the old man, looking up at him. "You were a bit hard on Drago back there."

"No I wasn't. He's trash, murdering trash. Look, a man can't help the way he was born, but Drago went on to forge his own destiny. He set out to be a killer and he succeeded. Because he's ugly and misshapen, he's at war with all of God's creation, blaming the world for his ills. Know what that means, John, to hate God and all he stands for? That's the very definition of evil."

McBride smiled. "Bear, for a mountain man you sure talk like a college professor sometimes."

"Damn right. I read books an' so should you."

The sleet of last night would have washed away Cortez's tracks and McBride said as much to Bear. The old man looked down at him from his lofty perch on the tall black and grinned. "Spoken like a true pilgrim. The land is always scarred by a man's passing and no amount of sleet or rain or wind will get shet of it. His mount's hoof scars a rock or crushes a wildflower and it always leaves dung behind. The dwarf said Cortez was heading west and he told you the truth. I reckon he swung south soon, toward the foothills of the Delawares. He's planning to cross the peaks and head for the flat, easy-riding country between the Apache Mountains and the Sierra Diablo."

Bear nodded, his face set and hard. "There's a heap of rough country ahead, but we'll find him."

"If he's still alive," McBride said.

"Well, if he ain't, we'll find his body."

"I can't be away that long," McBride said. "I have to get back to the cantina."

Bear drew rein and turned in the saddle, both hands flat on the horn. He spoke slowly, as though he were lecturing a child. "John, you told me Cortez rode out scared. Now, it could be he expected somebody to come after him, somebody who didn't want him to leave Suicide. If that is the case, he'd be gunned fairly close to town. His killer wouldn't waste time by hanging back and then tracking him all the way to the mountains."

The old scout's eyes reached across the grass and brush flats. Then he kneed his horse into motion. "One way or another, we'll come up on Cortez soon and you'll be back in Suicide in time for supper."

McBride felt a niggle of irritation. He was a trained detective and he should have figured all that out for himself. Finally he consoled himself with the thought that the rugged Guadalupe country was not New York. Out here it took a whole different set of skills to play detective, skills he had not yet learned.

But I'll learn them eventually, he thought. The promise rang hollow, even to himself.

An hour passed without further talk, the only sound the creak of saddle leather and the jangle of bits. The sun was climbing higher in a lemon-colored sky and the day grew a few degrees warmer. But there remained a chill in the air and, shivering, McBride turned up the collar of his coat.

Bear had dismounted several times, getting down on one knee to check the ground. In the distance, the sandstone ramparts of the Delaware Mountains were soaring gray against the sky when he drew rein and motioned toward several upthrust slabs of rock about fifty yards ahead of them. "Good place for a bush-whacking, huh?"

A narrow stream, bordered by crowded coyote willows each standing about fifteen feet high, ran between the rocks. A solitary buckbrush, trailing its fall plumage, struggled to survive nearby. A rifleman could have hidden among the willows or climbed to a perch in the rocks, trusting to the tree branches to conceal him.

"Cortez rode close to this place," Bear said. "If he's dead, he was shot from here. That's my guess."

"But an attacker would have had to get ahead of him."

"Cortez was riding a mule. A man on a fast horse could have passed him wide on the trail, then holed up here and waited until he got him in his sights." Bear nodded to the rocks. "John, you're young and spry—climb up there and see what you see."

McBride had been in the saddle for a long time. He clambered off the mustang stiffly, got his left foot tangled in the stirrup and fell flat on his back. He got up and brushed off his muddy pants, his face livid.

Bear was highly amused and it showed. "Nice dismount, boy. But that's not how it's usually done around these parts."

McBride swore, caught up his hat and jammed it back on his head, looking daggers at the old man.

"You know," he said, "I'm beginning to develop an intense dislike of horses."

"Hell, so would any man if'n he fell off them as much as you do." Bear grinned. "Now climb them rocks like I told you an' scout around."

Turning on his heel, McBride walked toward the rocks, but Bear's voice stopped him. "Hey, John!"

"What?"

"Be careful you don't fall."

It took only a few moments for McBride to scramble up the rocks, and he found the empty shell casing almost immediately. Bright and new, it lay in a gravel-filled crack angling across a flat stone slab that leaned against a second, forming an inverted V. The slab where McBride stood was about eight inches lower than the other. The drop made a handy place to rest a rifle while a man lay hidden behind rock and a covering screen of willow branches.

He scouted the area but found nothing else, no tracks or any other sign that someone had been here.

McBride regained the level and walked over to Bear who was now standing beside his horse. "Find anything?"

"Only this." He passed the shell to the old man.

"Sharps big .50," Bear said. He sniffed the casing. "And it was fired recently, maybe only yesterday." The old man's questioning eyes found McBride's. "Who do we know uses a buffalo gun?"

"Jim Drago?"

"Maybe." He studied the shell again and without

looking up said, "But I know for sure Allison Elliot uses one."

McBride shook his head. "I can't believe she'd have anything to do with this, a cold-blooded killing from ambush."

"Could be those five men lying in the ground beside her house thought the same thing."

"Bear, we don't even know Manuel Cortez is dead. The shell could have been used by a hunter after an antelope or a mule deer."

"That's a possibility," Bear conceded. He turned and moved his arm in a semicircular arc. "If Cortez was shot, I'm betting he's out there somewheres, and within a hundred yards of this spot."

"Then it shouldn't be hard to find him," McBride said. "Let's go look."

He and Bear split up and quartered the ground. The land around the rock pile was relatively flat, grassy in places, sandy in others, dotted with clumps of piñon, squawbush, mesquite and prickly pear.

Manuel Cortez's body was lying on its back near a thick stand of cactus. The man had been shot between the eyes.

Chapter 10

"Good shootin'," Bear Miller commented as he gazed down at the Mexican's body. His eyes lifted to McBride. "I reckon if you were to pace off the distance between here and the rocks, it's better than eighty yards."

McBride had examined Cortez's body and he calculated that the man had been killed sometime the day before, probably a couple of hours after he'd ridden out of Suicide.

Cortez's mule lay at a distance, its insides and flank meat torn away. The animal had been taken down during the night by wolves or coyotes. They'd be back for the leftovers.

The man's pockets were empty, McBride's money gone. He did not grieve for Cortez, but he did mourn for his five hundred dollars.

"What do we do with him?" he asked.

Bear shrugged. "We can't bury him and he's getting a mite too ripe to carry back with us. We'll leave him here. The coyotes will see to him."

"His cantina was the El Coyote Azul, the Blue Coyote," McBride said. "Funny that, huh? I mean in the light of what you just said."

"Yeah, real funny." Bear's glance shifted to McBride's saddle. "I see you brought your rifle."

"Yes, it's there."

"Well, that's good, John, because you're going to need it."

McBride's head snapped around. "What do you mean?"

"Look right ahead of you, at our back trail."

McBride shaded his eyes with the palm of his hand, his gaze searching the distance. "Smoke," he said finally. "It's a campfire."

"That's no campfire, boy, it's talking smoke. Mescalero Apache smoke."

"What's it saying?"

"It's saying, 'Hold on right there, blancos, we're a-comin'.'"

A spike of panic rose in McBride. "What do we do?"

"Well, we could try to outrun them, but they might be all around us. I don't recommend it."

"Then what do you recommend, Bear, for God's sake?"

"We hightail it back to the rocks and try to fight them off." Bear's smile was grim. "I don't like that either, but I've plumb run out of recommendations."

The two men mounted and headed for the rock pile at a gallop, Bear's leggy black outdistancing McBride's mustang. By the time he reached the rocks,

Bear had already found himself cover, his Henry up and ready.

A bullet split the air next to McBride's head as he found the slab where he discovered the shell casing and he hunkered down behind the drop. He looked across the plain, into vastness, then let out with a wild whoop.

"They're not Apaches!" he yelled. Bear was below him and to his left. "It's our brave boys in blue!"

McBride laid his Winchester aside and got ready to rise to his feet. But Bear's harsh shout stopped him. "Stay where you are! The gallant boys in blue who wore those coats are all dead. A coat of government wool is a valuable prize for an Apache when he knows fall is cracking down strong."

Then McBride saw the full magnitude of his error.

The necks of the Mescalero ponies were stretched, their quick gallop rapidly closing the gap between the Apaches and the rocks. There were at least a dozen warriors and six or seven wore tunics of soldier blue.

The roar of Bear's rifle slapped hard against the quiet, ringing echoes racketing around him and McBride. A horse and rider went down.

McBride fired at a warrior in a blue coat and cavalry kepi, his long black hair streaming behind him in the wind. A miss. He fired again. A miss.

A bullet whined off the rock in front of McBride and a second, even closer, sent him ducking for cover behind the drop.

Bear levered his rifle and looked up at McBride,

his face twisted in anger. "Keep firing, damn it! Even if you don't hit nothing, keep firing."

McBride got a knee under him and threw the Winchester to his shoulder. Too late. An Apache had climbed the rock face and was right on top of him. He fired as the man jumped from the higher slab. The Mescalero landed on McBride's belly with both feet, his rifle butt ready to crash down on his skull. McBride rolled and the Apache lost his footing and fell beside him, his rifle spinning away, clattering down the rock pile.

The Indian sprang to his feet, quick as a striking rattler. He had a knife in his hand and he swung the blade at McBride's head. McBride felt a burn across his cheek as the razor-sharp, strap-iron blade slashed him. He suddenly saw blood on the left shoulder of his coat, and, panicked, fell backward. The Apache, his black eyes flat, without emotion, the eyes of a man who had killed many times before, dived on McBride, his knife raised.

McBride had a split second to react—and he did.

As the Apache fell on him, he measured the distance and threw a straight right at the man's chin. The Mescalero's own impetus added power to the punch and he screamed as his jaw shattered. McBride threw the unconscious man off him and scrambled to his feet . . . to look at a ring of grinning Apaches, their rifles leveled on him.

Bear Miller had been dragged out of his hole and his head was bloody from the blow of a rifle butt. The old man looked defeated—and scared.

McBride had no illusions about what would happen next. The dime magazine he'd read back in New York described in terrible detail the fate of the stalwart frontiersman who fell into the hands of the dreaded Apache. He would endure days of unspeakable torture and in the end beg for death.

McBride doubted he'd last that long. He was far from being a frontiersman and the fight with the Mescalero, when he'd experienced both fear and panic, convinced him he was not much of a stalwart either.

"We were beat afore we even started, John." Bear was talking to him, his voice unsteady. "There was too many . . . caught out in the open like this. . . ."

McBride did not trust himself to speak. He said nothing. His heart was hammering in his chest and he heard a singing in his ears as blood rushed to his head. Now he wished that he'd let the Apache kill him.

That Mescalero had staggered to his feet, his busted jaw hanging loose. He looked around, found his knife and started toward McBride. His eyes were no longer emotionless. They were filled with black fire. He held the knife low, blade up, for a gutting slash.

A guttural command stopped him in his tracks. The man who'd spoken stood about five foot seven, tall for an Apache, his lean, whipcord body knotted with muscle. A blue calico headband held back his waist-length hair and his moccasins reached the midpoint of his thighs. Across his nose and cheekbones he wore red and white stripes, the traditional war paint of the U.S. Cavalry scout.

McBride looked into the man's eyes and was surprised to see more green than brown. But the Apache's glance was cold, cruel and as hard and unfriendly as tempered steel.

He hurled more words at the Mescalero facing McBride. The man hesitated for several moments, his face sullen. Finally he sheathed his knife and spat at McBride. He winced in pain and walked away, holding his jaw.

Bear had wandered closer to McBride. "The big Apache's name is Mingan. He's Mimbreno, not Mescalero, but he's loco and worse than any of them." Then, almost as an afterthought, Bear said, "He knows me."

The faint surge of hope that rose in McBride's chest was soon dashed.

Mingan, a Sharps carbine across his chest, stepped in front of Bear. He motioned to the old scout's pants. "You still wear the yellow stripe."

Bear's reaction was to display more grimace than grin. "No longer, Mingan. Now I seek a rocking chair and a fat woman." He made a circular motion with a forefinger near his temple and staggered. "Get drunk often with my friend the great warrior, hunter and scout Mingan. Maybe so."

The Apache shook his head. "You are not my friend, Bear. You are my enemy. All blancos are my enemy. Look at my face. See the red and white of the bluecoat cavalry? I wear those stripes not out of pride but to remind me that I must hate and kill those I once served. I will go on hating and killing until every white man is driven from our land."

"Hatred is a madness of the heart, Mingan," Bear said. "It injures the hater, not the hated."

The Apache smiled. "Always your words are as smooth as a young maiden's hair. How well will you talk when the fire is put to you?" Mingan waved a hand. "Out there lies the body of an Apache you killed. He has three wives and they will soon make you curse the day you were born and the mother who bore you."

Bear made no response and the Apache nodded. "Fear makes the wolf bigger than he is, but not to you. You fear because you know very well what is to come. I read your fear in your eyes. It is a living thing."

Mingan stepped away from Bear and yelled something to the other Apaches. McBride and Bear were roughly hauled from the rocks, their hands tied behind them and rawhide nooses drawn tight around their necks. Mounted Apaches took up the ends of the ropes, dragging the prisoners behind their ponies.

The sun was at its highest point in the sky and the day grew hotter. Acrid dust kicked up by the horses worked its way into McBride's mouth and eyes. As he shambled along he began to fantasize about water, the way they served it at Delmonico's in New York, brimming in a tall glass filled with crushed ice and a sprig of mint.

As if to remind them, the dead warrior, head down over his horse, was kept close to McBride and Bear. Flies buzzed around the bloody wound in the man's head and his long hair swayed back and forth, brushing the dust of the trail.

McBride turned his head, a movement that brought

him pain as the rawhide scraped cruelly against his neck. He spoke to Bear, his words muffled by a dry mouth and swollen tongue. "Where are they taking us?" he croaked.

Bear, older than McBride but toughened by a thousand hard trails in all kinds of weather, glanced up at the sun and then into the vastness of the plain. "The Delaware Mountains, I reckon. The Mescalero had a *ranchería* in a canyon there a few years back, then abandoned it. Now they're following the war drums, they may be using it again."

The Apache dragging Bear turned and angrily jerked on the rope. As the noose tightened and cut into his skin, the old scout yelped in pain.

His own anger flaring, McBride rasped at the Mescalero, "Hey you, quit that!"

Immediately the noose around his own neck tightened violently and he gasped in agony. After that he stayed silent.

The sun was hovering above the Delawares, touching the peaks with gleaming silver light, when the Apaches made a sharp turn to the west and rode into an arroyo, elderberry and dogwood growing on its slopes, prickly pear and other cactus scattered along its sand and gravel bottom. Months ago, in the spring, it would have been a rushing stream, carrying the rain and snowmelt washing off a mountain. Now it was dry and dusty and McBride's raging thirst grew. But here the air was cooler and the narrowness of the arroyo forced the Apaches to slow their pace, giving him a welcome respite.

But not for long.

The arroyo began to climb, up a gradual slope at first, then steeper, rocks and gravel making the footing difficult. McBride stumbled and fell several times, only to be roughly yanked to his feet again by a pull on the rope. His knees and the palms of his hands were scraped and bleeding, the spines of tiny, hidden cactus digging deep. Beside him Bear was in no better shape and the old man's face was ashen.

The last two hundred yards were flatter, the arroyo twisting its way around massive sandstone boulders that had toppled from the mountain in ancient times. Gradually the walls grew wider, opening up into a small clearing, the mountain looming a mile above them. The clearing was a hanging meadow of about thirty acres, bordered by scattered spruce and lodgepole pine.

Ten wickiups stood crowded together close to the pines and a small pony herd was picketed on the opposite side of the meadow. For an Apache ranchería, this one was relatively clean, but that testified only to the fact that the Indians had not been there long.

Within the shallow arc of the wickiups several cook fires burned, sullen flames flickering dull red in the fading light of the dying day. Near the picketed pony herd a dog barked heedlessly into the gloom, annoyed by the yips of prowling coyotes.

Almost as soon as they were dragged into the center of the village, McBride and Bear were manhandled to the ground. Their legs and arms were spread-eagled and staked out with rawhide ropes around their wrists and ankles. Then, inexplicably, they were left alone.

Bear Miller turned his head, pools of blue shadow in his eye sockets and cheeks. The old man was breathing hard, his skinny chest rapidly rising and falling. "John," he whispered, "I reckon soon we'll no longer be able to talk, so let's get it done while we can. Just remember that pain has no memory. When it's over and we're sitting in hell, you and me, it will be like this never happened."

Despite his growing fear and dread, McBride managed a weak grin. "Thanks, Bear, now I feel a whole lot better."

The old man raised his head and nodded. "Think nothing of it. You know, for a pilgrim you've got sand, John McBride. It's just a pity that you turned your back on your true calling and ended up here."

"You mean, I should have stayed a detective sergeant of police in New York?"

Bear cackled, a dry, raspy sound. "Dang me, is that what you was? I always took ye fer a lawman of some kind. But that wasn't your true calling or you wouldn't have headed west. No, boy, your true calling was to become a famous revolver fighter. You was headed in that direction until you got religion and decided to dish beans for a living. The Tenderfoot Kid, now he was on his way to becoming a man to contend with."

"Sorry I disappointed you, Bear," McBride said. His mouth was parched, his lips cracked and swollen, and it seemed that his whole body was crying out for water.

"Well . . . it don't matter a damn now, do it? We're done for."

McBride made no reply and after a couple of minutes Bear's voice came out of the darkness, a small, forlorn whisper that had a terrible finality to it. "Be brave, John McBride. Be brave."

"You too, Bear." McBride hesitated, trying to gather up his flagging courage. "You too."

Now the Apache women began to mourn for their dead.

From around the cook fires high, keening wails cut through the quiet dusk like razors, expressing a grief for the dead warrior that had a thousand shadows, each darker than the other. It has been said that the Apaches were filthy, emotionless creatures who cared only for killing. Nothing could be farther from the truth. They lamented the death of one of their own as fervently as any white man, and even more, since the Apaches were always few and their enemies many.

The cries of grief rose in volume, wavering from high screams to low, animallike moans. The women were weeping, believing that their god U-sen washed the eyes with tears the better to see the misty land of the dead where all pain and suffering ended.

The warriors were passing around and drinking deeply from a bulging water bag made from horse intestines. They seemed to be getting drunk very quickly.

"Tizwin, Apache corn beer," Bear whispered. "But it could be mescal. They're working themselves into a state, getting in the mood."

McBride told himself that it could not be much longer. He steeled himself for the torments to come, fearing that when the fire scorched and the knives cut he would scream like a woman in childbirth. He looked at the sky, dark and starless. A wind was blowing off the mountain, rustling among the trees, teasing him, whispering thin in his ears, mocking his cowardice.

Shuffling footsteps sounded near McBride and he turned his head to look. The warrior whose jaw he'd broken stepped beside him. The Apache's jaw was bound up in a strip of red tradecloth, knotted at the top of his head. For several moments the man looked down at McBride; then he pulled back his right leg and kicked his prisoner hard in the ribs.

The man's moccasin was soft, the buckskin chewed by his woman until it was the consistency of fine suede. But the toes in the moccasin were rock hard, the nails thick and tough as buffalo horn.

McBride gasped as sharp pain from the kick shrieked across his ribs. The Apache kicked him again, and again. McBride bit his lip until it bled, trying to bear the unbearable. He was certain several of his ribs were broken or at least cracked and he had to fight for every shuddering, agonizing breath.

Then the kicking stopped. But not out of any sense of mercy.

The Apache raised his foot and ground the filthy sole of his moccasin into McBride's face. Blood from his flattened nose, tasting like salt and iron, ran into his mouth, and his cracked, puffed lips were crushed against his teeth. For a wild, terrified instant, McBride thought he'd drown in his own blood.

Mingan ended it. He roughly pushed the warrior

away and he glanced down at McBride. The man's cruel face was expressionless, like it had been carved out of mahogany. Then he turned on his heel and walked away.

A couple of minutes later, as McBride's face was turned to let the blood from his nose and lips trickle away from his mouth, Bear Miller groaned.

It was not a moan of pain but part fear, part resignation.

McBride lifted his head to see what Bear was seeing.

Seven Apache women, their faces blackened with wood ash, dark eyes glittering, were striding toward them. Two of the women carried burning brands from the cook fires, the others knives or sharp-pointed sewing awls.

McBride let his aching head thud back to the ground. For the first time in his life he wished he'd never been born.

Chapter 11

The sky exploded.

Thunder slammed with titanic violence and lightning shattered the fabric of the night into millions of shimmering silver shards. Immediately, driven by the wind, a turbulent rain hammered down, drawing a shifting curtain of steel needles across the ranchería.

Their blazing brands sizzling into wisps of smoke, the Apache women, squealing, ran for their wickiups, chased by rain, thunder and the seeking, skeletal hands of the lightning.

McBride arched his back and opened his mouth, letting rain fall into the parched, shriveled tissues of his tongue and cheeks. He swallowed greedily, opened his mouth and swallowed again.

Beside him he heard Bear gulp as he drank, the rain falling on his buckskins with the sound of a hundred ticking clocks.

The mountain shook as thunderclaps racketed relentlessly around its peak, accompanied by lightning that scrawled across the sky like the signature of a demented god. Rain hissed like an enraged dragon and one by one the smoking cook fires winked out, leaving the ranchería to the darkness.

McBride's thirst was finally quenched but now he realized the danger of his present situation. Both he and Bear were soaked, spread-eagled in the middle of a flat meadow, lightning all around them. Searing bolts were spiking at the mountain, flaring wetly on gray sandstone, and once he saw a flash immediately followed by a roar of thunder over by the pony herd.

He arched his back and strained at his bonds until his wrists bled. The wet rawhide stretched, but not enough. The only way he would ever get free was to die as quickly as possible. In that case, the lightning, instead of a curse, could prove to be a blessing.

The storm raged for another hour. Then the thunder left, grumbling westward toward the salt flats. Lightning flickered dull scarlet within the departing clouds, touching their edges with burnished gold. The rain settled to an icy, steady downpour that fell straight from the night sky now that the wind had died to a sulky whisper.

McBride shivered and his teeth chattered. He had never been so cold in his life, not even in New York when the winter snows came and every window was etched with frost.

He turned his head and spoke to Bear. "How are you making out?"

The old scout's reply was long in coming and

when it did, his voice rattled. "I'm freezing. I reckon even the Apache women's fire would feel mighty good about now."

McBride smiled but let it go. If Bear could make an attempt at humor, he was all right. But come sunup, that would all change. The Apaches would be back. . . .

At some point in the night, he never knew when, McBride drifted into a restless sleep. He dreamed of fire.

The dark was just giving way to a gray dawn when he was shaken awake. A man crouched over him, dressed in a rubber poncho glistening with rain. He wore a cavalry slouch hat, crossed sabers on the up-turned brim, and he was smiling under a bristling dragoon mustache.

The man put a finger to his lips, then quickly cut McBride free. Another soldier already had Bear up on his feet.

"Captain Miles Fowlis, Ninth Cavalry," McBride's rescuer whispered. "Can you walk?"

McBride nodded. Over the officer's shoulder he saw black troopers silently deploying into two lines outside the wickiups. They were short men for the most part, since the U.S. Cavalry preferred its enlisted men small.

Fowlis nodded toward a pile of boulders at the edge of the meadow. "You and your friend get over there. You'll be safer among the rocks when the shooting starts."

McBride did as he was told, Bear trotting stiffly

behind him. They wedged themselves between a couple of boulders and watched the captain walk over to his troop.

The front line was kneeling, and had their Springfield carbines to their shoulders. The rear line stood. McBride estimated there were sixty officers and men in the troop and several Indian scouts. Every rifle was trained on the wickiups.

A minute ticked slowly by, the soldiers immobile in the teeming rain, then another. Captain Fowlis found himself a place at the end of the line and drew his revolver. He threw back his head and yelled.

"Fire!"

A shattering roar of rifle fire and a hail of .45-70 bullets rattled into the wickiups.

McBride heard women scream and then the scramble of moccasined feet as warriors reached for their weapons.

Now the troopers were pouring steady fire into the Apache shelters. Bullets flew so thick and fast that their clatter through willow and bear grass and the rolling thunder of carbines drowned out the sound of the rain.

Warriors threw aside hide doors and leaped outside, only to be immediately shot down. McBride saw the Apache with the broken jaw make a run for the horse herd. An officer tracked him with his revolver, then shot him. The man dropped, spinning, into the wet grass.

Mingan, the Mimbreno war chief, made it outside. His chest was covered with blood, but McBride could not tell if he'd been hit or if the blood belonged to somebody else. The Apache screamed his rage and threw a lance at the closest trooper. The iron point crashed through the soldier's chest and stuck out a hand's breadth from his back. Mingan grabbed for his holstered revolver but a dozen rifles immediately cut him down. He died, his face twisted in fury, the hate still strong in him.

A woman, a baby in her arms, saw Mingan's death. Her face terrified, she frantically tried to scramble out of her wickiup. She and her child were shot several times and they disappeared back inside. A trooper fell, hit by an Apache firing a Colt from his doorway. The Indian's chest blossomed scarlet as answering cavalry bullets found him and he crumpled onto his side.

The screaming from the wickiups had lessened, but the troopers kept up their fire, reloading steadily with practiced ease. After a few more minutes the screams of the women and children began to die away . . . then stopped entirely.

Captain Fowlis barked an order and the troopers began to tear down the wickiups. Scattered carbine fire followed as soldiers started to shoot the wounded and the dying.

McBride turned to Bear, his face gray with shock. "He's killing the women and children."

"He's killing everybody." The old man shrugged. "That's how it's done."

"No!" McBride yelled. He sprinted across the clearing. Captain Fowlis had his back turned to him. McBride grabbed the officer's shoulders and spun him around to face him.

"At least let the children go!" he yelled.

Fowlis' face was like stone, his blue eyes hard. "Nits make lice," he snapped. "My orders are to kill every Apache in this ranchería." He glanced icily at McBride's bunched fists on his shoulders. "Now unhand me."

McBride ran past the officer, toward the troopers. "Stop it! Stop it!" he yelled.

As the soldiers turned baffled eyes on him, McBride heard the captain snap, "Sergeant Johnston!"

McBride heard running boots behind him but before he could turn, something hard crashed into the back of his head . . . and the ground rose up and swallowed him.

McBride's eyes fluttered open. He was lying on his back near the boulders. The rain had stopped and he smelled coffee and frying bacon.

"Is he all right?" It was Captain Fowlis' voice.

"He's got a bump the size of a turkey egg on his head, Cap'n," Bear answered. "But I reckon he'll live. He's got a thick skull."

"Good," Fowlis said. "Excellent."

McBride sat up groggily, looking around him. There was no sun, but by the quickening light, he judged the time to be around noon.

"How are you feeling, McBride?" Fowlis asked. "I'm sorry for the unpleasantness, but interfering with an officer in the performance of his duty is a serious offense." He coughed. "But we're all a little overexcited and I'm willing to overlook your behavior this once."

McBride found it difficult to form his words, but when he did he refused to back down. "You killed the women and the children. What kind of man are you?"

"I'm the kind of man who becomes an officer in the United States Army and the kind of man who follows orders." He abruptly turned to Bear. "Are your horses with the pony herd?"

"I guess so, Cap'n."

"Then I suggest you cut them out. I plan to kill all the Apache ponies and the dogs. I was ordered to leave nothing alive in this stinking ranchería and, by God, that's what I fully intend to do." His eyes angled to McBride. "My troopers will feed you. Now I must bid you good day."

But the captain caught sight of one of his officers and lingered. "Second Lieutenant Armstrong," he yelled. "Come here if you please."

Armstrong was a fresh-faced young man who looked to be about nineteen and he still retained the spit and polish that suggested he was just out of West Point.

"What's the butcher's bill, Lieutenant?"

"Sir, Trooper Dewey is dead and I believe Corporal King won't last out the hour."

"And the Apaches?"

"Eleven warriors killed, sir, plus one other who may have already been dead before our attack."

"And the rest?"

"Twenty dead. Six squaws, the rest children. There were no old people."

Fowlis absorbed this for a few moments, then

smiled. "We've done an excellent morning's work, Lieutenant."

Armstrong snapped off a sharp salute, his face impassive. "As you say, sir."

After Fowlis left, Bear said, "Well, he did save your life, John. And mine."

McBride spat, as though to get rid of a bad taste in his mouth. "He's a murderer."

Bear smiled and shook his head. "No, John. Kill one man and you are a murderer. Kill hundreds or thousands or tens of thousands and you're a conqueror. Captain Fowlis will be hailed as a hero and get a medal for this."

"Maybe so, but I'd like to put a bullet in him."

"Ah, the worm turns. The pot scrubber becomes a gunfighter again."

McBride thought about that and said, "No, Bear, the worm hasn't turned. Now more than ever I'm all through with guns and killing. It's high time I got back to the El Coyote Azul and my fat ladies."

Later, as McBride and Bear rode into the arroyo, rifles were firing and the ponies were dying.

Chapter 12

McBride and Bear put their horses up at the livery stable. There was no sign of Jim Drago. But Bear insisted on stopping at the general store for tobacco, and when he and McBride stepped inside, the little man was standing at the counter.

Drago was examining a pair of expensive boots, hand tooled and adorned with the Texas star.

". . . standing on my shelf for a year or more," the store owner was saying. "Those boots were made for John Wesley Hardin himself, but he never picked them up and I bought them down Dallas way."

"How much?" the dwarf asked.

The gray-haired man behind the counter pretended to think about it, but McBride was pretty certain he already had a figure in mind.

"For a pair of boots like that, sixty stitches to the inch using an awl so fine the bootmaker could stick his finger with it and not bleed, for boots like that—"

"How much?" Drago snapped.

The storekeeper read something in the little man's eyes he didn't like. He said quickly, "A hundred dollars. And that's me letting them go to you at cost, Jim."

"You're a liar," Drago said.

For the first time the dwarf turned and looked at McBride and Bear. "Well, well, well, look what the cat just drug in." He smirked. "Been out riding, have you? Maybe you met Manuel Cortez on the trail, huh?"

Behind the counter the storekeeper looked like he'd been slapped, his lips white and pinched. In the West, to call a man a liar was the worst kind of insult, and a shooting matter. But the gray-haired man was afraid of Drago and it showed.

McBride decided to intervene, but Bear was on the prod and spoke first: "Drago, where does a dirty lowlife like you, a man who consorts with rats, get the money to buy boots like those?"

"That's for me to know," Drago said defensively. His right hand was inching behind his back to his waistband.

The muzzle of Bear's Henry rose a couple of inches until it was pointed right at Drago's navel. "In my life I've killed seven men, one very recently," he said. "I don't mind adding half a man to my score."

McBride was watching Drago's face. He saw something flicker in his eyes, anger certainly, and something else . . . wariness. The little man must know that if he drew on Bear Miller, he'd be dead before his gun cleared.

Then Drago confirmed it. "Not today, Miller," he said, letting his hand drop to his side. "Soon, but not today."

"Like I told you before, I'll be waiting," Bear said. He kept his gun on the man.

Drago swung away, reached into his pocket and dropped two shining double eagles onto the counter. He grabbed the boots. "Thanks."

"But that's only half what I asked for, you little—"

Drago swung the boots, the hard, two-inch heels slamming against the storekeeper's left cheekbone, opening a deep cut that bled immediately. "When I want lip from a damned grocery clerk, I'll ask for it," he snarled.

The dwarf, his face black with rage, elbowed between McBride and Bear and stalked out of the store. The man behind the counter was holding a wadded handkerchief to his face. It was stained red.

"Someday," Bear said, looking at Drago's receding back as he walked in the direction of the livery, "I'll kill that man."

"I'll dance on his grave when you do," the storekeeper said.

After Bear got his tobacco he walked to the cantina with McBride. They stepped inside and were immediately assailed by female wails from the kitchen.

The men exchanged puzzled glances. Then McBride crossed the floor and walked into the kitchen, Bear at his heels.

The two fat ladies sat at an empty table. McBride noted that all the shelves were empty as well.

One of the women rose to her feet, tears staining her plump cheeks.

"What's wrong?" McBride asked.

The woman looked at him blankly and Bear said, "¿Qué está equivocado?"

Throwing up her arms, the fat lady launched into a long tirade in Spanish, punctuated by sobbing and more tears. When she was all used up she flopped down at the table and buried her face in her hands. At once the other woman jumped to her feet and took up where the first one had left off.

Finally Bear, using a lot of cooing and tut-tutting noises, got the women calmed down. Then he turned to McBride, grinning. "You want the whole kit an' caboodle, or only the gist of it?"

"Break it down, for God's sake," McBride said, horrified.

"Well, near as I can tell, you ran out of food the day before yesterday. The young ladies say they're missing their last six meals and they're already fading away." Bear's grin stretched wider. "I'd say they're down to about three-fifty apiece, poor things."

McBride was not in the mood for humor. Having no food to cook for the paying customers was a disaster. "What else did they say?"

Bear looked down at the women, asked them a question in Spanish and listened intently to their answers. He turned back to McBride. "They went to the general store for supplies, but Jed McKay—that's the man Drago hit—refused to give them credit." Bear frowned. "After that it gets a tad hazy on account of how McKay don't have much Spanish. But, again, the gist of it is that Manuel Cortez skipped town owing McKay eighty dollars and he won't extend any more credit to the El Coyote Azul until the debt is paid." After a moment's hesitation he added, "In full."

McBride was stricken. He didn't have eighty dollars. He didn't have twenty dollars. Or ten. Without flour, beans, beef, salt, coffee, spices . . . mescal . . . beer—the list ground on remorselessly in McBride's head—he couldn't feed his paying customers.

Hope flared in him like a bright star. "Bear, ask them how many customers we've had since I've been gone."

Bear asked the question in Spanish and even McBride understood the women's answer. *"Nada."*

The star flared and blinked out.

"Boy, I'd say you're in a heap of trouble," Bear said, stating the obvious.

"I'll talk to McKay," McBride said.

Bear's face creased into a grim smile. "You didn't see him at his best today, John. The Poisoned Dwarf has a way of doing that to people. Ordinarily Jed McKay is a mean, grasping man who would wrench the last nickel out of a widow woman's hand and watch her orphans starve. He ain't about to forgive and forget an eighty-dollar debt."

"I'll talk to him."

Bear shrugged. "Suit yourself."

McBride stepped out of the kitchen and behind him the women's wails began anew. He would talk to McKay. But he felt like a man about to put his head in a hangman's noose.

* * *

The cut on Jed McKay's cheek had stopped bleeding, but the blow from Drago had left a nasty arc-shaped cut that looked red and raw. The skin around the cut was swollen and purplish blue in color.

McKay nodded but showed no hint of recognition when the big man stepped into the store. McBride was wearing his suit coat, freshly brushed, celluloid collar and tie and plug hat, hoping to present as businesslike an appearance as possible.

"What can I do for you?" McKay asked.

McBride smiled. He pointed to the cut on his cheek from the Apache knife. "I've got the same injury." He was desperately trying to form a bond with McKay.

It didn't work.

"What can I do for you?" the man asked again, disinterest in his eyes but a slight edge to his voice.

"I'm John McBride, the new proprietor of the El Coyote Azul."

"You've come to pay your debt, huh?"

McBride forced a grin. This was starting off badly.

"No, I'm here to ask you for an extended line of credit. Once the cantina starts to prosper, I—"

"Mr. McBride, you already owe me eighty dollars." McKay placed his hands on the counter beside the cigar case. He leaned forward. "Further credit is out of the question."

The man was as unbending as steel, but McBride tried again.

"Mr. McKay, that debt was owed by the former proprietor of the cantina, one Manuel Cortez, now deceased. As the new owner I am hardly responsible for his debts."

The storekeeper showed a spark of surprise. "Cortez is dead?"

"Yes, he sold his place to me, then left town and—"

"Say no more." McKay held up his hands, shaking his head. "It's forbidden for anyone to leave Suicide."

"I did, a few days ago."

"You are a newcomer and perhaps the rule doesn't apply to you."

His credit momentarily forgotten, McBride was intrigued. "Who made this rule?"

McKay's face closed down. "Will that be all?"

Further questions about the rule would go nowhere and McBride knew it. He changed tack. "About Cortez—"

McKay sighed, a long, drawn-out whine that rattled phlegm in his chest. "The state of Mr. Cortez's mortality is neither here nor there. The debt was incurred when I gave him credit to purchase supplies for his restaurant. Therefore it is the debt of the El Coyote Azul, which you, as the new proprietor, are duty bound to honor."

"Allow me just a little longer," McBride pleaded. "I'm sure the cantina will soon be prospering."

"Splendid! When it is, you can come settle your debt to me, Mr. McBride. Now, good day to you, sir."

Defeated, his pride sagging around his ankles like dropped pants, McBride turned and stepped to the door. McKay's voice stopped him.

"There is one thing."

"What's that?" McBride asked, fearing more bad news.

"Earlier today you witnessed my unfortunate incident with Jim Drago." McKay's fingers strayed to his damaged cheek. His gray eyes were hard and tight, like bullets peering out of the cylinder of a Colt. "The dwarf owes me fifty dollars. I want it."

"That's no concern of mine," McBride said, his run-in with the storekeeper still smarting. He turned to go.

"Wait, John McBride! I know who you are."

McBride smiled. "So do I. I'm the man who just asked you for credit and was refused."

McKay ignored that. "You're a gunfighter out of the Colorado Picketwire country, sometimes known as the Tenderfoot Kid. You're the man who killed Hack Burns, him who carried the Mark of Cain on his face."

"I'm the proprietor of the El Coyote Azul," McBride said stiffly. "Nothing more." He walked away and McKay called out after him.

"Get my fifty dollars back from the dwarf and I'll cancel your debt and extend you a six-month line of credit."

McBride stopped. For a few moments there was silence, McKay's chesty wheeze the only sound. "You're a vengeful man, McKay," he said suddenly.

"Yes I am. And you are a desperate one."

The truth cut McBride like a bullwhip. "I'll get your damned money," he said.

Chapter 13

Clouds crowded the sky, sending the sun into hiding, as John McBride walked to the livery stable, a cold wind pinching at his nose and ears. Echoing from the blacksmith's shop he heard the clang of a hammer on iron, and as he passed the saloon, a bald man with bushy sideburns stepped outside and threw a bucket of dirty water into the street.

The man glanced at McBride, looked again, then stood watching him for long moments before he turned back into the saloon.

For his part, McBride saw nothing. He walked, deep in thought, his head bent against the wind. The last thing in the world he wanted was a fight with Jim Drago. He planned to be polite, businesslike and above all show no aggression.

"Mr. McKay down at the general store would like the fifty dollars you owe him for the boots. He's sure it just slipped your mind."

Yes, something like that. To the point, but real neighborly, as though he were talking to kinfolk.

He conjured up a mental picture of Drago, the small, deformed body, huge head and the man's permanent, ferocious scowl. He was poison all right, but the very existence of the cantina was at stake and with it the fate of his young Chinese charges. He could not fail. One way or another he had to get the money from Drago.

One way or another . . .

The stable door creaked as McBride pushed it open. The interior was dim and no lamps were lit. The place was quiet, ominous, the shadows angled sharply and dark, full of mystery. Unarmed as he was, McBride knew he was hanging himself out to dry, but he breathed away his butterflies and hollered, "Drago! Jim Drago!"

The response was immediate. "What the hell do you want, McBride?"

Was the dwarf watching him or had he only recognized the Yankee twang?

"We need to talk, Jim," McBride said into the gray half-light, throwing his voice to reach to the rear of the barn where the black rats scuttled.

"We got nothing to say to each other."

"I need a favor, Jim." The words tasted like lye soap in McBride's mouth.

A long silence. McBride could sense the little man's astonishment. Then a laugh, a high, grating screech filled with scorn and malice.

"You want a favor from me? That'll be the day."

Drago emerged from the gloom. His left hand was stuck inside one of the fancy Texas boots and the other held a yellow polishing cloth. "I asked you before, McBride, what do you want?"

He had rehearsed it; now McBride said it aloud. "Jim, Mr. McKay down at the general store would like the fifty dollars you owe him for the boots. He's sure it just slipped your mind."

Drago stared at him coldly, without expression. He asked, "Did he send you here to collect?"

"I'm . . . ah . . . acting as his agent in this matter."

"The fifty I gave him was too much. These boots ain't even worth twenty-five."

"Still," McBride said, "Mr. McKay's price was one hundred dollars."

Drago let his hands drop to his side. He was holding the boot and cloth. "McBride, you go to hell. And take that other idiot McKay with you."

John McBride's pride had already taken a pounding that day and now something snapped inside him. "Listen, Drago, you piece of trash, give me the fifty dollars or I'll hammer you into the ground like a tenpenny nail."

He knew how it would happen and it did. Drago dropped the cloth even as his right hand was moving behind him. McBride covered the distance between them with a few long strides. He saw the Colt come up and chopped down with the blade of his right hand onto Drago's wrist. The little man squealed and the revolver dropped from his numb fingers, thudding into the dirt.

Displaying amazing speed and agility, Drago turned

and vaulted over a stall partition. He came up with a pitchfork in his hand and threw it like a spear at McBride. The big man stepped quickly to his right and the fork sang through the air where his head had been a split second earlier.

McBride charged, but Drago easily eluded him. The dwarf ran out of the stall and scrambled swiftly up the ladder to the hayloft. McBride went after him. Drago had found another pitchfork and as McBride's head appeared, he jabbed at him. The big man ducked and the tines of the fork rammed an inch into the timber frame around the opening.

Drago was desperately trying to free the pitchfork as McBride reappeared. He grabbed the fork and pushed it up and away from him, wood splintering as the tines ripped free. McBride threw the pitchfork into the shadows and began to climb into the loft. Drago screeched and aimed a kick at his head. The little man's feet were bare and McBride grabbed Drago's ankle as his foot swung toward him. He yanked upward and the dwarf crashed onto his back. McBride descended the ladder, dragging Drago after him. The little man's head hit every rung and he was dazed by the time McBride reached the ground.

Anger flared in McBride. Drago had tried to kill him twice and he felt no mercy toward him. He was a tall man, strong in the arms and wrists, and he bent, grabbed the dwarf's ankles and held him upside down, shaking him. Coins tumbled from Drago's pockets onto the dirt and McBride said, breathing hard, "When the pile reaches fifty dollars I'll stop."

Drago was screaming at the top of his lungs, angry curses mixed with threats. "I'll kill you for this, McBride!" he screeched. "I'll shoot you down in the street like a dog."

McBride shook Drago harder, an up-and-down motion that made the little man's head bounce and more money to spill from his pockets.

"Has it reached fifty dollars yet, Drago, huh?" McBride asked. His arms were tiring but his anger would not let him quit.

"Please, Mr. McBride, let that man go."

Startled, McBride turned and saw the biggest black man he'd ever seen in his life—or white man either, come to that. He stood almost seven foot tall with huge hands that dangled from the sleeves of a black frock coat that was three sizes too small for him.

The man, who looked to be around sixty, was smiling, teeth very white against a skin as dark as ebony. His hair was cut short, gray at the sides, and the expression on his broad face was one of benign concern. However, the cocked Greener scattergun pointed at McBride's belly was much less affable.

McBride let go of the little man's ankles and Drago thudded to the ground in a heap. Immediately he got onto his hands and knees and scrabbled in the dirt, searching for his gun. "I'll kill you, McBride!" he squealed. "I'll kill you!"

"That will do, Drago," the black man said. His voice was deep and pleasant, like the boom of a draped bass drum. "Give the gentleman his fifty dollars and run along."

Drago had found his gun. But he had no intention

of using it. Whoever the huge black man was, he had intimidated the Poison Dwarf, and that was not an easy thing to do.

The little man picked up the coins at McBride's feet and counted two double-eagles into his open hand. Like the ones he'd spent at the general store, the coins looked brand-new. McBride held one of them between his thumb and forefinger and checked the date. It read 1872. That was ten years ago, but the shining gold coin looked like it had never been used.

"Go now, Drago," the black man said.

The dwarf's glance lifted to McBride's face. He didn't speak. He didn't have to. Everything he wanted to say to the tall man was writ large in his blazing black eyes: "One day I'll kill you." The threat Drago's glance revealed was as simple as that.

The black man watched Drago leave. Then he eased down the hammers of his shotgun. "You can never be too careful around that man," he said. "Jim Drago can be notional." He smiled. "But then, so can you, Mr. McBride." He took a couple of steps closer. "My name is Moses. I work for Miz Elliot."

McBride stuck out his hand but the man called Moses backed away from it. "No, Mr. McBride, suh. I'm only a humble servant in the big house and it would neither be fitting nor proper for me to shake your hand."

There was an echo of remembered slavery in the man's statement and McBride did not push it. He dropped his hand and asked, "What can I do for you, Moses?"

"Miz Elliot presents her compliments and says

she'll expect you for dinner tomorrow evening at seven."

McBride felt a thrill of excitement. Finally he was going to meet the lovely Miss Elliot. If the evening went well he could elicit her opinion on the murder of Manuel Cortez and ask her about the mysterious rule that, once settled in Suicide, no one can ever leave.

"Tell Miss Elliot I'm delighted to accept her kind invitation," he said.

Moses nodded. Then he said, "As Miz Elliot's guest there are certain rules she expects you to abide by. I hope you don't mind." It seemed Moses didn't much care if McBride minded or not, because he added without pause, "You must come unarmed. You must not wear cologne or other perfumes and until tomorrow evening you should avoid contact with animals, including dogs and cats. While in Miz Elliot's house you should refrain from foul language, tobacco chewing or smoking and any comment that might be perceived by Miz Elliot as amatory innuendo. Nor will you discuss politics or religion."

Moses had obviously learned his mistress' house rules by rote, and now McBride smiled. "I shall be happy to avoid all those social miscues," he said.

Moses nodded again and tucked the Greener under his arm. "Until tomorrow evening, then."

He turned and left as quietly as he had come, a giant of a man who moved like a panther.

McBride watched Moses go and shook his head, grinning. Dinner with Miss Allison Elliot was shaping up to be an interesting experience.

Chapter 14

"I'm a man of my word, McBride," Jed McKay said. "I will cancel Manuel Cortez's debt to me and extend your line of credit for six months from this date." McKay gave McBride a sly glance. "Though I was hoping you'd put a bullet into that little piece of dirt."

"It didn't work out that way," McBride said. He was grateful for the credit but decided he didn't like McKay much. "I need flour, salt—"

"Hold on there," the storekeeper said. "We have another matter to discuss."

"We have?"

"Yes, a very pressing matter."

Feeling he owed it to McKay to be pleasant, McBride said, "I'm listening."

McKay had been arranging small burlap bags of ground coffee on the counter. Now he stopped and his eyes lifted to McBride's face. "I've called a meeting of the concerned citizens of the town for six o'clock this evening. It will be held here in my store."

McBride grinned. "I didn't think there were any concerned citizens in Suicide."

"Then you thought wrong," McKay snapped. He waited until the tall man's grin faded to a suitable look of interest and said, "Adam Whitehead the blacksmith is concerned and so is Clyde Kaleen the saloon owner. They'll both be here tonight. So will Nathan Levy who owns the hotel and a dozen or so other men who make their living in or around town."

"No women?" McBride asked.

"Conrad Heber has a wife and so does John Wright. Heber lives in a shack near the creek and brews beer for the saloon. Wright is a carpenter. We had another carpenter here, a man by the name of Weiss, but he was killed two years back."

McKay read the question in McBride's eyes and answered it. "He tried to leave Suicide."

"The rule, huh?"

McKay nodded. "Yes, the rule."

"Whose rule?"

"We don't know, but some of us have our suspicions. You'll learn more tonight."

"McKay, I really don't think—"

"You want the El Coyote Azul to prosper, don't you?"

"Of course."

"The men who will be here tonight can help you make that happen."

Knowing full well he was making up McBride's mind for him, McKay said, "Flour, salt . . . and what else can I get for you?"

*　　　*　　　*

A couple of cow ponies were standing three-legged outside the cantina when McBride carried in his supplies.

Two bearded men, who wore low-slung Colts and had a watchful wariness about them, were drinking mescal at the bar and divided their time between keeping their eyes on McBride and ogling the generous cleavage revealed by one of the fat ladies. After fifteen minutes they paid and left.

Business, McBride decided, was picking up. The money of outlaws on the dodge was as good as anybody else's.

McKay had promised to deliver a new barrel of mescal within three days, and, judging by the joyful reception of the supplies by the fat ladies, the stove fires would be lit very soon.

McBride smiled inwardly as he donned his apron, grabbed a corn broom and began to sweep the floor. Now he had a line of credit at the general store and the word was seemingly getting around to outlaws and drifters that his cantina was a safe place to visit, his business success was all but assured.

But then Papan Morales rode into town and suddenly all that changed.

"Senor McBride, please to step outside."

The summons drifted through the cantina door, vaguely polite but demanding.

McBride propped the broom on a table and walked into the street. A small, slender man sat a tall roan horse, his face shaded by a wide Mexican sombrero. The man wore the tight pants and short jacket of a vaquero, but no ordinary rider could have afforded the silver-plated, ivory-handled Colts that hung on his thighs.

"Ah, Senor McBride, it is so good we meet at last. My name is Papan Morales and I am your very good friend."

McBride was puzzled. He'd never seen this man before in his life. He gestured toward the door of the cantina. "There are mescal and food inside."

"Ah, yes, that is good. That is very good. But, alas, Papan is not in the fair town of Suicide to eat or drink mescal. No, I am here to discover if the generosity of the late owner"—here he made a hurried sign of the cross and raised his eyes skyward—"is excelled only by your own."

His confusion growing, McBride asked, "Are you collecting for charity or something?"

"Senor, charity begins at home." Morales' teeth flashed white under his thin mustache. "No, I am here for the angel's share."

McBride was aware that Jed McKay was standing outside his store, looking at him. Whitehead, the blacksmith, had laid down his hammer, his eyes also intent on McBride and the Mexican.

"I don't understand," McBride said, thinking that no good was about to come of this.

"Of course you don't understand," Morales said, his thin, hard face concerned. "How could you understand when you have only newly become the owner of this fine establishment?" The Mexican leaned forward in the saddle. "I will explain it to you.

"Senor McBride, this land around us is very dangerous, the haunt of outlaws and Apaches. Many people have died or been robbed of all they own. Now, my boss is a very great man. His name is Angel Guerrero and he pondered deeply and for a very long time about how he could protect the people of this town from bandits and Indians. After confessing his sins to a holy priest, he spent many days in prayer and then God came up with a bold plan.

" 'Angel, you yourself must protect the people of Suicide from all who would do them harm,' God said, smiling down on him.

"From that day forth, out of the generosity of his heart, that is what Angel has done. He has protected this town."

Morales smiled. "Now, even saints like my boss have to eat and he has many men to support. So God told him to collect a small fee for his services and call it the angel's share."

The Mexican settled back in the saddle and spread his arms, palms upward. "And that is why Papan is here. To collect the angel's share."

"How much might that be?" McBride asked.

"Ah, a good question, senor. Why, it might be five hundred dollars every month, but it is not. It might be two hundred, but it is not. No, Angel Guerrero is a generous man. He collects only from the business establishments in town and his fee is a pittance, a mere hundred American dollars every month."

Morales held out a hand. "And now, senor, if you will give me the angel's share, I'll be on my way."

"Papan, is that your name?" McBride asked, a slow-burning anger rising in him.

"Si, Papan, that is my name and the name of my father before me and of his father before him."

"Have you ever heard of New York, Papan?" McBride asked.

Now it was the Mexican's turn to be puzzled. "Sure, it is a big city, far, far from here."

"Know what they call the angel's share in New York? It's called a protection racket. Lowlife scum, just like you and your boss, use it to prey on the weak and the frightened and extort their hard-earned money. Well, mister, I'm not weak and you don't scare me a bit. Now, ride on out of here and tell Guerrero he won't get a penny out of me."

"Ooh, senor, this is very bad for you, I think," Morales said. "Angel will be very hurt and when he is hurt, he does evil things that he later regrets."

"Tell him I won't give the devil his due," McBride said. "Tell him that, and something else—tell him to go to hell."

Morales grinned, his eyes on fire. "I will tell him, senor. Soon Angel will talk to you himself." He swung his horse away and called over his shoulder, "With his gun."

Jed McKay walked hurriedly down the street and yelled, "McBride, wait up!"

A few drops of slanting sleet splattered against him as he stepped next to the tall man and said, "Angel Guerrero is one of the subjects we'll bring up tonight." He watched McBride nod, then added, "Be on your guard. You've just made yourself an almighty dangerous enemy."

Chapter 15

McBride was about to walk back into the El Coyote Azul when shouts from the street stopped him. McKay had also come to a halt. He was watching heavily loaded freight wagons slowly emerge through the blowing gray veil of the sleet storm.

The wagons, three in number, were carrying buffalo bones and dead men.

A bearded man was standing in the lead wagon, the lines of his eight-mule team in one hand, the other cupped around his mouth.

"Apaches!" the mule skinner yelled, a mindless hysteria spiking his voice. "Oh, my God, Huck Benson is dead. Ed Warner is dead. Ol' Bill Henry is behind us on the grass, kilt an' scalped. They took Zeke Bryant an' by now he's wishin' he was dead. Oh, God! Oh, God!"

McKay, who looked angry as his fear turned on him, grabbed the bridle of the lead mule and halted the team. "Get control of yourself, man," he hollered. "Where are the Apaches?"

The mule skinner looked down at McKay and waved a hand. "Behind us somewhere. We met a Tonto scout on the trail who was lighting a shuck for home. He said the Apaches ambushed a company of Negro hoss sodjers earlier today, killed five and wounded twice that many."

"Where is the cavalry now?" McKay asked.

"Skedaddled. The Tonto said they're headed south, carrying their captain over his saddle."

The wind was rising and the floppy brim of the mule skinner's hat was pushed up against the crown. His face was ashen and sleet whitened his mustache and beard, giving him the look of a frightened ghost. Several other mule skinners had left their wagons and were drifting closer. They were looking at McKay but their hollow eyes were seeing nothing, haunted by the memory of what had happened to them.

A fight with loco Apaches was not a thing a man could soon forget.

"Luke, you carryin' wounded?"

Bear Miller had stepped beside McBride.

The eyes of the man called Luke widened in recognition. "Oh, howdy, Bear. Yeah, we got a youngster in the last wagon. He's gut shot an' he won't live." The man's glance searched Bear's face as though he was seeking an answer to a question. Finally he said, "We lost three wagons, had a two-hour runnin' fight with them savages."

"You kill any?" McKay asked harshly.

Luke shook his head. "I don't reckon so. I think maybe I winged one, but I ain't sure." The mule skinner's eyes angled back to Bear. "Ol' Bill Henry is dead, Bear. You remember him, kinda quiet-spoken feller. He won't be playin' his fiddle no more."

"You still got your scalp, Luke," Bear said. "Be thankful for that." His glance shifted to the mule skinners standing by Luke's wagon. "You men, bring that wounded boy into the cantina. I've done a heap of doctoring in my time. Maybe I can do something for him."

It took a few moments for the old scout's words to register with the mule skinners. They stood looking at him dully, their eyes so expressionless they could have been painted onto their faces. At last several of the men turned and shuffled in the direction of the rear wagon.

Bear turned to McBride and said, loud enough for the mule skinners to hear, "John, these men look like they could use a drink. You still got mescal?"

"Enough." McBride's eyes lifted to Luke, cold, wet sleet lashing around him. "You and the other men come inside."

Both fat ladies tended bar, dishing out equal measures of mescal and sympathy to the stunned, speechless men crowding around them.

McBride had the mule skinners lay the wounded boy on a table. He was a freckled youngster who looked to be no more than fourteen. But he had sand. Gasping breaths hissed between his gritted teeth as he tried to bear a pain that was unbearable. In a world of hard men, he desperately wanted to prove that he was worthy to be counted among them.

"What's your name, boy?" McBride asked.

Luke stepped beside him, a cup of mescal in his hand. "That's no good. He can't hear you. He can't talk either, and if he has a name, I never knew it."

"He's a deaf mute?"

"If that's what you call it."

"Does he have folks, back where you come from?"

Luke shook his head. "Far as I can tell, he's an orphan. He signed on with us as a bone picker at our camp up on the Black River. That was six months ago an' he done his share without complaint."

The mule skinner lifted the boy's head and put the cup to his lips. "Drink boy," he said. "It will ease the pain." Luke helped the boy drink, coughing on the fiery mescal, then gently laid his head back on the table. "He don't know a word I said, but he knows what mescal is all right."

"Three dead and if Zeke Bryant ain't dead by now, and I hope to God he is, two dying," Luke said. "All we wanted to do was to hunt the plains for buffalo bones and take 'em to a railhead someplace to be ground up into fertilizer, make us a few dollars maybe." His troubled eyes searched McBride's face. "Why did the Apaches kill us for that? Do you know?"

"I don't think the Apaches need a reason for killing," McBride answered. "Or if they do, the fact that you were white men was reason enough."

The wounded boy had gone quiet and Bear Miller had been listening to McBride.

"It ain't that simple, John. Some Apaches want to live in peace with the white man, but most don't. There's already been too much killing to ever go back. When an Apache has seen his wife shot down by soldiers, his children tossed on the points of bayonets, he becomes a loco Indian and he'll fight the white man until one or both of them are dead.

"Now, with a few exceptions, the blancos don't want peace either. They've seen their cabins burned, their wives and children butchered, and they've become loco themselves. I reckon the fighting and killing will never end until all the Apaches are dead or all the white men. The trouble with that, as far as the Indians are concerned, is that there are few Apaches and a lot of white men. And the whites will keep on a-coming right at them, no matter how many are killed."

To McBride's surprise McKay was standing at his shoulder. "That is yet another topic of discussion for tonight's meeting," he said. "If the bone picker is right and the cavalry has retreated, Suicide is wide-open to attack. We need to form a militia."

Bear laughed without humor. "Look around this place, McKay. You don't have enough men to form a decent-sized posse, let alone a militia."

"The mule skinners might be persuaded to stay," McKay suggested, plainly irritated at Bear doubting him.

Luke shook his head. "Not us. We've had our fill of Apaches. After we see this boy buried decent, we're moving on."

"Then we'll have to make do with the men we have, that's all," McKay said. He turned to McBride. "I'll see you at the meeting."

After the storekeeper was gone, Bear said, "I don't like that man."

"I don't much like him either," McBride said. "But right now I need him."

The wounded boy began to groan, clutching at his belly, his lips white with pain. Bear slipped the youngster's suspenders off his thin shoulders and lowered his pants. The wound was a nightmare, a ragged bullet hole so large the intestines were coiling out of it.

McBride heard Bear's sharp intake of breath and realized the boy was beyond saving.

The old scout lifted bleak eyes to Luke. "In about another fifteen minutes or so, he'll start screaming. The pain will be bad, beyond anything he has ever imagined, and it could last for hours, maybe days." He hesitated. "Luke, you're the nearest thing to kinfolk he has."

Luke had seen the wound and he knew he was being asked a question. McBride saw the man's inward struggle and felt his pain. The mule skinner was a hard, uncompromising man and the life he led was one of backbreaking labor, few comforts and little joy. But even he was hesitant to make the final decision.

As it happened, the dying boy made up his mind for him. Brave as he was, he could no longer dam up the floodtide waves of pain that swept over him. As Bear had predicted, he shrieked in agony, a primal scream that turned every head in the room in his direction. And he kept on screaming.

The eyes of Luke and Bear met. The mule skinner swallowed hard, and nodded.

Bear drew his Colt and looked down at the youngster. Somehow the boy knew and he nodded, even struggling to form words he could not speak. Bear's brown, gnarled hand gently moved from the boy's sweating forehead, over his eyes, closing them.

Quickly he shoved the muzzle of his gun into the center of the youngster's chest and pulled the trigger.

The kid's last scream provided a fearsome counterpoint to the reverberating roar of the revolver, echoes of both chasing each other around the sudden, singing silence of the room.

Bear peered at the boy through a moving mist of powder smoke. "He's gone," he said quietly.

Over at the bar the fat ladies were sobbing and the eyes of every mule skinner were on Bear, neither angry nor accusing. To a man they knew he'd done what had to be done and they would not hold it against him.

McBride's ears were ringing from the closeness of the gunshot. Back in New York, just a few short months ago, he would have arrested Bear Miller for murder. That he understood and approved what the man had done was a fair indication of how far he had come.

This was not the city; it was the West, and out here how you took the measure of a man and judged his actions were very different.

McBride placed a hand on Bear's shoulder and squeezed, letting him know.

Chapter 16

A dozen men and two women were gathered in the back room of McKay's store when John McBride stepped inside. It was cold out and the sleet, driven by a blustering wind, had hardened into pellets of ice that stung the face and made breathing difficult.

A potbellied stove glowed cherry red in one corner of the room and as McKay made his introductions, McBride was grateful for its cozy warmth. A coffeepot bubbled on the stove, filling the room with its fragrance, and someone had brought a huge platter of doughnuts.

"Are the bone pickers gone?" Jed McKay asked him.

"Yes, they left an hour ago."

The storekeeper looked shocked. "They buried the dead boy already?"

"No, they took him with them. They said the youngster wouldn't rest easy near a town called Suicide, so they'll look for a likely spot on the prairie."

"Just as well," McKay said. "We don't need strangers buried here."

The women were using the only chairs in the room and McBride took a seat on an empty wooden crate. He accepted a cup of coffee and a doughnut from one of the women, who had been introduced to him as Mrs. Whitehead. Then he gave his attention to McKay, who was clearing his throat.

"I've called you all here tonight—"

"McKay, talk about the death of Manuel Cortez." The interruption came from John Wright, the town carpenter. He was a tall, string bean of a man with a droopy mustache and sad, hound-dog eyes.

"That matter is on the agenda for later, John," McKay said, irritated.

"Discuss it now," Wright said. "Cortez was an original, just as we all are here." The brown eyes moved to McBride, vaguely hostile. "Except for him."

"Later, John," McKay snapped, his annoyance growing. "We'll talk about Cortez later."

As though he hadn't heard, Wright said, "Sam Weiss, Charlie Hodges, Joe Beckwith, Slim Peacock, his wife Betty and their three youngsters, Dave Whipple and now Manuel Cortez. Every one of them an original and all of them murdered as they tried to leave Suicide."

The brewer Conrad Heber, a German with a round, pleasant face, massive belly and tree trunk legs, got to his feet, wheezing as he faced Wright. "John, my friend, it was the Apaches who killed poor Manuel." He turned his head to McBride. "That man found his body. Ask him who killed Herr Cortez."

Without further prompting, McBride said, "It could have been Apaches. Or it could have been person or persons unknown. Cortez was shot with a .50-caliber rifle and robbed. So far, that's all I know."

"So far?" Wright jumped on that. "What do you mean, so far? Are you investigating Cortez's death?"

"Of course he's not," McKay interrupted. "He happened to find the man's body. That's all."

McBride ignored the storekeeper and said to Wright, "You could say I'm investigating this so-called rule that no one can leave Suicide."

"That doesn't apply to you, McBride." It was Nathan Levy, small, plump and dark-eyed. "All the people who have been killed so far have been originals."

"What does that mean—originals?"

"It means the original settlers who accepted Tam Elliot's invitation to start a town here." Wright was answering for Levy. "Only it wasn't Suicide then—it was called Eden Creek. Suicide came later, after Elliot shot himself."

"Who changed the name?" McBride asked. "Surely not you originals?"

"Miss Elliot give it that name," Wright said, his face stiff. "She threatened to foreclose on all our businesses if we didn't accept it."

"What's in a name?" Jed McKay said. "Maybe by this time Miss Elliot has gotten over the death of her father and will let us change it back to Eden Creek."

"Who's going to ask her, McKay? You?" Wright asked belligerently.

"I'll ask her," McBride volunteered, mildly surprising even himself. "I have a vested interest in this town, and calling the place Suicide is bad for business."

Every eye in the room was turned to McBride, puzzled, trying to figure him out. "I've been invited to Miss Elliot's home for dinner tomorrow evening," he explained. "I'll ask her then."

"No one in this town has ever been invited to Miss Elliot's home," Wright said. "No one that is except the damned Poison Dwarf."

"Is Drago an original?" McBride asked, brushing doughnut crumbs off his mustache with the back of his hand.

"No, he came later. Not much later, but later."

"Then there's your answer. I'm not an original either."

But McBride was confused. What common ground could the beautiful, rich and presumably sophisticated Allison Elliot share with a homicidal dwarf who had the disposition of a wounded rattlesnake? Maybe he'd discover the solution to that and other questions tomorrow evening. . . .

Suddenly he became aware that John Wright was talking again.

". . . I'm through, McKay. I'm loading up and pulling out. I've had enough of Suicide to last me a lifetime."

"Don't be hasty, John," McKay said. "Things are going to change around here, I promise."

But the carpenter refused to be appeased and now he was addressing the entire meeting. "Look at us.

We're terrified to leave this place. This isn't a town, it's a corner of hell. Where are the children? How can you have a town without children? You women, Mrs. Whitehead, my wife Ann, why are there no children?"

Ann Wright was a slender, careworn woman with frightened brown eyes that seemed too large for her face. She twisted a small lace handkerchief in her white-knuckled hands. "John . . . please . . . not now."

"Tell them, Ann," Wright went on remorselessly. "Tell them how you refused to bring a child into the world that would be trapped forever in Suicide. And you, Mrs. Whitehead, didn't you have that same reason?"

Tall, thin, with an almost pretty oval face and black hair drawn back into a harsh bun, Joan Whitehead nodded, her eyes moist. "Yes, that was my reason, that and the deaths of the Peacock children." She hesitated as though trying to bolster her courage for what she had to say next. "I remembered them, all three of those children. Robert, aged nine, Marcia, aged six, little Virginia, just eighteen months. They weren't shot like their parents. Their throats were cut."

McBride saw something terrible in Joan Whitehead's eyes. The pale shadow of a dawning madness. "We all know who made the rule, who ordered the deaths of so many. And we all know that for some reason she wants to punish us." She pointed a bony forefinger in the direction of the house on the hill.

"Allison Elliot, that vile she-devil, that witch, won't be content until all of us are dead."

A stunned hush followed Mrs. Whitehead's accusation, punctuated only by her soft sobs as she buried her face in her hands. Her blacksmith husband, a man almost as big in the shoulders and chest as McBride, led her back to her seat, uttering soothing words in a language that was all his own.

Wright, his face black with anger, jumped to his feet. "I say we all leave, every man jack of us. The witch can't kill us all."

"No!"

Adam Whitehead was standing tall and terrible, one huge hand on his wife's shoulder. With his beetling eyebrows and long black beard he had the wild look of an Old Testament prophet. "Listen to me! We burn the witch. Now. Tonight. And we hang her evil familiars, the black Goliath and the hunched dwarf."

Most of the people cheered, a few even yelling, "Burn the witch!" But others, notably Nathan Levy and Conrad Heber, looked horrified.

The meeting was getting out of hand and McBride rose to his feet. Wright's idea of a mass exodus from Suicide would ruin him and he would not even consider Whitehead's mad plan. If he had to, he'd stop it.

But McKay waved at McBride to stay where he was and yelled, "Order! Order everybody! Listen, Miss Elliot harms no one except those who would rob her. She is in perpetual mourning for her dead father, no more than that. Listen to reason. She lives with grief and has no evil intent toward any of us."

"Then who is behind the rule, Herr McKay?" Heber asked.

"I don't know, but there is a man among us who could find out." Everybody looked at McBride as McKay continued, "The reason I called this meeting tonight was to offer Mr. McBride this"—he put his hand in his pocket and, with a dramatic flourish, produced a small silver shield—"the town marshal's badge."

That statement was met with another flat silence.

"But we don't even know the man!" This came from a pale figure in a black frock coat who had not spoken before.

"I know him, or at least I know of him," McKay said. "He's the new proprietor of the El Coyote Azul and he's good with a gun."

"Who says? He says?" the frock-coated man asked, smirking as he looked McBride up and down.

"He's the man who killed Hack Burns," McKay said, a hint of malice in his eyes. "Does that tell you something, Channing?"

It told Dave Channing plenty and it showed in his suddenly slack jaw and shocked eyes, but now he tried to salvage his composure. "He'd have to prove that to me."

"He doesn't have to prove anything to you," McKay snapped. "You're a professional gambler, Channing. You neither reap nor sow. Strictly speaking you shouldn't even be here tonight."

"I can leave anytime you say," Channing said. He

brushed his coat away from the handle of the Colt in his waistband. "Just be real careful how you say it."

"I've got something to say." McBride rose to his feet. "I don't want the job."

McKay smiled and nodded. "I thought that would be your response." He waved a hand around the room. "You've heard these people tonight. If they all leave, you'll be out of business. If they become a lynch mob and burn Miss Elliot's home, the law will come down on us, the outlaws on the dodge will avoid us and for all intents and purposes our town will cease to exist. Either way, Mr. McBride, you will be the loser."

Feeling trapped, McBride asked, "If I pin on the badge, what am I expected to do?"

"Nothing much. Just run undesirables out of town and preserve the peace."

"And preserving the peace means finding out who is behind the rule?"

"Yes, that's part of it. The most important part, I suppose."

"Then I'll wear the badge," McBride said. "But only until I discover who the murderer is."

"Better not take too long, McBride," Adam Whitehead said. "I propose we give this man five days to find out who killed Cortez and the others. If he doesn't, then we burn the Elliot witch and hang her familiars."

A majority wildly cheered this statement. McKay looked at McBride and said wryly, "You heard them. You've got five days, Marshal."

The gambler Dave Channing stepped closer to

McBride. "Where's your gun"—he smiled like a coiled snake—"Marshal?"

"I don't need a gun."

Channing struck a pose, his thumbs in his gun belt. "One time I knew a town marshal who said that very thing. A week later they cut off his head and paraded it around town on a pole."

"That won't happen here," McKay said quickly.

And just as quickly he handed McBride the badge.

Chapter 17

Compared to the ornate gold shield he'd worn in New York, the badge of the town marshal of Suicide was a crude piece of work. Tinned iron, McBride guessed, and it read, misspelled, SHERRIF, not MARSHAL.

He pinned the badge to his shirt, making him the only lawman in maybe twenty miles in all directions—an acting, unpaid lawman at that.

Watching him, Bear Miller was not impressed.

"All you've done is make yourself a target for every outlaw passing through," he said, talking around a mouthful of beef and beans. "And if Miss Elliot is behind the killing of the originals, she won't let you go poking your nose into her business."

They sat at a table in the cantina. Earlier McBride had told Bear what had been said at last night's meeting.

"Miss Elliot didn't make the rule," he said. He spooned sugar into his coffee. "It has to be somebody else, somebody here in town who has his own agenda."

"Agenda? What kind of agenda would that be?"

"I don't know," McBride admitted. "The whole thing doesn't make any sense."

Bear jabbed his fork at the badge on McBride's shirt. "Neither does that."

"It's only for five days. If I can't find out who is behind the rule, I'll be free of it."

"Wear your gun, John."

McBride shook his head. "This will be detective work. I don't need a gun for sleuthing."

"Wear your gun."

"You worry too much, Bear."

"I heard something yesterday. One of the mule skinners told it to me. I didn't want to worry you since you've already got you hands full with Angel Guerrero, but when I came in here and saw you wearing that badge I figured you might as well know."

"Know what?" McBride sipped his coffee, only half-interested, sizing up the possible take from the three breakfasters in the cantina. There were four, if he counted Bear, but Bear never paid for anything.

The old scout took a deep breath. "Roddy Rentzin has left the Brazos River country. The Texas Rangers are really worked up, talking on the wires to any tin-star lawmen who'll listen. I hear they're telling them to look out for Rentzin and to step around him if they can." Bear's eyes were anxious. "John, the mule skinner told me a drifter up from Texas told him the latest word is that Rentzin is headed in this direction.''

McBride laughed and laid his cup on the table. ''Bear, what in hell are you talking about? And who is Roddy Rentzin? An outlaw?''

''No, he's worse—a gun-slick kid on the prod. He has three gunfighting brothers and he wants to prove himself faster than any of them. Right now he's trying to build himself a rep. A few months ago he took a big step in that direction when he gunned Frank Bishop. I knew Bishop and he was a hard man who'd killed way more'n his share.''

Bear laid down his fork and pushed his plate away. ''John, word gets around fast because of the talking wire and the railroads that folks seem to ride all the time. You don't suppose Rentzin has been told that the man who killed Hack Burns is right here in Suicide and he's on his way?''

McBride was amused and it showed in his eyes. ''Now how would Rentzin know that? Nobody knows I'm here.''

''Is that a fact?'' Bear glanced around the room, his eyes lingering on each diner for a moment. Then he leaned forward in his chair and whispered, ''John, you're a named man. You came south from the Picketwire country, looking to buy a hardware store. Did you give your name to anybody?''

McBride nodded. ''Yes, a few times.'' He remembered the Zuni Plateau and the killing of Deer Creek Tom Rivers and his clan. News of that gunfight would have spread far and his name would have been spoken often.

Bear was talking. "When you're a named man, folks remember. Maybe saying, 'I'm John McBride,' meant nothing to you, but it meant plenty to them as heard it. Sure, they might have said nothing at the time, but as soon as your back was turned, tongues would start wagging. People ride trains, lawmen talk on the wires and newspapers tell stories. Word gets around."

The old man helped himself from the coffeepot on the table. "You may be right of course. Rentzin might not know you're in Suicide. But by now he'll have enough information to figure that you're holed up somewhere in this neck of the woods."

McBride was suddenly uneasy, but he angrily derided himself for being so foolish. Roddy Rentzin had left the Brazos, but the western lands were vast and he could be headed anywhere. He told this to Bear, then added, "Besides, with the Apaches out, he'd be a fool to come this far north."

The old man nodded. "That could be." He rose to his feet and looked down at McBride. "Wear your gun, John."

Bear passed Jed McKay at the door and the two exchanged a curt nod. McKay's glance swept the room and settled on McBride. He sat opposite him and said, "With all the excitement last night, I forgot there was something I wanted to talk to you about, Marshal."

"Talk away," McBride said. He picked up the pot. "Coffee?"

The storekeeper shook his head. "Listen, the

Apaches have driven out the Army, at least for the foreseeable future, and Suicide is wide-open."

McBride nodded. "It's a worrisome thing, all right. What about your militia?"

"A dozen men trying to protect every building in town? It won't work. We'd be scattered and the Indians could pick us off one by one."

"Then what do you suggest, McKay?"

"When you visit with Miss Elliot tonight, inquire of her if we can use her house as a citadel in the event of an attack by the savages. The house is solidly built and, as we well know, it has an excellent field of fire in all directions. A dozen riflemen, well provisioned, could hold out until help arrived or the Apaches got discouraged and left."

"That makes sense to me," McBride said. "I'll ask her. I'm sure she'll be agreeable."

McKay rose to his feet. "There's one thing more, Marshal, and it's troubling. John Wright and his wife pulled out this morning. It seems he has no faith in your finding the killer among us."

Alarmed, McBride sprang to his feet. "Why didn't you tell me earlier?"

"I just found out myself. Conrad Heber saw them go and took his own sweet time telling anybody."

"When did they leave?"

"At first light. Heber said they loaded their few sticks of furniture into a spring wagon and headed east. He said Wright told him that he'd rather take his chances with the Apaches than remain a minute longer in Suicide."

Rage spiked through McBride. Heber was so fat and lazy he probably couldn't be bothered making the effort to tell anybody until it was too late.

"I'm going after them," he said.

McKay nodded. "Bring them back, Marshal. Bring them back alive and well."

Chapter 18

There was no sign of Jim Drago at the livery as McBride saddled his mustang and led the animal outside.

The morning was cold, sleety rain driving from an iron gray sky, borne along by a north wind off the mountains that cut to the bone. The harsh, freezing air smelled of hardening ice and distant, frost-rimed trees. No comfort was offered by the day, only the uncaring promise of much worse to come.

McBride turned up the collar of his thin coat, his shivering breath fogging. He was wishful for a thick, sheepskin mackinaw but had none. He put his foot in the stirrup, swung his leg over the mustang and settled in the saddle.

A moment later he found himself flat on his back in the stony mud, watching the irritated, snorting mustang trot back into its warm barn.

McBride rose slowly to his feet, hurting. He picked up his hat, jammed it on his head and, his eyes ablaze, looked daggers into the gloom of the stable.

The mustang had bucked like a bee-stung mule, sending him flying. Well, he didn't want to go out in the cold either, but it had to be done.

He stomped into the barn, grabbed the horse by the reins close to the bit rings and let it outside again. But this time he was ready. He bunched his fist, held it close to the mustang's head where the animal could see it, and yelled, "Do that again and I'll punch you right between the eyes."

Whether it recognized imminent violence in its rider's tone of voice or had made its protest and was done, the mustang stood and allowed McBride to mount. He swung away from the stable and headed east. He was two miles outside of town before he finally finished cussing his mount.

McBride rode through high, rolling grass country with plenty of piñon and here and there thickets of gambel oak. Rabbitbrush, proudly displaying its golden fall blossoms, grew among the juniper on the slopes of the hills, adding streaks of color to the bleak landscape. This was open land, vast and lonely under the dark iron bowl of the sky, the passing of the plains tribes and the buffalo they once hunted here still remembered by the mournful wind.

Shivering in his coat of thin cloth, McBride scanned the distances around him. The falling rain mixed with sleet drew a veil over the Guadalupe peaks to the north, and ahead of him green hills and shadowed valleys stretched far, before fading into a hazy wall of gray.

McBride was slowed by the need to scout for wagon tracks. He quartered the ground, riding a mile to the north, then swinging back to the south again along the same line. After two hours he'd found nothing.

There was no movement on the plain except the long grass tossing in the wind and the slow, somber passage of slate-colored clouds across the ashen sky.

Breathing the icy air was like drinking long draughts of freezing water, and the cold tore at McBride's lungs. The land was gradually rising higher and he swung the mustang into a mixed thicket of gambel oak and juniper growing on a rocky hillside. Here, sheltered from the wind, it felt a few degrees warmer, but McBride was shivering uncontrollably and the mustang hung its head, making its own misery known.

He would have to turn back. If he stayed out much longer he could easily freeze to death, especially now that night was only a few hours away. Maybe tomorrow he could try. . . .

The shots carried in the wind, distant, faint, but McBride heard them: twice the flat statement of a rifle, then, after a few moments, a third. He guessed the firing came from somewhere ahead of him and to the north. Kicking the mustang into a shambling trot, he left the shelter of the trees and rode to the flat.

McBride lifted his reluctant mount into a canter, riding into a curtain of icy sleet that penetrated his clothing and seemed to reach the very marrow of his bones. He carried no revolver, but his Winchester was booted under his left knee. He slid the rifle free and his numb fingers fumbled with the lever.

A bullet split the air next to his head, another, a split second later, thudded into the saddle horn, tearing out a chunk of leather. McBride's head swiveled on his shoulders, seeking the rifleman. He was not confident enough of his riding ability or his marksmanship with a long gun to shoot off the back of a running horse. Slowing the mustang to a walk, he held the Winchester high, ready to throw it to his shoulder if a target presented itself. Was it Apaches? He considered that, then rejected it. Even an Apache wouldn't be out on a day like this when he could be sitting warm in his wickiup. It had to be a white man—a man who had good reason to travel in a sleet storm.

About fifty yards away to his left rose a steep ridge, its slope covered with stunted piñon and juniper. Patches of frozen sleet showed themselves around the roots of the trees and streaked the slope, clinging to ragged stands of bunchgrass. The ridge was about a quarter-mile long, crested with tumbled slabs of gray sandstone rock, clumps of bunchgrass and thickets of prickly pear. A fallen tree, its trunk white as bone, lay across a couple of rocks, stubby, broken-off limbs pointing to the sky.

McBride glanced quickly around him. The ridge was the only place a bushwhacker could hide. He climbed out of the saddle, hoping to make himself a less obvious target. Crouching low, he headed for the ridge, now shrouded behind a cartwheeling screen of sleet and chips of icy rain.

There was danger in the air. McBride felt it. He was exposed out there in the flat, and the hidden rifleman had come close twice. But if he'd tried to cut and run, his back would have been to the bushwhacker, giving the man time for a clean shot.

He was still bucking the odds, he knew, but he had a weapon in his hands and his face was to the enemy . . . if the man was on the ridge.

Fate is only a name for the result of a man's own efforts, and now it rewarded McBride for his cold, scared walk across open ground into the gun of a waiting marksman.

He was ten yards from the base of the ridge, his eyes scanning the rocks, when he stepped into a shallow hole scraped away by some animal. The depression wasn't deep, but it was unexpected. McBride's ankle turned and he stumbled awkwardly to his left. At that same instant a rifle shot slapped from the ridge.

As he fell, the butt of McBride's Winchester came up and the bullet slammed into the walnut, shattering the stock near the rounded end of the loading lever. The impact stung his frozen hands and the rifle spun away from him.

McBride rolled, got to his feet and dived for his gun. Grasping what was left of the stock, he fired into the rocks, racked the rifle and fired again. He saw his bullets chip fragments from the sandstone; then he was up and limping for the base of the ridge, his twisted ankle punishing him. He threw himself against the slope, his back coming up hard against its gravelly base. Again he levered a round into the chamber, the splintered butt of the Winchester clumsy in his hands as he looked up at the ridge.

The bushwhacker would expose himself to McBride's fire if he tried to shoot down the slope. The big man gulped icy air into his lungs and waited.

A few moments later he heard the hoofbeats of a galloping horse, loud at first, then fading fast. He jumped to his feet and struggled up the slope, favoring his throbbing ankle. Tree branches tore at him, and several times his feet went out from under him and he fell on his belly, each time losing ground as he slid back a few yards.

When he reached the ridge he saw a horseman in the distance, vanishing quickly into the gray gloom of the sleet-scourged day.

Sudden anger flared in McBride. Summoning up every cuss word he could remember, plus a few he made up right there and then, he roared at the top of his voice as he fired at the retreating bushwhacker, levered the Winchester and fired again. But he was shooting at shadows. Nothing moved on the plain but the sleet and the wind.

Thirty minutes later McBride found the bodies of John and Ann Wright.

Chapter 19

The wagon was stopped in a narrow valley between tree-lined hills. The old mare in the traces was standing head-down, facing into the worst of the sleet storm, frost on her back and head.

John Wright sat upright in the seat, a neat bullet hole between his eyes. He had a look of horror on his face, an expression he had carried into eternity.

Ann Wright had been riding in the back of a wagon and had covered herself with a blanket and a canvas tarp for warmth. She had been shot twice in the chest and lay half in, half out of the wagon bed, her long hair trailing on the ground.

McBride pieced it together.

Their killer had been waiting for them in the trees and when the wagon passed he'd come behind them at a gallop. He'd fired twice at the woman, the two fast shots McBride had heard. Then, when John Wright had turned his head to look, he'd been shot between the eyes.

It had been a cold, efficient killing by a man who

knew his business and had no conscience or had forgotten he ever had one.

McBride stepped from the saddle and walked to the wagon. Ann Wright's huge eyes were open, looking down at the grass where the sleet was gathering. But she was seeing nothing but darkness. As for her husband, he knew only for a single, horrified moment he was dying.

Casting around the wagon, McBride found what he knew he'd find—shell casings from a .50-caliber rifle. The man who'd murdered John and Ann Wright had also killed Manuel Cortez. He was sure of that.

But now he had a difficult decision to make.

Suicide was a tinderbox and anything could start a conflagration. If he took the bodies of the couple back to town, he doubted that Adam Whitehead and the others would wait the promised five days. They'd say the Wrights' deaths were confirmation of their suspicion that Allison Elliot was behind the rule and the murders. They'd storm the house, burn her inside it and hang Moses and Drago.

McBride was sure it would happen that way. The blacksmith and some of the others were on a witch hunt, possessed by the same, unreasoning fear that had made Salem, Massachusetts, a byword for madness and cruelty. A woman who was never seen, lived alone in perpetual mourning yet had killed five men to protect her vast fortune, was an obvious target.

Joan Whitehead had called Allison Elliot a devil, and it would be she and her husband who would provide the spark that would light the witch's execution pyre.

McBride knew he had no other choice. The bodies of John and Ann Wright must stay where they were. The chances of anyone from Suicide passing this way and discovering them were slight. McBride shivered, facing a thought that had just occurred to him—the coyotes, the wolves and the buzzards must be the couple's undertakers.

John McBride had never been a religious man, but he took off his hat, bowed his head and whispered what few words he remembered from the Bible. Then he racked a round into his shattered Winchester, his heart heavy in him.

If he turned the Wrights' mare loose, the chances were good that she'd return to the only place she knew where there was food and shelter, her barn in Suicide.

The return of the horse could be enough in itself to start the kind of vengeful reaction he feared.

McBride would not let himself think about it any longer. He stepped quickly to the mare and shot her dead in the traces.

The dark day dying around him, McBride, gladly surrendering to a darker night, rode into Suicide. He was chilled to the bone and could no longer feel his feet or hands. A few oil lamps burned outside of the businesses along the street and he noted with pride that one glowed on the wall near the door of the El Coyote Azul.

Again there was no sign of Jim Drago at the livery stable.

McBride rubbed down the mustang with a piece of sacking, then scooped the little horse a generous amount of oats with its hay.

He slid his ruined rifle from the saddle boot, stepped outside and walked toward the cantina. He checked his watch. It was close to six. He would meet Allison Elliot in another hour. Maybe after talking to the young woman he would be able to convince Whitehead and the others that she was not the ogre they thought she was. He sure hoped so. It would be an excellent way to head off further trouble until he found the real killer.

Then, as he drew close to the cantina, a nagging doubt: What if Whitehead was right? What if Allison Elliot was the person behind the rule and the murders?

As soon as the thought entered his head, McBride dismissed it. What did Allison have to gain by keeping a few very drab and ordinary people here in Suicide? Why would she have a hand in killing those who tried to leave? There was no sense to the accusation and as he stepped into the El Coyote Azul, McBride had already let it go as worthless.

He had no customers and he headed directly for the warmth of the kitchen. The two fat ladies were eating as usual, the table piled high with food. McBride spread his hands to the fire of the stove, frowning. At this rate the help was eating more than the customers and there was little profit in that.

One of the women rose, smiled and bobbed a

curtsy. She waved a hand to the table, inviting him to eat. But McBride shook his head. He would save his appetite for dinner with Allison.

The fat ladies shared a cabin on the edge of town and McBride had been spreading his blankets on the kitchen floor after they left. Now he needed to wash and shave, but that required at least a small measure of privacy. With one last despairing look at the table, he took down the scrap of mirror he kept near the door and walked into the restaurant. He found a basin behind the bar and stepped outside into the freezing cold and sleet. The well was at the side of the building and he pumped a couple of inches of icy water into the basin and fled inside.

He carried the basin to the bar, then realized he'd forgotten his razor. He stepped into the kitchen again, but this time the women, engrossed in their gorging, ignored him. McBride found the razor and went back to the bar. He spared a glance for the kitchen door and let out a yelping little sigh. The fat ladies were eating him out of house and home, putting away vast amounts of groceries that he hadn't even paid for yet.

As he scraped the razor down his stubbly cheek, McBride decided that things had to change around the El Coyote Azul. But what that change might be, he had no idea.

Shaving with cold water and no soap was a chore and when he checked his face in the mirror he saw that he'd nicked himself in several places. There was an old newspaper behind the bar and he tore off small pieces from the corners and stuck them on the cuts. He'd remember to take them off before he reached Allison's house.

McBride's third trip to the kitchen for his celluloid collar and tie again brought no response from the fat ladies. For the moment sated, they were leaning back in their chairs, eyes closed, their elaborate Spanish fans fluttering near their flushed faces.

Irritated beyond measure, McBride stomped back to the bar, studded his collar in place and knotted his tie. Tomorrow he'd let the women know that the food was for paying customers, not for the help, and he'd get Bear to translate for him. Then he remembered that slightly mocking grin the old man got on his face when he told the ladies what their employer was saying. Most of the time he wasn't even sure Bear accurately repeated his words. For all he knew, he'd tell them what a great job they were doing.

McBride brushed off his coat with his open hand. Well, maybe enlisting Bear's help wasn't such a good idea. He'd have to come up with something else. But come up with something he would.

Mirrors of any kind were rare in the West and all McBride had was a polished scrap of steel. Still, when he looked at his distorted image he decided he presented a respectable appearance, except for the pieces of bloody paper stuck all over his face and his untrimmed mustache.

"I guess you'll do, McBride," he whispered to himself as he turned away from the mirror.

It was important that he make a good first impression on Miss Elliot.

*   *   *

McBride left the outlying shacks of Suicide behind him and walked toward the Elliot house. The sleet had stopped and the clouds, driven by a bullying wind, were flying apart, scudding tattered and black across the sky like monstrous ravens. A bone white moon, almost full, spread an ashen light, deepening the shadows, filling the night with dark omens.

The only sound was the crunch of McBride's feet on frozen slush and the hiss of his breath, smoking briefly in the icy air, only to be snatched away by the wind.

He glanced at the moon and, a man of imagination, saw that same moon shining on a wagon out in the plains to the east, shading still, pale faces to deathly white. By now the coyotes would be talking and their shadowy shapes would be skulking closer to the wagon like gray ghosts. . . .

McBride shook his head, clearing the image from his mind. He'd done what had to be done. But try as he might, he found little consolation in that thought and no easing of his conscience.

Lights burned in the Elliot house and in a single turret room. A gravel path wound like a serpent up the hillside to the front door and all the trees had long since been cleared from the slope. A good rifleman would have an open field of fire from the house and nothing could live on this part of the hill once he started shooting. Projecting pillars of gray rock, each rising several hundred feet to the crest of the hill, flanked the house and a massive shelf of sandstone overhung the roof.

Allison's father had chosen the site for his house

well. The place was a fortress, obviously built where it was to hold off Indian attacks, and in that it had succeeded.

If the Apaches struck at Suicide, the men of the town could retreat here and fight them. McBride realized he might lose his cantina and the others their stores and businesses to fire, but they'd keep their scalps. The house was well nigh impregnable and the Apaches were not ones to lose men in a battle where all the odds were against them. Indians were first-rate fighting men, but they did not throw away their lives unnecessarily.

As he got closer, McBride noticed that despite the raw cold of the evening every window in the house was wide-open, lace curtains billowing into the rooms. The door of the house surprised him even more. He'd expected etched glass maybe, and a polished brass handle and knocker. But it was a massive affair, studded with iron, the knocker a heavy circle of green, mildewed bronze.

McBride stopped just before he reached the door and polished his boots on the legs of his pants. Looking up at the building, its soaring turret rooms with their narrow, arrow-slit windows and the steeply pitched roof, he was overwhelmed by a sense of foreboding. For all its gingerbread decoration and white paint, there was a pervading gloominess to the place. The house didn't sit on its foundation; it crouched like a great hawk, as though ready to swoop on what lay below. It seemed to McBride that the place could suddenly rise in a flutter of wings, descend on the town, pick it up in its talons and carry it to the crest of the hill to be devoured.

He had the feeling that this was not a happy place and it never had been. The house seemed alive, full of malevolence . . . watching him. Hating him.

McBride shook his head. He was tired and his imagination was working overtime. A house that sheltered a woman rumored to be as beautiful as Allison Elliot must surely be happy.

Smiling at his own foolishness, he stepped to the door . . . and it swung open just as he reached it.

Jim Drago, swaddled in a black cloak of some kind, a fur hat on his huge head, threw McBride a venomous look of intense dislike, then brushed past him without a word.

The giant figure of Moses stood silhouetted in the doorway. "You are three minutes late, Mr. McBride," he said accusingly. "Miz Elliot awaits you in the drawing room."

McBride stepped inside into a small foyer floored with marble. Ahead of him was a wide hallway with rooms leading off on both sides. Beyond soared a grand staircase that led to the second story. A massive, crystal chandelier hung over the first landing before the stairs branched in two directions, but it was not lit. In fact, the only light came from six oil lamps placed on small tables against the corridor walls.

Moses led McBride to a room at the end of the hall. "Wait here," he said. He tapped on the door and stepped inside, closing it behind him.

The house was cold, as cold as it was outside, and McBride shivered as he looked around him.

A huge portrait in a heavy oak frame dominated the hallway. It hung on the wall opposite McBride and reached almost from ceiling to floor. The painting had been done in oils and was of a stern, middle-aged man with a mane of iron-gray hair, a thick mustache adorning his top lip. The man's gray eyes looked down at McBride and no matter where he moved in the hall, the eyes followed him, disapproving and faintly contemptuous. A thriving city with tall buildings, sprawling suburban mansions, a railroad yard, churches and schools formed the background of the painting. There were also busy stores and people either strolling or riding streetcars, all under a bright blue sky without a hint of cloud.

McBride smiled. No city in the world looked that clean and uncrowded—certainly not New York with its constant pall of factory smoke, chaotic traffic and dirty, teeming streets. This was one man's fantasy of what the ideal city should look like, and it was far divorced from reality.

"I see you've met my father, Mr. McBride. And his utopia."

McBride turned, saw Allison Elliot standing in the drawing room doorway looking at him—and his heart almost stopped beating.

Chapter 20

Allison Elliot's father had dreamed of creating a beautiful city, but that was fantasy. However, he had created a beautiful daughter and that was reality.

The woman burned like a candle flame, a creature of blinding loveliness who possessed the delicacy, almost fragility, that goes hand-in-hand with true feminine beauty.

Her glossy auburn hair was piled on top of her head. Her eyes were large, a lustrous smoke gray like her father's in the portrait. Her lips were full, scarlet, delicious as ripe cherries waiting for a hungry man to devour them. She wore a floor-length kimono of watered yellow silk that did nothing to conceal the voluptuous curves of her body.

Allison regarded McBride with a smile on her lips and a twinkle in her eyes, a woman in her midtwenties who knew very well the effect she had on men.

She glided toward him. "It's nice to meet you at last." A man would have gladly died for her smile. "I've been hearing quite a lot about you."

McBride tried to talk, gave up the struggle and awkwardly extended his hand.

"Forgive me. I don't shake hands," Allison said, the smile fixed on her luscious mouth. "It bothers me."

Feeling too big, too ungainly and too out of his depth, McBride swallowed hard and said the first thing that popped into his head. "You have a lovely home, Miss Elliot."

"Thank you. I like it. And, please, call me Allison. I shall call you John."

It pleased McBride greatly that the woman knew his name. "Cold tonight," he said, then swore at himself for being so transparently gauche, like a teenage boy.

"Yes, yes it is. But then I don't feel the cold. You obviously do."

"I, I mean I—"

"Your hat?"

McBride snatched the plug hat from his head, feeling his cheeks redden. "I'm sorry."

"No harm done."

Allison moved closer to him and she looked up at the portrait. "My father built this house. He was a wonderful man, a great man. Tam Elliot was a giant, a visionary. Unfortunately smaller men could not share his vision and it died with him. It died and rotted into a town named Suicide."

"Your father founded the town," McBride said. It was a statement, not a question.

"Yes, he did." She flashed her dazzling smile again. "But more of that later. A sherry before dinner?"

Finding himself again, McBride smiled. "Yes, I'd like that."

Allison led him into the drawing room. The room was ornately furnished. A low coffee table and two large, leather wing chairs fronted a wide fireplace. But no warm and cheery log crackled in the fire. An embroidered screen stood in front of the grate and the entire interior of the fireplace had been blackened and polished. All the windows were wide-open, letting in gusts of icy wind that tossed the curtains and made the candle flames in the candelabras placed around the room gutter and smoke.

As though she didn't notice the freezing cold, Allison led McBride to one of the leather chairs and she took the one opposite. A crystal decanter and two glasses stood on the table and she poured sherry for both of them.

"A poor sherry, I'm afraid, John, but in Suicide one must take what one can get."

Trying his best not to be too obvious in his shivering, McBride tried the sherry. It was vinegary and long past its best. "It's just fine," he said, choosing a small lie over a truth that might offend.

"You're too kind." Allison sipped her sherry and her eyes sought McBride's over the rim of her glass. Her kimono had slipped from one shoulder, showing the upper swell of a milk white breast. "Did I tell you about my father?" she asked.

McBride was surprised. "Why yes, when we were admiring his portrait."

As though she hadn't heard, the woman said, "He was a great man, an intelligent man, full of passion and restless energy. I have known many men, but not one has ever come close to comparing to him."

Including me, I guess, McBride thought glumly. He knew he'd already made a grievous faux pas. Damn it all, he should have taken his hat off as soon as he entered the house.

Allison was talking again. "After he struck it rich in the goldfields, Father had a dream, call it a vision. He wanted to build his own town, a utopia where people could live in peace, prosperity and harmony."

McBride smiled, knowing he was sunk anyway. "In the middle of Apache country?"

If Allison was offended she didn't let it show. "The savages were quiet then, and besides, they would never have attacked the kind of city my father planned to build." She lifted her glass and sipped. Then she said, "It took my father five years of searching before he found this place. There were no other towns close and his city would have had plenty of room to grow."

She laid the glass carefully back on the table. "Father's idea was that his city would attract the railroad and he'd make Eden Creek a great cattle shipping center." She smiled. "Think about it, John. Why should the Texas ranchers drive their herds all the way to Kansas, running off tons of beef, when they could ship them east from here?"

"Seems like a good plan." McBride was shivering and he fought to keep his teeth from chattering. "What happened?"

"Father first built this house as an anchor for all the rest to come. That was ten years ago, just after my mother died. I was at a finishing school back east at the time and he invited me to join him here."

McBride brightened. "I have four young charges and I plan on—"

"Father began by erecting the buildings you see in town," Allison said, as though she hadn't heard. "They were but a tiny acorn from which a mighty oak would grow. He invited people passing through to settle here, men like Jed McKay and Adam Whitehead and others. But they were unworthy."

"In what way?" McBride asked, now that his attempt to shift the conversation had failed.

"They were a lazy, shiftless bunch and they did not or could not share Father's vision. Instead of growing, Eden Creek stagnated. No more settlers came and the railroad turned far to the north." The woman took a deep, shuddering breath. "Three years ago, in utter despair at the failure of his dream, Father shot himself."

"Why didn't he go someplace else? Try again?"

"He was discouraged and sank into a deep depression. He no longer had the will to try again. Tam Elliot was a broken man. The people of Eden Creek destroyed him and because of that it was I who renamed the town Suicide."

McBride tried another tack. There were tears in Allison's beautiful eyes and the present line of talk was going nowhere. "I've heard that there's a fortune in gold in this house."

The woman gave McBride a sidelong glance. "Father did not believe in banks."

"And the five men who tried to steal it?"

"No doubt you've heard I killed those men. I did not. Greed killed them."

"But they say you pulled the trigger, Allison." Even as he said it McBride wondered how this slender woman could have handled the weight and punishing recoil of a Sharps big .50.

"I didn't pull the trigger. Men who protect me, protect this house, did."

"Who are they?"

A gong sounded somewhere in the house and Allison rose quickly to her feet. She was smiling again. "Ah, it's time for dinner." Her eyes lifted to McBride's face. "Perhaps your cuts are healed?"

Now he remembered the scraps of newspaper all over his cheeks and neck. Flushing, he picked them off one by one, dried blood making them stick to his skin. When the papers were all gone he didn't know what to do with them, so he shoved them in his pocket.

"Much better," Allison said approvingly. "You must be more careful with the razor, John."

McBride said nothing, feeling foolish.

The woman led the way to a door at the end of the hallway near the stairs. She entered first and McBride followed. A long, mahogany dining table ran almost the whole length of the room, but there was a setting for two at the end near the cold fireplace. All the windows were open and the room was icy.

Allison stood at the head of the table and waited until McBride helped her with her chair. She waved to the place next to her on her right. "Please be seated."

The woman waited until McBride took his seat, then said, "You will find that Moses is an excellent cook."

A freezing draft assailed McBride's back and his fingers and toes were numb. He managed a smile. "Has Moses been with you for long?"

"Ten years, and before that he was with my father. He was once a slave, you know, a field hand on an Alabama plantation. Wine?"

McBride nodded and Allison poured from another expensive crystal decanter. "I'm afraid you'll discover that the wine is no better than the sherry."

The woman was right, McBride told himself as he placed his glass back on the table. He was no expert on wines, but the stuff was terrible.

"May I ask you a question, Allison?" he asked. Through the open windows he heard the coyotes talking, their mad yips carried along by the wind.

"Why, of course you may."

"Have you ever heard of the rule?"

Allison smiled and McBride again found himself devastated by her stunning beauty. She said, "Well, let me think. I've heard of the golden rule, the rule of thumb and the rule of King Henry the Eighth of England. Are you referring to one of those?"

Refusing to be sidetracked, McBride said, "Unfortunately not. The rule says that no one is allowed to leave Suicide."

Allison's laugh rang like a silver bell. "Who told

you such a silly thing, John? People come and go in Suicide all the time, a lot of them outlaws on the dodge."

"I'm talking about the originals. The first settlers invited here by your father."

The woman studied McBride for some time. Finally she said, "I suspect they made the rule story up to cover their own stupidity and idleness. Not one of them has the gumption to leave and try to start a new life somewhere else."

McBride would not let it go, even as he saw a look of irritation in Allison's wonderful eyes. "I'm told that some have tried, and all of them were found murdered on the trail, including women and children." He thought about mentioning the Wrights but decided against it. For the time being he'd keep that a secret.

Allison looked startled. "John, the people you're talking about packed up slow-moving wagons and headed into Apache country. Of course they were murdered. Man, woman or child, it doesn't make much difference to a savage whom he kills."

"Manuel Cortez was one of them." McBride watched Allison's face for a reaction. The woman didn't flinch.

"I heard about that. I'm told you found his body and had a narrow escape yourself. It only proves what I just said—you can't go gallivanting into Apache country and expect to survive for long."

Dinner was a long time coming and it seemed to McBride that the room had grown even colder, the cutting wind stronger. Beside him, Allison Elliot didn't seem to notice. He grinned and changed the subject. "Will you ask me for my rent for the El Coyote Azul before I leave?"

Allison didn't smile. "It's a nominal sum—a hundred dollars a month."

"Have you ever heard of a man named Angel Guerrero? He recently tried to shake me down for that much protection money, or at least, one of his men did."

"Guerrero has been around these parts for years," Allison said. "He's a bandit and an all-round scamp." Now she was smiling.

That, McBride decided, was putting it mildly. It seemed Allison did not object to the man's criminal activities in the least. He was still pondering that fact when Moses entered with a loaded silver tray.

He laid a shallow bowl of what looked like thin chicken broth in front of Allison, then passed a huge platter with a thick steak, roasted potatoes and peas to McBride.

The woman picked up her spoon. "Please eat, John," she smiled.

Western men, surrounded by the best prime beef in the world, burned their steaks to the consistency of old boot leather. McBride, to his surprise when he cut into his meat, discovered that it had been cooked medium rare, the way he liked it.

"The food is to your liking?" Allison asked. She had yet to try her soup.

"Wonderful," McBride said, chewing. He was

eating fast before the coldness of the room chilled his steak. "How did Moses know how I like my beef cooked?"

"I think he heard your"—she smiled, taking any possible sting out of it—"'Noo Yawk accent and drew his own conclusions. And you are from New York, aren't you, John?"

McBride nodded, his head bent over his plate. "Yes I am."

"And you were a police officer of some kind."

That surprised him. McBride lifted his eyes to Allison's. "How did you know?"

"There's something about you that speaks lawman to me. Maybe that's why you agreed to become our new town marshal."

"You know that too?"

"There's little that happens in Suicide I don't know about." She hesitated a heartbeat. "What kind of police officer were you?"

"A good one, I hope."

"I didn't mean that. I meant, what did you do in the police force?"

"I was a detective sergeant. A shadow as we were called."

Allison considered this, then said after a while, "John, can I depend on your protection?"

McBride was surprised again. "Of course, but protection from what?"

"From those who would do me and this house harm."

"I won't let anything happen to you, Allison," McBride said, meaning every word.

The woman reached out and placed her slender white hand over his huge scarred paw. "Thank you, John. Just know that I may need you sooner than you think."

"Better eat your soup," McBride said softly.

But Allison pushed her bowl, untouched, away from her. "I eat very little," she said, frowning. "I have an absolute horror of getting fat and ugly."

Chapter 21

After dinner Allison suggested they withdraw to the drawing room while Moses dealt with the dishes.

For an hour they talked of inconsequential things, the woman questioning McBride closely about how large the bustles of New York's fashionable belles were and how tiny their hats. He in turn asked about Allison's finishing school and finally got a chance to tell her about his young Chinese wards and how he hoped his cantina would help provide them with a good education.

Finally Allison pulled her kimono closer around her and rose to her feet. "John, the hour grows late. You've been an excellent guest, most gracious, understanding and erudite, and I wouldn't dream of making you walk home in the dark and cold. You may stay here tonight."

She pulled a cord hanging by the fireplace and said, "Moses will show you to your room."

"That's very kind of you, Allison," McBride said,

feeling vaguely disappointed. "But I don't want to be any trouble."

"No trouble at all. I'll sleep better knowing you are under my roof." The door opened and she said, "Ah, here Moses is now. Then I'll bid you good night."

After Allison left, the haunting memory of her perfume lingering, Moses picked up a candelabra and said, "This way, please."

They climbed the staircase, then turned along a balcony, the giant's moving shadow an enormous, hulking shape on the wall. The balcony led to a short hallway with a door on either side and a narrow stairway at the end. Moses opened the door on the left and ushered McBride inside. There was a large, four-poster bed, a dresser and a single overstuffed chair. Both windows were open, the curtains blowing.

Moses laid the guttering candelabra on the dresser and turned to McBride. The man's eyes were hidden in shadow. "Breakfast is at six sharp," he said. "I'll wake you then."

Then he turned and was gone, taking the candles with him. McBride heard a key turn in the lock—on the outside of the door.

Left in darkness, he stumbled across the room and shut the windows. He made his way back to the bed, removed his elastic-sided boots and placed them and his hat on the carpeted floor beside him. He took off his coat and pants, let them drop, and climbed between the sheets, pulling the patchwork comforter higher around his neck. The sheets felt damp, clammy, but he was tired out from his long ride earlier in the day and from the large meal he'd eaten, and sleep found him quickly.

McBride woke to the sound of voices.

The room was still dark and he guessed he'd been asleep only for a couple of hours. He lay on his back, hands behind his head and, his ears straining, listened.

Recalling the layout of the house, his bedroom must be directly under one of the turret rooms. The voices were muffled, but one was a woman's; the other, harsher, lower, belonged to a man.

Did Moses live in the turret room and was Allison up there talking to him?

But as he listened, McBride realized that the male voice did not belong to Moses. It was a strained rumble, interrupted by long pauses, the intonation of a sick man or a man in pain. The woman's voice, Allison's voice, was higher and more distinct.

McBride listened but heard only tattered fragments of speech, the man's voice saying, ". . . dangerous . . . no good . . . best alone . . ."

Then Allison: ". . . need him . . . get rid . . . move on . . ."

The male voice coming back: ". . . this town . . . time . . . I want . . . finish it . . . get Guerrero . . ."

McBride rolled out of bed, the springs shrieking under him. The voices suddenly stilled. He crossed to the door, floorboards creaking under his weight, and listened. He heard hurried footsteps on the stairs outside the wall of his room, then silence.

He waited at the door for several long minutes, then made his way back to bed.

With whom had Allison been talking? And about what? McBride had no answer for either question and for the time being he dismissed them from his mind.

Right now he needed more sleep.

The love beautiful women have for candlelight dates back millennia, and candlelight loves them passionately in return. But in the cold, gray dawn there is no candlelight, only reality. There are no mysteries, no hidden things; everything is revealed.

When Allison Elliot, dressed in a demure morning gown of brown taffeta, took her seat beside McBride in the dining room, he noticed a hardness about her mouth and fine lines between her eyebrows that suggested a woman who frowned much and laughed little. He had not seen either the night before. All the womanly softness had fled from her with the morning, revealing steel.

Now McBride could imagine Allison Elliot using a Sharps rifle.

"Did you sleep well, John?" she asked, fluttering a napkin onto her lap.

"Very well. Like a log, as they say."

"The coyotes complained all night. I thought they might have disturbed you."

"I heard nothing," McBride said, his face expressionless.

Allison held his eyes for several moments; then she smiled. "Coffee?"

Moses served McBride a huge breakfast of bacon, eggs and sourdough biscuits. To his amazement the man poured three fingers of whiskey, laid the glass in front of Allison and beside that a long, black cheroot.

"May I beg your indulgence?" the woman asked, holding up the cigar between two fingers.

"Of course," McBride said, his fork poised midway between his plate and mouth. Allison Elliot was turning out to be a strange woman.

Moses thumbed a match into flame, lit Allison's cigar, then bowed and left.

"A good cigar and bonded bourbon was a morning ritual of my father's," she said. "I follow in his footsteps."

McBride nodded. He didn't know what to say. He bent to his plate again just as the woman blew a cloud of smoke into his face—whether by accident or design he could not tell.

After breakfast Allison rose and said, "It was so lovely having you visit, John. We must do it again sometime." She smiled. "Moses will see you to the door."

McBride remembered the Apache threat and McKay's request that Allison allow her house to be used as a redoubt in the event of an attack. Now he told her that much.

The woman's back stiffened and a cold blaze kindled in her eyes. "The Apaches have never bothered this house. No, what you suggest is out of the question. And you can tell that to Jed McKay and the others."

Allison turned on her heel and swept out of the room, leaving McBride to dangle his hat in his hands and feel small, like a poor relative who'd just been turned down for a handout.

When McBride walked through the gray morning and stepped into the El Coyote Azul he was pleased to see that the place was busy. Every table was taken and the fat ladies were so busy cooking and serving they didn't notice him come in. But Adam Whitehead did.

The big blacksmith rose and blocked McBride's path, standing so close he smelled coffee on the man's breath. Whitehead got right to the point, his black eyes hostile. "Did you find John Wright and his wife?"

Lying did not come easily to McBride and he tried to sidestep the issue. "Who told you I was going after them?"

"McKay. Well, did you find them?"

Whitehead's voice was loud and every head was turned in McBride's direction, even, he noticed, Bear, who was standing at the bar, a cup of coffee in his hand.

Knowing he was backed into a corner, McBride swallowed and said, "No, I didn't. That's a lot of country out there."

"No matter," the blacksmith said. "They're dead by this time anyhow."

One lie building on another, McBride felt trapped. "I wouldn't say that. If they avoided Apaches I guess they'll be all right."

Whitehead studied McBride's face for several moments. He said, "I see the lie in your eyes."

"Whitehead!" Bear's voice, an angry bellow. The old scout stepped away from the bar. "You call a man a liar—that's gun talk."

"Bear Miller, I'm not a gunfighter like you," Whitehead said. "But I see what I see. I think this man is lying to cover for the Elliot witch."

There was a murmur of agreement from the others in the cantina and McBride knew he had to defuse the situation fast. Bear took loyalty to a friend seriously and his hand was close to his Colt, the devil dancing in his eyes.

"Sit down and finish your breakfast, Adam," McBride said. "If I get news of John Wright and his wife, you'll be the first to know."

"The only news you'll get of Wright is that he's dead," Whitehead said. "You know it, I know it and the witch on the hill knows it." His head turned to Bear. "I've got no quarrel with you. Hell, I was leaving anyway."

The big blacksmith brushed angrily past McBride and stepped out of the cantina door.

A split second later his brains were blown out the right side of his skull as he was hit by a heavy caliber bullet. Then came the echoing blast of a rifle.

Chapter 22

Led by McBride, men stampeded for the door. Behind them, Joan Whitehead screamed and kept on screaming.

McBride glanced briefly at Whitehead, knowing the man was beyond help. He looked wildly around him and saw Jed McKay standing outside his store.

"Who fired the shot?" he yelled.

McKay raised his shoulders. "I don't know."

"Where did it come from?"

"I don't know that either. I heard the rifle and ran out here." McKay started to walk toward McBride. "Who is it, Marshal?"

"Adam Whitehead."

"Oh my God!" McKay started to run.

The blacksmith's brains were seeping into the dirt, his blood spreading around his head in a dark pool. Joan Whitehead was elbowing her way through the gawking men and McBride yelled, "Keep her away! She doesn't have to see this."

The woman's hand dived into her purse and she

came up holding a .40-caliber Deringer. "John McBride, you try to keep me away from my man and I'll kill you."

"She is his wife, John." Bear was looking at him, a small plea in his eyes.

McBride nodded. "Let Mrs. Whitehead pass."

The woman threw herself on her husband, sobs racking her thin body. Then she raised her tear-streaked face to the cold sky and screamed, "She did this! It was the witch!"

More people had gathered and there were loud mutterings. It doesn't take much to turn an assembly of angry, frightened men into a lynch mob, and already they were taking their first steps along the ragged edge between rationality and madness.

"Listen men, I'll find out who did this," McBride said, holding up his hands for quiet. "Just give me time."

"We all know who killed Adam Whitehead," a man yelled. "It was the Elliot woman or one of them that works for her."

"You have no proof of that," McBride said. "It could even have been an Apache hidden up there in the hill."

"No Indian can shoot that far," the man said. "But Allison Elliot can."

"Or her dwarf," another man hollered. "He's killed men before with a rifle."

"Kill him, kill that evil creature . . . that thing." Joan Whitehead was looking up at the men around her, her face a twisted mask of grief and hate. "The man who murdered my husband was no savage. It was Jim Drago, following the witch's orders."

"Let's get him!" somebody yelled.

"String him up!"

"You men stay right there!" McBride shouted. "I'm the town marshal and I'll arrest the first man who makes a move toward the livery barn."

A tall, towhead with a broken nose and hot eyes drew a gun from his waistband. "McBride, you step away or by God I'll drop you right where you stand."

"Maddox, the marshal ain't heeled," Bear said mildly. "But I am."

The man called Maddox hesitated, aware of the old scout's reputation. But another voice, soft, melodious and amused, ended it.

"McBride, I can drop . . . oh . . . say seven or eight of them pig farmers. You only have to give the word."

Every head turned to the speaker, a young man sitting a paint pony. Unshaven and wearing dusty range clothes, he looked like anybody else. But the two silver-plated Remingtons he held muzzle up at each side of his head, his thumbs on the hammers, gave the lie to his ordinary appearance.

The youngster grinned. "McBride, what say I drop the big towhead just to prove my bona fides?"

"And what the hell are your bona fides?" a voice yelled.

"These." The youngster shook his guns. "And my name. Down in the Brazos River country where I hail from, they call me Roddy Rentzin."

A ripple went through the crowd and men were already climbing down, dropping their eyes. Even Bear looked uneasy, and McBride saw him slowly move his hand away from his gun.

The kid was grinning again. "You, towhead, are you planning to use that gun? If you ain't, drop it."

Maddox was either stupid or brave or both. He turned to face Rentzin as other men moved away from him. "Maybe you was the one who murdered Adam Whitehead, the man you see lying there. You shot him with the rifle on your saddle and then rode into town bold as brass."

Rentzin smiled and nodded. "Maybe. But I'm calling you a damn liar."

"Enough!" McBride said. "You two let it go." He moved to step between the men. But he never made it.

Maddox's face was wild, scared, but he knew he could not step away from an insult like that, not if he wanted to hold his head high in the company of men. His gun came up as he eared back the hammer with the palm of his left hand. Too slow. Rentzin's guns were already hammering. Hit twice, then twice again, Maddox slammed back against the wall of the cantina, his shirtfront crimson. He tried to bring his Colt on target but couldn't lift it to his eyes. He dropped to his knees, his eyes shocked and unbelieving, then fell facedown in the dirt.

A sullen drift of gray gun smoke coiled among the onlookers. One by one, few sparing a glance for the two dead men, the crowd faded away until only

McBride, Bear and Mrs. Whitehead remained. The woman was staring at Rentzin as though he was some kind of wild animal she'd never seen before.

Rentzin spoke to McBride. "Fair fight, Marshal. He didn't give me a choice." He nodded in the direction of Whitehead. "Who done for him?"

"I don't know yet," McBride said. "But I will." He moved to Joan Whitehead and put his hand on her shoulder. "Mrs. Whitehead, do you want us to take Adam home?"

The woman nodded and rose unsteadily to her feet, McBride helping her. "I'll wash him and bury him in his Masonic apron so he'll be decent when he meets his Maker," she said.

The two fat ladies stepped out of the cantina doorway and flanked Mrs. Whitehead. Tears were rolling down their chubby cheeks as they tried their best to console her in a language she did not understand.

McBride called some of the men back, including McKay and Nathan Levy, and they carried the dead man to his cabin. His wife, supported by the fat ladies, followed behind them. Maddox had no family but he too was carried to his shack on the edge of town. Suicide had no undertaker, but Levy filled that role and he would take care of Maddox. His fee for a man who died without family was everything the man owned.

Rentzin watched the grim processions leave, then grinned and holstered his guns. "Well, Marshal, are you going to arrest me?"

McBride thought for a few moments, then shook

his head. "No, it was a fair fight, just like you said." He lifted cold eyes to the kid's face. "But you pushed him into it."

The youngster shrugged, swung gracefully out of the saddle and gathered up his pony's reins. "I couldn't just stand by and let a pig farmer gun you, John McBride." He smiled. "I mean, on account of how I plan on killing you myself."

Chapter 23

Bear Miller's eyes were hostile. His rifle hung in his hands, but he was ready. "And just when do you plan on killing Marshal McBride?"

Rentzin struck a pose, his thumbs tucked into his crossed gun belts. "Well, let me see. Is there a newspaper in this godforsaken burg?"

"No," McBride answered.

"Too bad. They could have written a story about me like they do for that Billy the Kid feller." Rentzin's face screwed up in thought. He looked like a cherub from a Renaissance altar fresco, with mild, baby blue eyes, blond hair and a full-lipped mouth that any woman would have envied.

But what came out of the youngster's angelic mouth was pure evil. "Lemme see, you got two dead men who will start to stink by nightfall, so they'll be buried tomorrow." He grinned. "Now, it's been my experience that after a buryin', men head for the saloon to drown their sorrows and celebrate their still being alive. So there it is, John McBride—I'll gun you tomorrow. Best you come to the saloon so I don't have to go looking for you. If you make me do that, I'll gut-shoot you and you'll die real slow." The smile widened. "I mean, on account of me being so upset an' all."

"I won't fight you, boy," McBride said. "I don't even carry a gun."

Rentzin stroked his pony's nose. He was grinning widely, like somebody had just told him a good joke. "Ah, but see, that don't matter none. Heeled or not, when the smoke clears and you're lying dead in the sawdust, I'll still be the man who killed the man who killed Hack Burns. See how it works?"

McBride made no answer, his anger rising, but Bear spoke up. "Kid, you came all the way from the Brazos, through an Apache uprising, just to kill a man?"

Rentzin laughed. "Sure I did, and it took me a spell to find this place, let me tell you. But I'm not here to kill just any man. I'm here to kill John McBride, the Tenderfoot Kid." His eyes slid to McBride. "Though right now in that city-feller plug hat an' necktie you sure don't look like much."

"Maybe not," Bear said. "But he's my friend."

Rentzin's grin slipped. "You keep out of this old man. My fight ain't with you, so don't go making any mistakes."

"You scared of me, boy?" Bear asked.

The youngster was genuinely astonished. "Scared of an old coot like you? Are you crazy?"

"Well, you should be."

Bear swung up his Henry to waist level and fired.

He was aiming for the belly and that's where he hit. Rentzin was a small man and the shock of the big .44-40 bullet rocked him, tearing a scream out of his lungs. Right then he knew he was dead, but he drew with flashing speed and both his Remingtons leveled— at McBride!

The big man saw the danger and threw himself to his right. He heard the vicious *pop! pop!* of Rentzin's guns, loaded light to reduce recoil. As McBride hit the ground, two bullets chipped the cantina's adobe wall where he'd been standing.

Bear levered the Henry and fired again, this time an aimed shot from the shoulder. He was patient. The bullet hit Rentzin at the bottom of the V made by his open shirt collar. Rentzin gagged and staggered back, his Remingtons lowering. Bear shot him again.

Rentzin went to his knees, blood staining the cupid mouth, trickling down his chin. His eyes were on Bear, angry, accusing. "You dirty old . . . you old . . ."

Then he died.

The old scout stepped beside the dead kid. He shook his head almost sadly. "Boy," he said, real quiet, "somebody taught you real well, but they didn't teach you that when killing's to be done, you don't talk, you shoot."

McBride rose to his feet and Bear turned to him. "Now there's another man to stink before sundown," he said. He smiled. "Three dead men and it ain't even noon yet. This burg is sure getting some snap."

His face stiff with shock, McBride looked at Bear. "You didn't have to kill him."

"Yes I did. He would have killed you, John. His mind was made up, and you aren't near good enough to shade a man like that. You wouldn't even be close."

"I could have talked him out of it."

"Roddy Rentzin was a talkin' man, sure enough," Bear allowed. "But when his talkin' was done he'd have drawed down on you and put a bullet through your brain pan."

Dave Channing walked to the cantina from the door of the saloon. He looked at Bear, a slight smile on his lips. "You didn't give him much of a fair shake, did you?"

The old man's dislike of Channing bubbled to the surface. "You saying I should have politely asked him to draw down on me?"

Channing shook his head. He was still smiling. "I'm not saying that. You kill a man any way you can. The bottom line is, fair shake or no, he's dead and you're alive."

"Damn right," Bear said. "First sensible thing I've ever heard you say."

Men were gathering around the cantina again, one of them Jed McKay. His horrified eyes widened when he saw Rentzin sprawled dead on the ground. "My God," he whispered, "another one. What is happening to us?"

"His name is Roddy Rentzin, a fast gun out of the Brazos River country," Bear said. "At least he was until very recently. He came all the way up here"—the old man grinned—"to gun your town marshal."

McKay's eyes moved to McBride. "Why?"

"Because I'm the man who killed Hack Burns," McBride answered, his voice bitter. "That's all the reason he needed."

A silence fell over the crowd, each man busy with his own thoughts. It was Bear who broke it.

"Just to cheer everybody up," he said with a grin, "I got more good news. Young Roddy there has three gunfighting brothers. There's Reuben, Rufus and Ransom, and Ransom is the worst of them, fast with the iron and a man-killer from way back." The old scout paused for effect. "They could come here a-lookin'."

A man in the crowd said, "I seen you kill the kid, Bear. If them Rentzin boys come here, it's you they'll be a-looking for."

"Could be," Bear said. "Only thing is, when the Rentzins gather for a killing, they don't much like leaving witnesses behind. Catch my drift?"

"They can't kill everybody in town," McKay scoffed.

Bear grinned. "Oh yes they can. The Rentzins are hell on wheels and they'll play hob. And they won't do it alone. Them boys ride with a dozen hard cases that make the worst bronco Apaches look like a bunch of maiden aunts."

McKay thought that through; then he made up his mind. "Nobody knows that gunfighter was ever in Suicide, do they?" He was talking to McBride.

"All I know is he came up from the Brazos after me. Maybe he told his brothers where he was headed, maybe not."

"Even if he did, he wouldn't have mentioned this town by name. Up until today he probably didn't even know we existed."

McBride nodded. "I'd say that's the case."

"Then he was never here, and that's what we'll tell the Rentzins if they come. We'll get rid of any trace of him." McKay talked beyond McBride to the crowd. "You men, grab picks and shovels from my store and come with me. We'll bury this man deep, well away from town. We'll bury his guns and saddle with him." The storekeeper's eyes moved over faces and stopped at Nathan Levy. "Nathan, take his horse into the hills and shoot it. The coyotes will soon clean up the mess."

"Nice horse," Levy said, patting the animal on the neck. "I've always liked paints."

"Just do as I say. Take the damn thing far away and shoot it where it won't be found."

Levy nodded. "I'll shoot it."

McKay clapped his hands, his breath clouding in the cold air. "Right, then let's get started. We're going to kill Roddy Rentzin all over again and bury him where he'll never be found."

John McBride stood at the door of the El Coyote Azul and moodily looked out at the hammering rain kicking up Vs of yellow mud in the street. It was noon, but there was no sun, the clouds thick and black, casting a gloomy, dark pall over the town and the surrounding land.

"Do you think they'll come?" McBride asked without turning his head.

"Who?"

"The Rentzin boys."

From inside the cantina, Bear said, "I'm sure of it. That is, if they can find their way."

"Maybe McKay is right. If people say Roddy Rentzin wasn't here, they might ride on."

"They mought. But you better not be here, or me."

"You mean hide out until they're gone?"

"Something like that."

McBride shook his head. "You know, so far my profit from the cantina has been three dollars and seventeen cents, and all of that goes to McKay. I'm beginning to think I made a mistake buying this place."

"You mean you've only begun to realize that?"

In the distance thunder rumbled, coming off the Guadalupe peaks. As though he hadn't heard Bear, McBride said, "I've got the people of Suicide to worry about, who's killing them. I told Allison I'd protect her, but from what? Throw in two fat ladies who are eating up all my profits, Angel Guerrero and his bandits and now the Rentzin brothers. I'd say I have more woes than a man should reasonably be expected to handle."

The old scout joined McBride at the door, a glass of mescal in his hand. He glanced outside and spat into the mud. "You could always go home. Go back to New York."

McBride turned his head and smiled at the old man. "I'm not exactly a stalwart frontiersman, am I?"

"You do all right, John. Your trouble is, you have a reputation as a gunfighter you don't deserve and that will haunt you wherever you go. Leave this place, change your name and give the hardware business a try. Or go be a detective again in the big city.''

McBride suddenly felt defensive. ''Hey, I'm pretty good with a gun.''

The old man nodded. ''Yes, I'd say you're handy with a revolver, fair to middling with a rifle. But you lack the one thing a gunfighter needs.''

''What's that?''

''You're not a born killer.''

''Like you?''

''Exactly right. Just like me.''

''Did gunning Roddy Rentzin today trouble you?''

''I did what I had to do. I had to kill him.''

''Bear, did it trouble you?''

''No.''

''It troubled me. He was so young, just a kid.''

''He was grown enough to carry a gun and take his chances. He would have killed you, John.''

''Suppose I'd been carrying my self-cocker?''

''He would still have killed you.''

''If it came down to it, how would I stand with the Rentzins?''

''On his worst day, the slowest of the brothers could outdraw and kill you.''

Despite his gloominess, McBride laughed. ''Bear, you surely know how to cheer a man. According to you, just about anybody in the West who carries a gun can shade me.''

The old scout's eyes held no humor. ''I'm just telling you how it is, John. Or how it's going to be.''

Chapter 24

Wearing Bear Miller's slicker, John McBride climbed the hill toward the Elliot house in a heavy downpour. The ground was slick and muddy underfoot and made walking difficult. Thunder crashed and lightning reached Jack Frost fingers across the sky, flaring a mother-of-pearl brilliance that momentarily banished the murkiness of the day.

A cold wind drove rain into McBride's face and drummed on his plug hat as he angled away from the house for fifty yards, then stopped at a flatiron-shaped shelf of red sandstone that jutted from the hillside. Sagebrush grew thickly around the base of the rock along with a few stunted juniper.

McBride looked back at the cantina. A rifleman hidden in the brush would have had a clear shot at Adam Whitehead. He could then have climbed higher up the hill to where the juniper was thicker and disappeared from sight. A small man, if he was dressed right, would have blended with the brush and rocks, especially in the gray, early-morning light.

A man like the dwarf Jim Drago.

McBride scouted around the rock and delved into the sagebrush. He found nothing. Thunderclouds were rolling overhead and now lightning cracked every few seconds. A gusting wind hammered icy rain at McBride, heedless of his discomfort, reminding him that he was alone on a hillside where every roar of thunder could be followed by instant, flashing death.

He left the rock and retraced his steps, his feet slipping on glassy mud.

All the windows but one were open at the Elliot house. The window of the turret room where he'd heard Allison talking with a man was tight shut. McBride did some mental calculations, looking down the hill again. A rifleman in the turret room would also have a clear shot at Whitehead. All he'd have had to do was make the kill, quickly shut the window and vanish into a rectangle of darkness.

His mind working, McBride wiped rain from his eyes. Adam Whitehead and his wife had made no secret of the fact that they wanted to burn Allison as a witch and hang Moses and Drago. The woman had motive and she, or someone close to her, could have waited in the turret room with a rifle until Whitehead showed in the street.

McBride acknowledged to himself that Allison, though stunningly beautiful, was strange, almost to the point of mental illness. But did that make her a cold-blooded killer? She'd told him that someone else had killed the men who had tried to rob her. The man who pulled the trigger could have been Drago or Moses. Or was it someone else, someone McBride would never suspect?

The answer to McBride's questions could lie within the walls of the house. Somehow he had to get inside without being seen. He needed to search the turret room.

The open windows!

He could wait until dark and climb through a window into the house. It would be risky, but worth it. The answer to a lot of questions might lie in that tiny room . . . and put him on the trail of a killer.

As he made his way back down the hill, McBride made up his mind. He would do it tonight.

The late afternoon was trying desperately to hang on to the feeble light of day in a futile attempt to hold off the coming of darkness. The thunder had passed but the rain fell steadily, turning the street into a sluggish river of yellow mud.

McBride had no customers, little hope of customers, and even the normally cheerful fat ladies seemed depressed, picking unenthusiastically at their food in the kitchen. The El Coyote Azul had all the warmth of a tomb, the only sound the steady plop! plop! plop! of water from the leaky roof falling into the tin buckets McBride had scattered around the floor.

Restlessly, he stepped to the door and looked outside through the shifting shroud of the raking rain. He was waiting for the death of the day but it seemed it would never come. Down at the saloon someone was picking out the tune of "Buckeye Jim," a lonesome jangle of discordant notes tinkling from a tinny piano. Jed McKay had already shut his store, its single window dark. Smoke from wood fires hung in the air, acrid and sharp, and over by the cottonwoods the first of the night birds were calling.

McBride was about to go back inside when he caught sight of a lone horseman splashing across the rain-swollen creek. The rider sat slumped in the saddle, his chin on his chest, the posture of a tired man or a dead one.

It took McBride a while before he recognized Bear Miller's tall horse and his buckskin shirt black with rain. Worry in him, he stepped out of the cantina into the downpour, watching Bear come.

The old man had turned toward the livery, but he spotted McBride and swung his black toward him. Bear drew rein at the cantina door. His face was gray, a man teetering on the brink of complete exhaustion.

"They're coming, John," he said, his eyes far away, still somewhere back on the trail he'd ridden. "I smelled them all morning and left on a scout, and now I know—they're coming."

McBride stepped to Bear's stirrup. "Who is coming?"

"Apaches. Maybe twenty-five, thirty bucks. All of them painted for war. No women or children."

"Bear," McBride said hurriedly, panic spiking in him, "are they headed here? Now?"

"Not now, later. Maybe tomorrow. But Apaches are notional. They could come anytime." Bear swayed in the saddle. "They're camped about ten miles back, in an arroyo just east of Guadalupe Peak. I got close, John, real close. They were drinking tiswin, getting loud, and I heard a fair piece of what they were saying. The young warriors are real worked up about the massacre of the women and children we saw at the ranchería. They've got so much blood in their eyes, it could be some of them lost kinfolk."

For a moment Bear's face was hidden in shadow under the brim of his hat; then he raised his head again. "I heard them, John, heard them plain. They're coming here. Burn this town and kill everybody . . . revenge raid . . . coming here . . ."

The old man's story was breaking into pieces. He reeled in the saddle and McBride caught him as he fell.

The fat ladies rushed to Bear's side after McBride laid him out on a table. "Coffee," he said. "And whiskey."

That much English the women understood. Within a few minutes they had the old scout sitting up, holding coffee spiked with bourbon to his lips, cooing over him like amorous turtledoves.

"Feeling better?" McBride asked.

Bear nodded, grinning. Displaying the incredible resilience of the frontiersman, he was looking better. "I'm drinking coffee and whiskey and I'm surrounded by about seven hundred pounds of female. How would you feel?"

Normally McBride would have laughed, but right then he was hard-pressed to see humor in anything. "How long do we have?" he asked.

"Like I said, John, an Apache is mighty notional. Sometimes he doesn't even know what he's thinking his ownself and that makes him hard to read. I'd say tomorrow, the next day or when the rain lets off, whatever comes first."

"Bear, you know Apaches. What do we do?"

The old man answered without hesitation. "Get everybody in town to the Elliot house. Maybe we can hold them off from there."

"Allison told me that's out of the question. She says the Apaches are our concern, not hers."

"That won't cut it, John. We'll just march up there and take the house from her."

"Men might die doing that."

"Hell, a lot more men will die if we don't. I reckon Miss Elliot has no say in the matter."

McBride hesitated a moment before saying, "Bear, tell your lady friends to go back to the kitchen. We need to talk."

"Sure, John." The old man said something to the women in Spanish, pausing every now and then to nod toward McBride. Whatever he told them didn't go over well because they glared daggers at McBride, then flounced into the kitchen, their noses in the air.

Surprise at the women's attitude widening his eyes, McBride asked, "What did you tell them?"

"Nothing much. I said you were a straitlaced, long-faced Yankee from the big city and you hated to see other folks having fun."

"Bear, if the Apaches kill me, please don't write my obituary."

"Pity," the old man grinned. "I'd have written you up real nice." He swung his legs off the table and flopped into a chair. "Now, what do you want to talk to me about that's so all-fired private?"

Briefly, McBride told Bear about his visit to the Elliot house and how he heard Allison talking to a man in the turret room. Then he described how he'd scouted the hill that afternoon but failed to find any evidence of a bushwhacker.

"The more I think about it, the more I'm convinced the bullet that killed Adam Whitehead was fired from the turret room of the house," he concluded. "I plan on taking a look at that room tonight."

"How are you going to do that?" Bear asked. His sour expression revealed that he didn't think much of the plan.

"Allison leaves all the windows in the house open. I'll climb in a window and then make my way to the turret room."

"And get your damn fool head blown off. If Miss Elliot doesn't do it, her man Moses will or somebody else. Maybe the man you heard her talking with."

"You got a better idea, huh?" McBride's question was edged with irritation.

"Yeah. You and me walk up to the house and shoot our way inside if we have to. Then we step over bodies and head for the turret room."

"Suppose it's empty? Suppose Allison had nothing at all to do with Whitehead's death?"

Bear shrugged. "Then all we've done is waste a few cartridges."

"I think I'll do it my way," McBride said.

"Suit yourself." Bear drained his cup. "I need more

coffee." He rose to his feet and glanced toward the kitchen where the fat ladies were giggling. Then he said, "John, do you think you could stable my hoss? I'm feeling right poorly."

McBride smiled. "Sure, Bear. I can see you're feeling peaked."

The old man stepped toward the kitchen, then turned and said, "Rub him down real good, John. And feed him some oats, mind."

Before McBride could answer, Bear disappeared behind the curtain and the fat ladies squealed with excitement.

It was now full dark, made darker by cloud and rain. Wearing Bear's slicker, McBride led his horse toward the livery. He glanced behind him and saw no light in the turret room of the Elliot house. It looked like whoever had been there was now gone. But he could have left evidence of his identity behind and McBride was determined to find it. The mystery man might be the one who enforced the rule, who had murdered so many, including women and children.

Or he could be just a visitor or a lover, guilty of no more than talking loudly.

The thought of Allison Elliot with a lover would once have upset McBride. Now it did not and he felt oddly relieved.

The stable was dark and smelled of damp hay. McBride looked around for a lamp but couldn't find one. He groped his way forward and led the black into a vacant stall. He stripped the black's saddle and bridle, and as his eyes grew accustomed to the gloom, he spotted a piece of sacking hanging over the stall partition. He began to rub down the horse.

A bullet smashed into the timber divider close to where he was standing, showering splinters. Another split the air next to his head. He dived for the ground, hit the dirt hard and rolled. He stayed where he was, hardly daring to breathe.

A soft, mocking voice came from the hayloft: Jim Drago's voice.

"I told you I'd get you, Miller. You dead yet?"

Then McBride understood. He was wearing Bear's slicker, leading his horse. In the dark, the dwarf had mistaken him for the old man.

"I think you must be dead, Miller. But I'm coming down there to look."

Feet scuffled through hay in the loft, stepping toward the ladder. Bear's Henry was still in the scabbard, strapped to the saddle. Carefully, trying to make no sound, McBride rose to his feet. He felt around the saddle, found the rifle and slid it free. Drago was almost at the stairs. McBride cranked a round and fired at where he guessed the opening for the ladder was. He heard a startled shriek, then the pounding of running feet that sent hay sifting through the cracks of the loft floorboards.

McBride levered the Henry and fired. He worked the rifle again and again, dusting shots into the hayloft. Then he ran for the ladder and climbed quickly.

Drago was gone.

The wooden shutters that closed the loading door just under the roof peak were wide-open. McBride looked outside. The little man must have jumped and then fled into the darkness. There was no sign of him.

"John, are you alive?"

Bear had walked into the stable and McBride heard other voices, one of them McKay's. It seemed that his rifle shots had roused the whole town.

"I'm here," McBride yelled. "And I think I'm still alive."

He climbed down the ladder into a pool of faded orange light. McKay was holding a lamp above his head. "You hit?" he asked.

McBride shook his head. "No, he missed me."

"Who missed you?" asked another man standing in the shadows.

"Drago. He mistook me for Bear." McBride stepped closer to the old man. "I was wearing your slicker and leading your horse. He planned on making good on his threat to kill you."

In the lamplight the hard planes of McKay's face were angled and harsh. "The attempted murder of a town marshal is a hanging offense."

"He didn't know it was me," McBride said. "I guess he still doesn't."

"That's neither here nor there," McKay said. "When we catch him, we'll hang him."

There was a murmur of approval from the other men.

"If I don't see him first," Bear said.

McBride walked past the old man and into the street. He looked toward the Elliot house. Every window showed light, including the turret room. The racket of rifle shots travels far and Allison and Moses would be alert for trouble. He would not be searching the turret room that night.

Bear stepped out of the barn, and heedless of the rain, stood next to McBride. He cocked his head to one side, like an inquisitive bird. Listening.

"Hear that, John?" he asked.

McBride heard only the steely hiss of the rain. He shook his head.

Bear glanced behind him. "You, McKay, and the rest of you men. Step out here."

McKay led the others outside. They were talking among themselves until Bear hushed them into quiet. "Hear anything?"

"How can we hear in this downpour?" McKay asked.

"Damn it, man, listen!"

Then McBride heard it . . . the dim throb of drums in the distance of the night.

Bear read McBride's face. "Drums, right?"

The younger man nodded.

"The Apaches heard the gunshots," Bear said. "They're answering us, telling us to be patient and not to go wasting ammunition. They want us to know they'll be coming very soon."

McKay had listened with disbelief, his eyes wide, horrified. His sharp intake of breath was palpable in the sudden quiet and the circle of light from his lantern danced on the muddy ground as his hand trembled.

Chapter 25

McBride watched Jed McKay fight to regain his composure. There were other men present and he did not want to show yellow. When he did, he laid the lamp at his feet and in his best take-command voice told the others that Apaches were not his immediate concern.

"Our first task is to hunt down Drago," he said. "You men get your guns and spread out over town. Find him."

It was Nathan Levy, dressed in a tattered robe he'd thrown over his long johns, who voiced the concern of the others. "Jed, in the dark we could walk right into Drago's gun. The Poison Dwarf has killed his share and I don't want to end up just another notch on the handle of his Colt."

Other men agreed and Conrad Heber said, "Jed, Herr Levy is right. We wait until first light. Then we go after Drago. This is a better plan, ja?"

Bear had been listening in silence, and now he said, "Listen to these men, McKay. Drago is a snake and he'll back-shoot you if he gets a chance. Wait until morning. At least then you'll get a fair shake."

McKay looked relieved. He'd shown that he had backbone and now he was willing to let it go. "All right, we wait until sunup. You men gather at my store and bring as many others as you can find. We'll track down that little assassin and string him up from a cottonwood down by the creek."

"You won't find him, McKay," Dave Channing said. The pale gambler was still dressed in his frock coat, frilled shirt and string tie. He looked like he hadn't slept in days. "I'd guess he's already tucked up in Allison Elliot's best guest room."

The Apaches still stalked like demons through the dark recesses of McKay's mind where fear dwelled, and now he pounced on a chance to mention them again. "Marshal McBride, talking about Miss Elliot, did you mention to her about using her home in the event of an attack by the savages?"

"Yes, I did. She turned me down flat."

"Turned me down flat," Conrad Heber repeated. "What does that mean?"

"It means if the Apaches attack, we're on our own."

Heber was agitated and his English began to slip. "Dat ist ein outrage! Dat vill not stand!"

The German looked to others for support and found it from Channing. "Heber is right. It won't stand. If the Apaches attack, we'll all be up that hill anyway. I don't know if Miss Elliot has ever seen drunk, screaming Apaches on the warpath, but when she does she'll open her doors fast enough. Now, I'm getting out of the rain." He touched his hat, smiling. "Good night, gentlemen."

McBride watched Channing go, wondering about the man. His frock coat and linen were expensive, but much patched and frayed, and his shoes were scuffed and down at heel. The gun he wore showed signs of considerable use and McBride had no doubt he could handle it well when pushed. But there was an air of defeat about the man, as though at some point in his life he'd taken a wrong turn and lost his way. The gambler seemed to have known better times in places where men and manners were very different. He did not belong in a hick town like Suicide. But then, where exactly did he belong?

Men were saying good night to McBride, and Channing faded from his mind, just as the man was now fading into the darkness.

He handed Bear the Henry and the two men walked in silence down the rainy street before splitting up, McBride to the El Coyote Azul, Bear to the hotel.

By the time he reached the door, McBride had made a decision. His brush with Jim Drago had woken him up to some harsh realities about life in the West. From now on he would wear his gun.

By morning Suicide was on a war footing. Apache smoke was talking among the hills to the west of town and McKay, helped by Bear, had pickets out.

The hunt for Drago was forgotten as half-a-dozen men took up positions at the creek and several more climbed the hill where they could act as lookouts.

McBride had no customers for breakfast until Bear stopped by and ordered coffee. "Seen the smoke?" he asked, laying his rifle on the table.

McBride nodded. "You have any idea what the Apaches are saying to each other?"

The old scout shook his head as he spooned sugar into his cup. "I never could read smoke, but what it's saying is plain enough. It's spelling out trouble for Suicide."

"Bear, are you staying or going?"

"Been thinking about it, John. I don't owe this town a damn thing and there's nothing to stop me moving on."

"But you won't." McBride was reading Bear's eyes.

"No, I won't." The old man tried his coffee and added more sugar until McBride thought the spoon would stand up in the cup. "One reason is that I don't want to leave Jim Drago on my back trail. I want to settle with him before I leave."

"And the other?"

Bear jerked a thumb toward the kitchen. "Them two. They don't want to leave. They say Apaches are men like any other and living with them can't be any worse than it is among the blancos."

McBride smiled. "I thought you'd convinced them otherwise."

"Not yet, but I'm working on it."

A shot echoed from the creek, then another. Bear scowled. "Damn fools are so scared, they're shooting at shadows." He rose to his feet. "I'd better get down there."

"I'll come with you," McBride said. He stepped

behind the bar and found his shoulder holster and gun.

"Changed your mind I see," Bear said.

"Drago changed it for me. Well, him and the Apaches."

The six townsmen, under the loose command of Nathan Levy, were strung out along the creek bank. They were hunkered down and had a fairly uninterrupted field of fire for several hundred yards; then the flat climbed higher into rolling hills cut through by shallow arroyos where piñon and juniper grew. A steady drizzle was falling and the clouds were so low they hazed the crests of the higher hills with gray mist. The morning was cold, the wind raw, the air smelling of mud and rain.

McBride and Bear dropped down into the creek, then splashed across ankle-deep water to the far bank. Levy saw them and rose to his feet. His nose was red, a drip perilously suspended at the end, and his cheeks were pinched, tight to the bone.

"Levy, who fired?" Bear asked.

Before he could answer, a lanky man farther down the bank yelled, "I did."

"Was it an Apache?" This from McBride.

"Darn tootin' it was," the man said. "He was over there behind that nearest mesquite bush. I think I winged him, because he ain't made a move since."

McBride's eyes reached out across the distance. The land was dotted with mesquite and cat's-claw and wide expanses of sand streaked by patches of low grass. He turned to Bear. "I'll go take a look."

"That isn't wise, John," the old man warned. "There's nothing more dangerous than a wounded loco Apache."

"If it is an Apache, there will be others close by," McBride said, "and we can't hold them here. Bear, you see me waving, order everybody back to the hill, fast." He glanced beyond Bear to the rise. "Are those lookouts asleep up there?"

Bear smiled. "If an Apache don't want to be seen, then you don't see him."

McBride spoke to Levy. "Nathan, tell your boys to cover me. If you see me hightailing it back here, I want to hear rifles killing Apaches."

"You can count on us, Marshal," Levy said. But McBride saw no confidence in his eyes. Close-up, Apaches could put the fear of God in a man. This McBride knew, because he was scared to death himself.

He turned to Bear. "Keep your rifle handy."

The old man nodded. "John, know this—if I see the Apaches carrying you away, I'll scatter your brains with a bullet."

"Thanks," McBride said. "As always, you're a great comfort to me."

"Damn right," Bear said, pleased.

Chapter 26

McBride scrambled up the creek bank and, every nerve in his body jangling, crouched low and headed for the mesquite. He had drawn his Smith & Wesson and he held the .38 up and ready. His mouth was dry, the thud of his heart loud in his ears, and his breath was coming in short, sharp gasps.

The rain was now heavier and within moments his coat was soaked. He transferred the revolver to his left hand, wiped the wet, sweaty palm of his right on his pants, then took up the gun again.

He was less than twenty-five yards from the mesquite and out in the open.

McBride thought about firing into the bush, flushing out anyone who might be hiding in there. But he decided against it. If the Apaches were lurking close, the sound of his gun could bring them running.

Twenty yards . . . ten . . . five . . . McBride's skin was crawling in expectancy of a bullet.

He rounded the mesquite—and found nothing. If an Apache had been there, he was long gone. He scouted around the bush. After several minutes he found a single smear of blood clinging to the underside of a yellowish green leaf. If there had been more, it had been washed away by the rain. Dropping to one knee, McBride's eyes searched the muddy ground. Then, close to the base of the mesquite where it had been protected by the thick growth of branches, he saw a partial track. It had not been made by an Apache moccasin. The imprint of a boot heel was plain and it had sunk two inches or so into the soft dirt. The heel had been high and small in area, suggesting the boot of a man who rode much and walked little. A Texas puncher could have worn this boot . . . or Jim Drago.

The more McBride studied the heel print, the more he was convinced that Drago had been wearing his fancy boots when he jumped from the livery window. Fearing a manhunt, he'd either hid out behind the mesquite or had been making his way back to town at first light when he was mistaken for an Apache.

It didn't look like the little man had been hit hard, but where was he now?

McBride rose to his feet. The dwarf was a welcome guest at the Elliot house and if he was wounded, he might seek refuge there. The man was dangerous, especially if he found himself cornered, but McBride quickly made up his mind. He was going after him.

McBride returned to the creek and told the others what he'd found, and his suspicion that the dwarf had headed for the Elliot house. Levy and the man who'd fired the shots insisted it had been an Apache, but Bear would have none of it.

"Apaches don't wear boots," he said. "Maybe it was Drago, maybe it wasn't, but I'm walking up the hill to find out."

"No, you're not, Bear," McBride said. "For what it's worth, I'm the town marshal. It's my job to arrest Drago."

"Then I'll go with you. The little man's handy with a gun and he'll kill you any way he can."

"I'll go it alone, Bear," McBride said, a note of finality in his voice. He smiled at the old man. "If the Apaches come this way, we need your rifle right here at the creek."

Bear thought it through and apparently found some logic in what McBride had said. "All right, do it your way, John. But if I hear shots from up there, I'll come a-runnin'."

McBride grinned. "Run fast, old timer. Run real fast."

When he reached the cantina, the fat ladies stripped off McBride's wet coat and held it to the stove fire to dry. They giggled as he stood for a few moments, gloomily watching the coat steam. It was all but ruined and he had no money to buy another.

Since he was making an official visit to the Elliot house he wiped off his celluloid collar with soapy water before attaching it to his shirt. Then he knotted his tie. His coat was still damp and smelled of scorched cloth, but the two women helped him into it, looking proud of themselves. He smiled and said nothing.

McBride adjusted his shoulder holster, then pinned his marshal's badge to the lapel of the coat. After he settled his bowler hat square on his head, he decided he looked official, like one of New York's finest and not the marshal of a one-horse town.

The giggling of the fat ladies wafted him out the cantina door. He bent his head against the rain and headed for the hill.

Aware that he was a wide-open target should Drago be waiting at a window with a rifle, McBride increased his pace along the path leading to the house. But he reached the massive door without incident and swung the heavy bronze ring. He heard the hollow boom of metal on wood echoing through the house like the dull tolling of a mourning bell—then a dead silence that echoed louder.

McBride stood in the rain for a couple long minutes, getting wetter. He was about to try the door again when it swung slowly open, creaking on its iron hinges. Allison Elliot stood there, smiling at him, and McBride's heart lurched. For all her strange ways the woman had a devastating effect on him. There was a wild, untamed sexuality about her that hinted at boudoir delights a man could only dream about.

"How nice to see you again, John," she said with a soft purr that made McBride weak at the knees. "Please, come inside out of the rain."

McBride stepped past the woman, smelling her perfume and an undertone of whiskey and cigars. "I'm so sorry to trouble you, Allison," he said.

"Ah . . . that stern tone of voice suggests an official visit by an officer of the law. Am I correct?"

"I'm afraid so." McBride suddenly remembered to remove his hat. "I'm looking for Jim Drago."

Allison seemed genuinely shocked. "Goodness, whatever for?"

"He tried to kill me last night. Mistook me for Bear Miller."

"I can't believe that. I'm sure you're mistaken."

McBride smiled. "Allison, when a man takes shots at me I remember him real well."

Allison's hand flew between her breasts. "Oh dear, that's very distressing. Poor little man, he was probably scared to death of this Miller person and that's why he shot at him—or rather shot at you by mistake."

"Allison, Jim Drago can make mistakes, but he doesn't scare easily. Is he in the house?"

"Why no. He hasn't dropped by since you were last here."

"He may have gained entry without your knowledge. Mind if I look around?"

"Normally I would say no to that request, but since this is an official police visit, then of course." She waved a hand toward the interior of the house. "Where would you like to start?"

McBride jumped at the chance. "Let's start at the top and work our way down. I'd like to see the turret rooms first."

Allison smiled. "Ah, the servants' quarters, except I don't have any servants." She gathered up her skirt. "Follow me, John."

The woman led McBride to the staircase, but when they reached the landing she turned right, away from the turret room he badly wanted to see. An identical narrow stairway angled from the hall and led to a small landing and a door. Allison pulled the door open and stepped inside.

"I use this for storage, as you can see," she said. "One day I must get around to throwing out half of this stuff." The room was littered with boxes of all shapes and sizes; a few pieces of furniture and a thick layer of dust covered the floor. The dust had not been disturbed and McBride guessed this room had not been used in years.

"I'd like to see the other turret room," he said.

"That room has been empty for a long time, John. I doubt Jim Drago would have made his way up there."

"Nevertheless, I'd still like to see it."

"As you wish."

Allison made her way to the other wing of the house, McBride following her. They walked past the bedroom where he'd slept and climbed the stairway. Allison opened the door and motioned McBride inside.

The room was empty, the window tightly shut.

McBride immediately noticed two things: The floor was free of dust—and the tiny room entombed a stench that hit him like a fist.

In New York he'd smelled that smell many times in the course of his career. It was the sweet, cloying stink of rotting flesh.

Chapter 27

"My God, Allison," McBride said. "Do you keep dead bodies in here?"

For a fleeting moment the woman looked stung. But she recovered quickly and said, "We're close to the roof, John. It's probably dampness. Nobody has lived in this room for years."

"But I'm sure I've seen a light in here."

"And I'm sure you haven't. Sometimes Moses leaves doors open. You probably saw light from the hallway reflected up here." She smiled. "Shall we continue?"

McBride nodded, but he walked to the window and looked out. The window had three wide panes that wrapped around the front and sides of the turret. From here a rifleman could cover the entire slope and every corner of the town. A watchful man would see everybody who came and went in Suicide and, if his eyes were keen, far out into the plains in three directions. It was the ideal watchtower. Only to the rear was there no window because the hill itself obscured the view.

"Shall we continue our search?" Allison asked again.

This time, grateful to get away from the dreadful stench, McBride crossed the room and stepped through the door. He didn't breathe again until he and Allison were back in the hallway.

"I'm sorry the smell disturbed you," the woman said. "I'll get Moses to clean the room right away."

McBride was watching her eyes. "It smells like something died in there."

"Many things have died in this house, including dreams," Allison said. "Sometimes the death of a dream leaves a foul odor for those sensitive enough to detect it." She smiled. "Now, the rest of the house?"

McBride searched the basement last. It was empty but for a couple of dozen stacked barrels. Thick cobwebs hanging from the rafters and corners told him that no one had been down there in a very long time. He had expected to find nothing and he had, but still, disappointment tugged at him. Allison walked him to the door.

"The next time you visit I hope you'll come as John the good friend and not John the stern marshal."

"I'm sure that will be the case," McBride said, half smiling.

The woman was silent for a few moments. Then she said, "I will be leaving this house soon. Circumstances— things—are coming to a head and all my reasons for staying in Suicide will soon be gone. I will call on you then, John. I will need your help."

"What kind of help, Allison?"

"When the time comes I'll tell you. Then you will have to make a choice. I will offer you money, power, influence . . . and me."

"And my other options?"

"There is only one. If you wish, you can choose poverty, obscurity, a useless life and a meaningless death."

"Easy choice to make." McBride grinned.

"Let's hope you choose the right one." Allison held out her hand. "Good day, Marshal McBride."

McBride took the woman's hand. It was cold—like ice.

It was not yet noon and the rain, falling hard and smelling of mildew, showed no sign of letting up. The plains around Suicide were shadowed with gray, the clouds hanging so low there was no horizon, only a merging of the dark land and the darker arch of the sky. As he walked away from the creek in the direction of the El Coyote Azul, McBride saw a small herd of antelope trot toward water, then veer away, frightened by the man smell. They trotted into the murk again, and distance and a shifting mist swallowed them.

McBride was concerned. The men manning the creek were passing around a jug and a couple of them were already half drunk. It was a bad omen. Drunken men, filled with whiskey courage, should not fight Apaches.

McBride sat with a cup of coffee in front of him, swearing in a slow whisper. If the Apaches attacked, he'd pull the pickets back to the hill. Hopefully he could save enough of them to mount some kind of defense.

His thoughts turned to Allison Elliot. What kind of help would she soon ask him to provide, and what did she mean that things were coming to a head in Suicide? And why did the empty turret room stink like a charnel house?

Try as he might, McBride could not tie it together. All he could do was wait, and see how events unfolded. Maybe then he—

Bear Miller stepped into the cantina, words tripping over themselves as they tumbled from his mouth. "John, Texas Rangers a-comin'. Carrying their dead."

McBride walked outside into the downpour. The Rangers were riding from the creek, seven mustached men sitting hunched on good horses. Several of them wore bloodstained bandages and three others were draped over their saddles, heads swaying with every step of their mounts.

Bear's tight face revealed his concern. The Rangers looked like they'd tangled with Apaches and had come off a poor second best in the fight.

The riders drew rein at the cantina and a big man wearing a yellow slicker looked over the place, lingering for a moment on the painting of the blue coyote. His eyes settled for a moment on Bear, dismissed him, then turned to McBride. "You own this place?"

McBride nodded and the big Ranger said, "Will you feed my men?"

"Of course. Step down, all of you, and come inside." McBride turned to Bear. "Tell your ladies to put on some grub and pour mescal." His glance moved to the dead men and the Ranger read the question in his eyes.

"They're not going anywhere," he said.

The big man swung stiffly and wearily from the saddle. He let the reins of his horse trail, stripped off his glove and offered McBride his hand. "Sergeant Ed Walker, C Company, Texas Rangers, out of El Paso."

McBride took the man's hand. "Name's John McBride, out of New York and other places."

Walker shot a glance at McBride, a flash of recognition showing in his tired eyes. "Heard that name back on the trail a piece. Mr. McBride, I'd say you either got trouble headed your way or some mighty interesting kinfolk."

Before McBride could question the Ranger, he turned and waved to his men. "Inside, boys, there's grub and mescal."

McBride stood by the door as the Rangers filed past. There were a couple of old hands, men with hard faces and cold eyes, but the rest were very young, little more than boys. One had a bandaged shoulder, a brown bloodstain seeping through. Another had a thigh wound and limped badly and a third had a fat bandage wrapped around his head. All of them looked exhausted, as though they'd been through the mill.

The fat ladies rose to the occasion and spread the tables with huge platters of frijoles, onions and beef. The women got a lot of attention from the younger

Rangers, especially after they got a few shots of mescal inside them, and their giggling and hand-slapping helped lift some of the gloom from what was a crowd of beaten men.

McBride and Bear sat with Sergeant Walker. After the Ranger had eaten and built a cigarette, the old scout asked, "What happened out there? Were you hunting Apaches?"

Walker lit his smoke and sipped mescal before he answered. "Yeah, we were hunting Apaches. The Army has pulled out, waiting for infantry and artillery they say, though what good either will do against Mescaleros is beyond me. I was ordered to round up any hostiles we could find and herd them back to the nearest army post."

Walker's eyes wandered to one of the women and held there as he said, "We were ten, twelve miles east of Diablo Plateau when they hit us. That's broken country back there and we were spread out considerable. I lost two men in the first volley, then a third as we tried to retreat into an arroyo."

The big Ranger took off his hat and laid it on the table. He was almost bald, a few strands of black hair brushed back from the widow's peak on his forehead. "Look at these men," he said. "A year ago most of them were plowboys walking behind a mule's butt. They were no match for Mescaleros."

"You're here," McBride said mildly. "They must have stood."

"Oh, they stood all right. But none of us would be here if the Apaches hadn't suddenly quit the fight and left."

"I'd guess that's because they're headed for here," Bear said. "Why fight Rangers when you can loot a town where there's women and mescal?"

"Figured that much. We rode right through them in the dark—heard their drums. I reckoned they were working themselves up to attack this place. I rode through here a few years back and I recollected that it's the only settlement for miles around." Walker's speculative eyes tore away from the fat lady to McBride. "Are you kin to the Rentzin brothers, huh?"

Alarm flared in McBride. "Is that who you met on the trail?"

"Yeah, the day before the Apaches hit us. The three brothers and a bunch of hard cases riding with them. Ransom said his brother Roddy wired him that he was visiting a man called John McBride in a town south of the Guadalupe Ridge. Ronson says he and the others talked it over and decided it might be fun to join the party. That's why I had you pegged as long-lost kin."

"I'm no kin of the Rentzins," McBride said stiffly.

"Glad to hear it. Roddy Rentzin is a mean one and he badly wants to be a heap meaner. Is he here?"

"No." Bear jumped in quickly. "We haven't seen him."

"Strange that, because the Rentzin brothers know all about Suicide, it being the only settlement south of the ridge an' all. They were mighty sure Roddy was headed this way. Seems that one of their hard cases passed through here one time when he was on the dodge from the New Mexico law. The brothers were real interested in millions in gold he said was stashed somewhere in that abandoned old house up on the hill there. They asked me if I'd heard a rumor to that effect. I said I had, but told them not to put any stock in it." The big Ranger smiled. "Like anybody worth that amount of money would ever have lived in this dung heap." He looked quickly from McBride to Bear. "No offense intended."

"None taken," Bear said cheerfully. "Only, the house isn't abandoned. A woman lives up there with an old manservant."

Walker laughed. "Better tell her to look out for her fortune then."

McBride and Bear laughed with the Ranger, joining in the good joke. Then Bear's crafty eyes angled to McBride. "Where are the Rentzin boys now?"

"Behind us a ways. Like I said, it's rough, broken country back there and they had a mule wagon with them. That will slow them down some, even if the Apaches don't."

"Why the wagon?" McBride asked.

"To carry the gold they hope to find, I guess," Walker said, grinning. "Hell, I always figured the Rentzin boys were smarter than that."

"Well, gold can make a man take leave of his senses," McBride said.

Walker nodded. "I reckon so."

"I'm the town marshal here," McBride said.

"Saw that."

"Sergeant, the Apaches can attack this town at any

time. Once your Rangers are rested up, I'd like you to deploy three of them at the creek and the others on the hill."

"I'd sure like to help you, McBride," the man said. "But my boys are all used up and they're in no shape to fight. I'm headed home and I plan to take the long way around. You can get everybody in town together and I'll escort them as far as El Paso. I could use the additional fighting men anyhow."

"Sergeant, as a Texas Ranger your duty lies here," McBride said.

"No, my duty lies with my men. I told you they're in no condition to fight Apaches. Sorry, Marshal, but that's the way of it."

The Rangers had been listening and there were murmurs of agreement, the wounded among them displaying their bloody bandages.

McBride realized further argument was useless. With a sinking heart he also knew he was honor bound to give the citizens of Suicide the option of leaving with the Rangers.

How many of them would choose to stay?

Chapter 28

The men by the creek and those on the hill had seen the Rangers come in carrying their dead, and most had suddenly lost their appetite for fighting Apaches.

In the end, only Jed McKay, Nathan Levy, Conrad Heber and his wife, Clyde Kaleen and Dave Channing agreed to stay. Surprising McBride, Mrs. Whitehead refused to leave her home, saying that she would not desert her dead husband.

Counting Bear Miller and himself, McBride had only seven men to defend Suicide. It wasn't enough. It wasn't near enough.

The Rangers pulled out at dusk, the other townsmen walking or riding whatever mount they could scrounge. Sullen from whiskey and shame, the dozen departing citizens spoke to no one as they left and kept their eyes on the trail ahead, looking straight in front of them.

Joan Whitehead, an unholy light in her eyes, picked up horse dung and threw it after the departing townsmen. "Cowards!" she screamed. She looked around, picked up more, but McBride took it from her.

"Let them go," he said gently. "They're not worth it."

Mrs. Whitehead's eyes met his, vague and uncertain, as though she was trying to remember who he was. The woman was flirting with insanity, teetering very close to the edge.

"Now she can kill the rest of us," she shrieked. "Only the originals are left and the witch will destroy us one by one." She ran from man to man, stabbing at them with her finger. "Levy . . . dead! Heber . . . dead! Kaleen . . . dead! Channing . . ."

The gambler grabbed the woman and held her close, patting her thin back as he would a child. "It will be all right, Mrs. Whitehead. Trust me, it will be all right."

Joan Whitehead broke down completely. She sobbed uncontrollably, her face buried in Channing's shoulder, her unbound hair, wet from the rain, curling around her neck.

Watching the woman, McBride was filled with an impotent rage. He felt a wild urge to cross the creek, walk into the night and yell at the top of his lungs, "End it, damn you! Attack us and get it over with!"

Bear had his eyes on McBride, studying his face. The scout had seen that trapped, frenzied expression before, always before men cracked under the strain of an impending Indian attack. He remembered a young lieutenant, fresh from the Point, who had fled the field during a battle with Comanches. Bear had found his body a week later. The nineteen-year-old had shot himself. And he had known others, hardened veterans with the highest medals for bravery, who had shown yellow and later could not explain the reason why.

Now he was worried about McBride.

He stepped beside the big man and put a hand on his shoulder. "Easy, John," he whispered, not wanting the others to hear. "Take it easy, my friend."

McBride turned to Bear, staring at him without blinking, his jaw muscles working. He was fighting his own fear, searching for a way out of a dark tunnel where only madness lurked. He wanted to run—run far and fast—all the way back to New York, to his apartment, where he'd pull down the blinds, curl up in his bed and be safe.

"Easy, John," Bear said again. The thick-veined hand on McBride's shoulder was trembling. He watched the man battle the coward, stumbling to find his way. It was only a matter of moments now before he made his decision and it would be a close-run thing. Very close.

McBride blinked, like a man waking from sleep. He scrutinized the old scout's face and recognition dawned slowly in his eyes. "Bear, I'm all right," he said. "I'm all right." His voice cracked, but he had to say more. "I was running away from the Apaches. In my mind, I was running away."

"But you're still here," Bear said. "It takes courage to stand."

McBride glanced at the others: McKay, Kaleen, the rest, a dispirited bunch, soaked by the hammering rain, looking to him with hollow eyes for direction.

"You men," he said, loud, confident, like a Tammany Hall politician giving an election-day speech, "we'll fight the Apaches on this ground. We will not allow a bunch of savages to take what's ours and destroy it."

Dave Channing gently released Mrs. Whitehead, guiding her into the huge arms of Conrad Heber. "McBride, you may not have noticed, but there's only seven of us," he said. "How do you propose we fight them?"

"We'll take up positions on the hill and if things go bad, retreat to the Elliot house," McBride answered.

"Things will go bad, McBride," Channing said. "Count on it."

"Dave, do you have a better idea?" This, ominously soft, from Bear.

"No. No, I don't."

"Then you should have gone with the others while you had a chance," Bear said.

Channing smiled. "Go where? I could only go back to places I've been and nobody would be glad at my coming or sad at my leaving."

Nathan Levy, small and wound tight, stepped forward, the rain falling around him. "The marshal is right. We must make our fight here. I will not leave my beautiful hotel to be burned."

McKay, more pragmatic than the rest, spoke directly to Bear Miller. "You've fought Apaches before. How do you rate our chances up there on the hill?"

The old man smiled. "Slim to none, an' slim is already saddling up to leave town."

McKay took that like a punch to the gut, then

turned his gaze to the darkness where the plain began. "Maybe we should have left with the others."

"It's too late, McKay," Bear said. "Too late for you and too late for them."

McKay suddenly looked old, tired. "I don't catch your drift."

"It's easy enough to understand. You got a bunch of shot-up Rangers carrying their dead and a dozen scared rabbits from here with them. I don't think they'll make ten miles before they're ambushed and slaughtered to a man."

Bear's words sobered the group, and even Channing's pale face wore a shocked expression.

"What do we do, Marshal McBride?" Kaleen asked, his voice plaintive, like a child seeking reassurance from an adult.

McBride knew what he said in the next few seconds was vital. Above all, these men needed hope, at the very least a small expectation that they'd come out of this alive.

McBride chose his words carefully. "I want you men to get a few hours' sleep, then take up rifle positions on the hill before sunup. Channing, you're a gambler and don't need sleep. See that everybody is awake in three hours and on the hill."

"The women as well?"

"Yes. Mrs. Whitehead and Mrs. Heber and the two ladies who work for me."

Channing shook his head. "I sure hope you know what you're doing, McBride.' "

McBride wanted to say, "So do I," but he kept his mouth shut.

"Where will you be, Marshal?" Levy asked.

"Bear and me will scout around and see if we can locate where the Apaches are at. Then we'll swing to the south and maybe find out if the Rangers and the others got clear."

"We'll need you on the hill come first light," Channing said. "Just make sure you come back."

"Are you implying something, Dave?" Bear asked, his blue eyes hard.

McBride wondered at the old man's hostility toward Channing. Did he sense danger in the man like he had Roddy Rentzin?

Channing smoothed it over. "I'm implying nothing. Just be here, that's all."

"We'll be here, count on it," McBride said. "One of you men escort Mrs. Whitehead home. The rest of you get some shut-eye."

After the others were gone, vanishing into the steely pall of rain, Bear turned to McBride, his eyes burning. "I don't like that man, Dave Channing."

"Why?"

"He's a gunfighter and he's killed a few in his day."

"How do you know?"

"I know," Bear said, looking into the darkness as though seeking the gambler. "Trust me, I know."

Chapter 29

McBride and Bear approached the livery stable cautiously, guns drawn. There had been no sign of Jim Drago, but the little man was still a threat and one to be feared.

But the dwarf was not there and McBride and the old man quickly saddled their horses. Remembering what had happened the last time he tried to mount the mustang, McBride led the animal outside and shook his fist at it. "Remember this?" he said. "Well, it's still here."

The little horse did not seem intimidated but it didn't object either when McBride clumsily climbed into the saddle. McBride was vastly pleased. He figured he'd found the secret to horse training—the threat of a punch in the head.

Bear was not impressed. "I swear, John," he said, his eyes amused, "you mount a horse like an old lady with the rheumatisms." He watched McBride knee the mustang into motion. "Ride like one too."

McBride was stung but said nothing. He knew that was one argument with Bear he could not win.

An hour later they were well into the wilderness, riding through a vast tunnel of darkness. Lightning flashed violet in the sky but there was no thunder, and the unseen land around them lay quiet but for the hushed whisper of the falling rain.

Despite his age, Bear had eyes like a cat and led the way, though now and then he rode among prickly pear and cholla that tore at McBride's legs. They were riding through hill country, some of the slopes crowned with craggy mounds of rock and stunted juniper.

Bear drew rein on the shoulder of a grassy ridge, peering into the darkness. He raised his great beak of a nose, reading the wind. "We should have smelled them by this time," he whispered. "Hell, a few times back there I expected to ride right into their camp."

"Maybe they've pulled out," McBride suggested hopefully.

"Maybe." Bear sat his saddle, his head bowed, thinking. Finally he said, "The Apaches would have had scouts out, keeping their eyes skinned for the Army. Could be one of them seen the Rangers leave town and reported back here. The whole shebang might have up and gone after them." The old man smiled without humor. "Like I told you before, Apaches are notional, and I reckon they just changed their mind about attacking Walker and his men. Any Apache worth his tizwin would consider that a better option than sitting around a smoky fire in the rain.

And the Rangers have good horses, horses worth fighting for."

McBride was relieved. "Then they won't attack Suicide?"

"Oh yes, they will. Unless the Rangers and them others use them up real bad, which I doubt, they'll swing north again and hit the town. An Apache will ride two hundred miles out of his way to get into a good fight and Suicide isn't near that far."

McBride looked around him, his eyes straining to reach beyond the black wall of the night. "I think we might have missed them in the dark," he said. "Could be they're still around."

"Well, let's go see," Bear said.

"How are we going to find them? We're riding blind."

The old man touched his nose. "We'll follow this."

Ten minutes later they rode up on the abandoned Apache camp.

Bear swung out of the saddle. He stepped to the muddy ashes of a campfire and took a knee. But because of the rain it told him nothing. The old man scouted around, stopping every now and then to examine the ground. Finally he walked back to McBride.

"Hard to tell for sure, but I'd say they pulled out a couple of hours ago. Maybe thirty bucks, riding west."

"Then they are going after the Rangers."

"That would be my guess."

"What should we do, Bear? Go help the Rangers or head back to town?"

"I'd say the Apaches have already hit the Rangers and them other hayseeds. There's not a damn thing we can do to help them now, except sing their death songs—and ours."

McBride's teeth gleamed white as he smiled grimly in the gloom. "I don't have a death song."

"Me neither," Bear said. "But I've got a feeling I should be working on one."

The rain faded to a fine drizzle as McBride and Bear rode through the deepening night, a dank darkness crowding around them. They crossed a low saddleback; then the ground fell gradually away from them for a mile, ending in a tangle of brush and trees that began to climb another shallow hill.

When they reached the trees, Bear drew rein. "Smell that?" he asked.

McBride lifted his head and tested the wind. After a few moments he said, "Smoke. Apaches?"

Bear was looking to the south, as though he was thinking something over. "Could be Apaches, but I doubt it. There's a heap of smoke in the air and only white men make a fire that big."

"The Army maybe?"

The old scout said nothing, staring into the night. Lightning lit up the sky, flaring blue on the faces of the two men, deepening the shadows that pooled in their eyes under the hat brims. Restlessly, Bear's big black tossed its head, the jangling bit loud in the silence.

As though he were waking from a trance, the old man said, "The Apaches couldn't have failed to smell that fire, but they rode around whoever is out there. An Indian won't attack unless he figures the odds are in his favor, and that means they saw more white men than they cared to handle."

"It's got to be the Army, Bear."

Again the old man made no answer. He stepped out of the saddle and told McBride to do the same. "John, I've got a hunch about who's sitting around that fire," he said. "And if I'm right, we're in a heap of trouble."

Bear led the way into the darkness, moving south on cat feet. Only once did he speak, and then in a low whisper. "Step light. They're close."

Every twenty steps Bear dropped to one knee, listening, letting the night talk to him. McBride followed a few paces behind, hearing nothing but the silence singing in his ears. They avoided areas where the shadows were thin, keeping to the darkest reaches of the plain, seeking out the shallow valleys between the hills where lay waist-high lakes of blackness. The wet grass muffled their footsteps and they made no sound. Only the flashes of lightning that shimmered silver and lilac in the sky sought to betray them.

After ten endless minutes the rolling country gradually gave way to higher hills, crested with twisted rock formations and wild stands of cactus. Ahead of him, McBride saw a patch of darkness stained with pulsing red. Bear tapped him on the shoulder, then put a finger to his lips.

The old man made a gesture with the flat of his hand, telling McBride to stay where he was. Then he dropped onto his belly and glided like a snake, stealthy and silent, into the menacing night.

The darkness pressed on McBride. He could feel it wrap around him like a dusky cloak, smelling of damp earth and danger. He stared into nothingness, his ears straining for any sound. The rain began to fall heavier, a hushed rustling in the stillness, and far away the coyotes were talking.

Twenty minutes passed and McBride began to worry about Bear. Then he saw the old man, crouching low, only a few feet away. Once again Bear pressed a finger to his lips, then whispered into McBride's ear. The big man nodded and followed him, creeping slowly into the gloom.

Bear didn't talk until they reached the horses. Even then he kept his voice low. "I figure fifteen men, maybe a couple more or a couple less."

"Who are they?"

"It's the Rentzin boys. A few times I heard Reuben and Ransom called by name. They've got a wagon with a busted axle and right now they're forted up tight in the rocks. If the Apaches passed close they would have taken a look-see and decided to ride on by. Even loco young bucks know they'd lose too many men trying to push fifteen hard cases out of a strong position. Every man jack of them is a named gunfighter and I got close enough to recognize a couple of them. Ed Foster is there, kills with a scattergun, and Fish Allen, a two-gun lunatic who rode with a wild outlaw crowd up in the Nations."

McBride knew this day would come, but now the

shock of it punched him in the gut. "How long before they ride into Suicide?"

"As long as it takes them to fix the busted axle. They won't leave the wagon behind. It's a big freight drawn by six mules, sturdy enough to carry all the gold they hope to find at the Elliot house and other spoils besides."

McBride spoke aloud, but he was talking to himself. "Say, later today or early tomorrow." He felt like a man stepping onto a boat that was about to set sail and sink.

"That seems about right," Bear said. "If I had to guess, I'd say them boys will be on our doorstep tomorrow—right after sunup."

Chapter 30

McBride and Bear rode into Suicide as the night died around them. But no warmth attended the coming of the light. The rain was snarled with sleet and a cutting wind shredded the day into tatters, leaving the dawn naked to the cold.

The town was deserted, an unwelcoming, friendless place. The two men rode through a gray cavern of silence, the only sound the rusty iron creak of the sign hanging outside McKay's store and the constant banging of a door somewhere behind the saloon.

McBride headed for the hill, Bear following behind, but drew rein when a man stepped from the door of the cantina, a shotgun in his hands. "Halt, who goes there?" he demanded in heavily accented English.

"Damn you, Heber, who does it look like?" Bear yelled, cold and a lack of sleep making him testy.

"Advance, *kameraden*, and be recognized."

Now the old scout was really worked up. "Heber,

I swear I'll put a bullet in your fat belly if you don't stand aside and let us pass."

"I can't help it, Bear," the German whined. "Herr McKay said I'm part of a militia and that I should act like a soldier. He ordered me to take my post here and told me what to say."

McBride heard Bear's angry snort and headed off more harsh words. "Where are the others, Conrad?"

"On the hill, Marshal. Dave Channing woke us all in the middle of the night and marched us up there." Heber let the shotgun drop to his side. "We heard shooting to the south about an hour ago. It did not last too long. Channing says it was Apaches attacking the Rangers and the men who left us. He said to be on our guard because we'd be next. "

"He was right about that," McBride said, "unless the Apaches got licked by the Rangers."

After a bit, Heber said, hope in his eyes, "Do you think that's what happened?"

McBride shook his head. "No. I don't think that's what happened."

Bear jumped at the chance to talk. "Heber, if we'd been Indians you'd be dead by now. You don't walk out in front of Apaches and say, 'Halt, who goes there?' That's a sure way to lose your hair."

"Bear's right," McBride said. "Conrad, you'd better get up the hill with the rest."

The German looked relieved, then concerned. "But Herr McKay—"

"I'll talk to McKay. Get going. We'll follow you."

McBride and Bear rode after Heber to the base of

the hill. Channing came down to meet them. He had shed his gambler's finery and was wearing boots, canvas pants and a ragged checked mackinaw. He was wearing two guns in crossed belts.

"Glad to see you back, McBride," he said. "See any Apaches?"

"Saw their sign. They're around."

"We heard shooting just after sunup. It came from the south."

"I know, Heber told me. I guess the Apaches tangled with the Rangers."

McBride's eyes scanned the hill. "Your men in position?"

"Yeah. I've told them we'll fall back to the Elliot house if the Indians look like they're taking the hill."

Bear leaned forward in the saddle and asked, "It's cold and getting colder, Channing. Will they stick?"

"I reckon. They've got nowhere else to go."

McBride turned to the old man. "We'll put up our horses, and then I want to check on the El Coyote Azul." He looked at Channing. "My ladies here?"

The gambler shook his head. "I woke them, but they haven't showed yet. Neither has Mrs. Whitehead."

"I'll round them up."

McBride swung away from the hill and dismounted outside the cantina. Followed by Bear he stepped inside. To his surprise the place was warm and he smelled bacon frying.

Bear grinned. "Breakfast!"

He walked into the kitchen and appeared a couple of minutes later, carrying a coffeepot, cups and a platter piled high with thick sandwiches of bacon and sourdough bread. "The little gals say they knew we'd come back hungry. When they saw us ride in, they got out the fry pan."

McBride took a chair, picked up a sandwich and nodded in the direction of the kitchen. "After you eat, tell them to get up the hill with the others."

"I will, John, but they won't do it. They reckon it's better to be an Apache's squaw than get all shot to pieces on the hill. And they're right. An Apache is right partial to a gal with plenty of meat on her bones—proves he's a great hunter." Bear grinned. "Partial to a fat gal my ownself."

"Then at least we can get Mrs. Whitehead up there."

"Maybe. But she doesn't want to leave her husband's body. I don't think she'll go."

As McBride had learned, eating was a serious business in the West where food was hard to come by and restaurants were few and far between. He and Bear ate in dedicated silence and afterward McBride used the tip of a forefinger to pick up the last of the bacon and bread crumbs.

"Bear, tell the ladies thanks for the grub and tell them I wish they'd change their mind about staying."

"I will, John, but—"

Bear stopped, listening to the thud of hooves and jangling of harness outside in the street. A wizened, scarred old man who moved like a cougar, he rose to his feet, picking up his rifle. "Trouble, I think," he said.

"The Rentzins?"

"Could be."

No, McBride's mind protested, it's too soon, way too soon.

He got to his feet, put some distance between him and Bear and waited. If they rushed the door, he could drop several of them and make it more difficult for the others to get inside.

The curtain pushed aside . . . and a huge man wearing a long fur coat and wide sombrero stepped inside. He grinned like an amiable alligator. "John McBride, my good friend, it is I, Angel Guerrero, come to visit you at last."

Chapter 31

Six other men piled in behind Guerrero, one of them Papan Morales, his hands very close to his guns. The man was looking at McBride with hard eyes, his mouth creased in an I-told-you-so grin.

"There is a little matter we have to discuss, Mr. McBride," Guerrero said. "It is called the angel's share." He spread his hands. "It is a small matter, I know, but one I hold very dear." He smiled, his teeth white under his thin mustache. "I will take my hundred dollars now and trouble you no more. Well, no more until a few weeks have passed."

Out of the corner of his eyes McBride saw that Bear was tense and ready. But if it came down to it, this would be a gunfight they could not win. Desperately, he clutched at a straw.

"Guerrero, help us fight the Apaches who are threatening to attack this town and then we'll talk about the money."

"Ah, yes, the Apaches," Guerrero said. "Their leader is Goyathlay. He is a great warrior, mighty in battle, and he is my good friend. Alas, his wife and children were killed when soldiers attacked their ranchería. Now my friend thirsts for revenge against the blancos. All this he told me.''

The bandit's black eyes crawled over McBride's face. ''Mr. McBride, you know Papan who stands near me, my good right arm. He wants to kill you very badly. But last night I prayed for guidance and this very morning I told him, 'No Papan, violence is not the way. McBride will pay me my money and then we will ride on in peace.' '' His head turned to Morales. ''Papan, my friend, were those not my words?''

''*Sí*, you said those words to me this morning.''

Bear, looking agitated, could not contain himself. ''Guerrero, if the Apaches kill us all, there will be no more angel's share. Suicide will be gone.''

''This is very true, old man,'' Guerrero said. ''But I saw your riflemen on the hill. Perhaps you will win the fight and our business arrangement will go on as before.''

''Not without your help it won't,'' McBride said.

''That cannot be. I am a friend of the Mescalero. You see, at heart I am a simple trader. I supply the Apache with rifles and ammunition and sometimes mescal, and they pay me in good Mexican gold coins. They are my friends as you are my friend, McBride. Angel Guerrero does not kill his good friends.''

Morales said, ''Pay us our money, McBride. It is your rent for this fine cantina and our due.''

"He speaks the truth, McBride," Guerrero said. "You must pay your rent. It is the honorable thing."

"And if I don't?"

"Then Papan will kill you. Or I will. Later I will regret killing a friend, but what must be done, must be done."

McBride's back was to the wall. He didn't have a hundred dollars and saw no way out. Guerrero now had ten men behind him and they were as eager for the kill as wolves stalking a wounded elk. In the narrow confines of the cantina no one would miss and McBride knew he and Bear were tiptoeing very close to death.

Then he had a flash of inspiration. Even as the thought hit him, he realized it was a desperation play, the last roll of the dice, but it was all he had.

He hung his head, his voice strained. "Angel Guerrero, my friend, I have lied to you. I gave your money to another bandit. He is a fearsome man and says he is taking over this territory. He told me I must pay him for his protection. I was very afraid and I said, 'But the hundred dollars belongs to Angel Guerrero.' But this man, he would not listen. He took the money and told me, 'When I see this Guerrero I will send him to join the angels, with a bullet in his belly.'"

An angry muttering went through the bandits and Guerrero looked outraged. "Who is this man?"

"His name is Ransom Rentzin," McBride said, trembling, playing his role to the hilt. "He rides with his two brothers and a dozen other bandits. They are all hard, determined men and wish to take what is rightfully yours."

"Where can I find this thief?" Guerrero demanded, his black eyes glittering.

"He is camped to the west of here. He has a wagon, drawn by mules, to carry the loot he plans to take from Suicide—and from you."

McBride uneasily shifted his feet. He knew he was dangling a hook in front of Guerrero, a hook without a worm. Would the man go for it?

The bandit took a step toward McBride and grabbed him by the front of his coat. "I will go find this man, Rentzin, and kill him. But if you are lying to me, McBride, if there is no such man, I will turn you over to my Apache friends. You will scream for a bullet until your throat bursts, but they will not listen. They will laugh and torment you all the more. McBride, my good friend, it will take you a long time to die, I think." Guerrero shook his head. "Oh, a very long time."

"I do not lie. Ride to the west—you will find him as I told you." McBride hung his head again, and the bandit asked suspiciously, "Is there more? Something you have not told me?"

"I can't say it. You are my friend."

"Say it or I'll cut out your tongue and you'll never speak again."

McBride trembled again. "He says you are the son of a two-peso whore and that you were spawned in a brothel in Hermosillo by a one-legged—"

"Enough!" Guerrero screamed. He drew his gun and waved it under McBride's nose. "If you are lying to me about what he said about my sainted mother . . ."

"I told you I did not want to repeat what Rentzin told me."

The bandit stood in silence for a few moments, staring hard at McBride. Then he turned to his men. "We ride to the west, *muchachos*. I have a man to kill."

Guerrero's men crowded out of the cantina, but their leader stood for a moment in the doorway, staring back at McBride. "If you have lied to me, you will curse the day you were born."

"Good luck, my friend," McBride said, trying to look pious. "I will pray for you."

After a final, hard look, Guerrero stalked outside and McBride waited until he heard the pounding hooves of departing riders before he flopped, completely used up, into a chair. He realized his hands were shaking for real and green butterflies chased each other around his belly.

Bear's eyes were on him, hard and calculating. "John, all you can do now is hope Guerrero and the Rentzins wipe each other out."

McBride shook his head. "That's unlikely. All I've done is bought us a few more hours of life. Instead of dying now, we die later. The end result is the same."

The curtain parted and Dave Channing stepped inside. "I saw Angel Guerrero ride away. Did you pay him his money like everybody else in this town does?"

"No, at least not yet." Briefly, McBride told Channing how Bear had seen the Rentzins west of town.

Then he said, "I sent Guerrero after the brothers, fed him a story that they planned on taking over his protection racket. With a lot of luck, maybe they'll kill each other."

Channing smiled. "Angel Guerrero is a hard man to kill."

"I need a man like him. I thought he might help us fight the Apaches," McBride said. "I was wrong about that."

"He's half Apache himself," Channing said. "Gets on just fine with Indians. He's raided into Mexico with the Apaches and a couple of years back he helped the Comanche wipe out a company of U.S. infantry on the Staked Plains. Guerrero won't help us fight Indians."

McBride rose to his feet. "Bear, maybe you and Dave can try again to convince the ladies to come with us. Then round up Mrs. Whitehead. I'll stable the horses and join you both on the hill."

McBride forked the horses a generous amount of hay and all the oats that were left. He stepped beside the mustang and patted its neck.

"If I don't see you again, it's been real nice knowing you." He smiled. "And I didn't mean what I said about punching you in the head."

The ugly little horse munched on oats, its nose to the ground. McBride walked to the stable door and turned. The mustang was watching him. He waved a hand and the horse looked at him steadily for a moment, then lowered its head and went back to eating.

As horses went, the mouse-colored mustang wasn't much, but McBride felt he was taking leave of an old friend forever.

Thirty minutes later, in a driving sleet storm, the Apaches attacked.

Chapter 32

It was Dave Channing who saw the Apaches first. "McBride!" he yelled. "They're coming!"

McBride left the cover of the rocks where he'd been crouched and made his way to the gambler.

"Down the hill to the left about fifty feet," Channing said. "Behind that dead juniper you see there."

Bear was suddenly and silently at McBride's side. "They won't rush us," he whispered. "Apaches are too savvy for that. They'll pick us off one by one and try to wear us down."

An Apache showed himself for a split second at the white base of the juniper. Bear raised his Henry and fired. The bullet chipped wood from the trunk of the tree, but the Indian was gone.

"You got him!" a man yelled. It was McKay. He was farther up the hill, concealed in a shallow gully overgrown with sagebrush. Above him, around the base of the rock shaped like a flatiron, were Heber and Kaleen.

"Hell no, I didn't," Bear growled. "I missed him clean."

The sleet was being driven by a west wind, spattering into the faces of the defenders on the hill. Low black clouds hung motionless in the sky, spreading an ashen light that made it difficult to see, turning the Apaches into fleeting shadows.

Heber and Kaleen began firing at darting, bobbing figures that never stayed in sight for more than a second. Both men yelled, claiming hits that didn't exist, their bullets chipping rock and rattling through brush where an Apache had been but was no longer.

Heber, a large target, fired, fired again, then rose to his feet, pumping his rifle above his head. "I winged another one!"

A bullet chopped into the meaty part of his left shoulder, spraying blood, and he yelped in pain and surprise. The German ducked down at the base of the rock and was quiet for a long time.

Channing fired his Colts slowly, taking his time. He did not boast of hits, but his shooting helped keep the Apaches from getting closer.

McKay and Kaleen were also firing, too fast, unsure of their targets. Bear swore loud and long, then said to McBride, "I'm going up there. Tell them boys you don't shoot when there's nothing to shoot at."

Crouching low, the old scout climbed the hill. Soon afterward the fire from McKay and Kaleen slowed.

McBride took a snap shot with his .38 at heavy brush cover that might conceal an Apache. He was rewarded by a shriek, then the noise of a man making his way back down the muddy hillside.

He turned and glanced up at the Elliot house. The window of the turret room was open, but no one was shooting. It seemed that Allison and Moses did not care to join in the fight.

He turned to face the enemy again and instantly realized that his single, quick glance may have cost him his life. He saw the blur of a painted face, blue headband and upraised lance. The Apache was less than twenty feet away, running toward him, screaming his hate. McBride tried to get to his feet, slipped on mud and fell on his haunches. He raised his revolver. The Indian was right on top of him, the eight-inch-long iron blade of his lance gleaming in the gray light. McBride fired and the Apache's left eye disappeared in a burst of scarlet.

The lance head buried itself in the dirt inches from McBride's chest, and the Apache fell heavily on top of him. The man's blood splashed over his face and he cried out in disgust and fear.

McBride rolled the Indian off him, aware that Channing was standing, his legs spread, both Colts hammering. He saw an Apache start to go down, then another. Wounded in both legs, the Apache dropped to his knees, bringing his Sharps to his shoulder. Channing shot the man in the head and the Indian screamed and fell flat on his face.

As quickly as the wild rush had begun, it was over. Rifle fire forced Channing to take cover and McBride crawled to his side. "Good shooting, Dave," he said.

The man nodded, his lips tight and grim. "Thanks. It's been a while."

The Apaches had been burned. They had lost three men and now they settled down to sniping at the men among the rocks. McKay was burned by a bullet and Kaleen had his rifle stock shattered.

Then Heber was killed.

The big German was moving to another position lower down the hill when he was hit. His head was shattered by a heavy bullet and he dropped without a sound.

Bear saw it and yelled to McBride, "John, up here!"

McBride turned to Channing, aware that the man occupied the most exposed position. "Will you be all right alone?"

The gambler nodded. "If the Apaches get any closer, I'll hightail it up the hill."

"Good luck," McBride said.

He crawled higher, attracting shots, but he reached Bear unharmed. "Heber is dead," the old scout told him.

McBride took the loss hard. Heber had showed himself to be game enough and they could ill afford to lose him. "I'll get Channing up here," he said.

A bullet hit a rock near Bear and spat stinging chips into the old scout's cheek. He put fingers to the wound, looked at the blood without interest, then said, "The Apaches didn't kill Heber. He was shot in the back of the head"—Bear nodded toward the Elliot house—"from up there."

McBride felt ice in his belly. "Are you sure?"

"Saw smoke drift from the high-up window. The wind carried it away pretty quick, but it was there all right."

The shot had come from the turret room.

Bear was talking again. "John, somebody in the house is bent on killing white men."

McBride was torn. He had to get into the house, but that would leave only five men to defend the hill, a couple of them wounded. So far they'd managed to keep the hostiles at bay . . . but if they came all at once . . .

Bear saw his concern and read him correctly. "John, we're caught in a cross fire. We can't hold out for long against those odds. Somebody has to get into the house and silence that rifleman."

Bear was right. There was no other way.

McBride called to Channing to climb the hill, then yelled to McKay, Levy and Kaleen to give him covering fire. The gambler waved and began to make his way up the slope. An Apache leaped to his feet and snapped off a shot at Channing, kicking up dirt at his feet. Bear fired, unbelievably fast, and the Indian was shot high in the chest as he dived for cover. The Apache knew he was hit hard, but he had no intention of dying alone. He screamed and jumped to his feet, rushing at Channing. The Apache fired from the waist, lips bared from his teeth in an enraged snarl. The bullet opened up a crimson slash across the left side of Channing's neck. Shocked, for a moment he dropped his hands, his guns pointing at the ground. The Apache came on fast, heavy rifle swinging above his head like a club. Channing saw the danger too late. His guns came up but the Apache was on top of him. The rifle chopped downward as the gambler moved to his right. The stock missed Channing's head by inches, but smashed into his left shoulder. Higher up the hill though he was, McBride still heard the sickening crack of shattered bone followed by Channing's wild shriek of pain. Beside McBride, Bear's rifle roared and the Apache's face disappeared into a crimson mask of blood and bone. The Indian was dead, but his body stood where it was for a moment, then toppled backward and sprawled over a jagged stand of cactus, arms and legs flung wide.

Apache bullets were hitting the dirt around Channing. McKay and the others were shooting back, but their targets were flitting shapes in the sleet storm that was now quickly gathering strength. A howling wind tossed the trees and brush on the hillside, and sleet splattered venomously against the rocks, soaking everybody.

"I can't see a damn thing!" Levy's voice was panicky, his shouted words torn from his lips by the wind.

"Damn it, Levy," Bear yelled, "if you can't see, neither can the Apaches."

Somebody, maybe Kaleen, fired, shooting at a shadow. Then a scowling, sullen silence fell over the hillside.

McBride's eyes, stung by sleet, searched the hill, trying to find Channing. It was like looking through a frosty window spiderwebbed with cracks.

"Channing!" he hollered. "Can you hear me?"

The wind mocked him, scattering his words. The sleet wheeled around McBride, so thick he could barely make out Bear's crouched form just a few feet away from him. He moved closer to the scout and yelled in his ear, "I'm going after Channing."

Bear nodded. His eyebrows and mustache were white with sleet and he looked a hundred years old.

McBride made his way down the hill, sliding on his rump most of the way. He could see only a few yards in front of his face, and brush and cactus tore at him.

Channing was conscious, his eyes strained. The man had always been pale, but now his skin was ashen and he breathed in short, sharp gasps, battling his pain.

"Dave," McBride yelled, trying to be heard above the ceaseless roar of the wind, "I'll help you get up the hill."

The gambler nodded, saying nothing.

"How is the shoulder?" McBride asked.

Channing moved closer. "Bad . . . all . . . busted up."

Shouting above the storm, McBride said, "We have to go, Dave."

The gambler gritted his teeth as McBride grabbed him by the collar of his mackinaw and began to drag him up the slope. McBride was a strong man but after a few yards he was breathing hard, his heart thudding in his chest. There was no letup in the sleet. If anything it was falling thicker, and the wind was relentless, punishing both men, but Channing worst of all.

A bullet probed the hillside, followed a moment later by another. Both shots went wide, hitting low and to the right of McBride. But he knew these were

not Apache bullets. They were coming from the Elliot house.

Bear left his place on the slope and helped McBride
manhandle Channing the rest of the way. Together
they got the gambler into the comparative shelter of
the rocks. Channing was in considerable pain, but he
managed a weak grin as he spoke to McBride. "Who
shot the Apache off me?"

"Bear did."

Channing turned his head, looking at the old man.
"Thank you. I guess you saved my life."

"Call it professional courtesy," Bear said. "Men
like you and me should die on a barroom floor, like
we're supposed to."

"And your friend McBride?" the gambler asked.
He was still smiling.

"He's not like us," Bear said. "He'll die in his bed,
or in church."

"If the Apaches don't get me first," McBride said.
He leaned closer to Channing and told him what had
happened to Heber. "Dave, I have to get into the
house and find out who is shooting at us from the
turret room. Can you still handle a gun?"

"I shoot a rifle off my broke shoulder. But I can
still use a revolver." Talking was an effort, but Channing fought back his pain and said, "While it lasts,
this storm will keep the Apaches away. I reckon
they're probably sheltering already. You best get
going and find that killer."

Bear moved close to McBride, his faded eyes shrewd.
"John, suppose it's Allison you find up there?"

"I just hope to God it isn't," McBride said.

Chapter 33

Studying the Elliot house just fifty yards away across open ground, John McBride kneeled behind a clump of thick-growing sagebrush. Marching straight up to the front door would be inviting a bullet from the turret room. Only if he approached the house from the back would he have a chance of getting close enough to gain entry.

The turret room window was open, but he saw no sign of movement. Without taking his eyes from the window, he broke open the Smith & Wesson and reloaded. He snapped the revolver shut, then moved to his right, picking his way through brush and juniper. The sleet storm still raged unabated and the day was edged sharp with cold. McBride felt tension in the air and the presence of danger.

Here the slope of the hill was more gradual and, though crouched, he could walk easily. McBride made his way around a tree fall and quickly crossed an open area of grass. Ahead of him, half-obscured by manzanita that still showed a few red berries, were the mounded graves of the five men who had tried to steal Allison Elliot's gold. McBride felt a chill as he walked past the graves and headed quickly for a barn that backed up to the slope of the hillside. Expecting a bullet at any time, he reached the side wall of the barn and crouched behind a water barrel. All the windows at the back of the house were open, but he saw no sign of life.

Beyond the barn were some outbuildings and a pole corral. An old surrey, missing a wheel, angled into the dirt, its tattered canopy flapping in the wind. Nearby lay the top half of a broken plaster statue, a woman with large breasts and no arms.

The back door to the house was to the right of the building. McBride decided to walk behind the barn, then keeping to the shelter of the corral, make a run for the door. He hoped it wasn't locked.

Leaving the cover of the water barrel, he backed to the end of the barn, then ducked around the corner. His back hit a solid wall of stone. Startled, McBride turned. The wall facing him was made of gray sandstone and stood about ten feet high. The blocks were neatly cemented in place by a man who knew his business. He stepped back and looked up. The top of the wall curved into a high, arched roof, and that had also been expertly crafted.

McBride was puzzled. Why build an archway connecting the rear of a barn to the slope of the hill where none was needed?

His path blocked, he made his way to the front corner of the barn and looked around. He saw and heard nothing but lashing sleet and the howl of the

wind. The barn doors were closed, secured by a
wooden beam that passed through a couple of massive iron clamps. McBride slid back the beam and
stepped inside.

Away from the roar of the sleet storm, the barn
was fairly quiet and warm. The structure creaked in
the wind and a single gray shaft of daylight angled
from a window in the roof and spread like wood
ashes on the floor. Depending on the whim of the
passing clouds, the light glimmered from silver to
dull slate and back again, now and then capturing
dust motes that danced like fireflies.

As McBride's eyes became accustomed to the
gloom, he headed for the back of the barn, walking
through the stream of overhead light that gleamed
on his shoulders and hat. As far as he could tell, the
timber wall was solid. Nails had been driven into the
wood where odd pieces of tack and a rusty collection
of worn-out horseshoes hung. He moved closer, his
probing hands traveling over the rough boards.

"Push it, McBride."

Jim Drago's voice came from behind him and
McBride froze. His .38 was in the shoulder holster
and he'd have to draw, turn, find his target and fire.

The dwarf read his mind. "Don't even think about
it. I'd kill you before you skinned the iron." After a
moment's hesitation he said, "Push it, damn you."

McBride did as he was told and a section of the
timber wall swung away from him. It was the door
to a concealed entranceway that opened easily on
oiled hinges hidden on the opposite side.

McBride heard Drago clump toward him in his

fancy boots. There was a smile in the little man's voice. "Don't turn around, McBride. Now, two things: With your left hand shuck your gun and drop it on the floor. Then walk into the tunnel."

"Tunnel?" McBride asked, surprised.

"No questions. Just do as I told you or I'll drop you right where you stand."

Drago was good with a gun and at that range he would not miss. McBride lifted his gun from the leather and let it thud to the floor.

"Now, into the tunnel."

McBride stepped through the door into the arched stone passageway and stopped. A dim light filtered through from the barn but beyond he saw only darkness.

"On your right, see the lamp on the stone shelf? Light it."

"I don't have a match."

"There are matches beside the lamp. Light it, McBride."

He found the lamp, thumbed a match into flame and lit the wick.

"Carry the lamp into the tunnel and start walking. And remember, I'm right behind you and I ain't sitting on my gun hand."

McBride knew Drago wanted to shoot him real bad but for some reason the little man was in no hurry, probably savoring the moments before the kill. But despite the obvious danger from the dwarf's gun, McBride was intrigued.

He was walking through a natural cave that burrowed deep into the hill. The sandy floor angled slightly downward, and all around him, weird in the guttering lamplight, stood tall pillars of rock. When he looked upward, McBride could not see the roof of the cave but he guessed it was very high. The air was cool, but not cold, and it was thick with a sharp, acrid smell.

As though answering an unspoken question, Drago said, giggling, "Smell the bats, McBride? Get used to it. You'll be sharing the cave with them for a long time, until the water drips from the roof turn your bones into stone."

The cave gradually widened out into an open area about fifty feet square. The expanse was surrounded by thick rock pillars that looked like the columns of a Gothic cathedral, soaring upward until they were lost in darkness. But it was the beautiful horse that surprised McBride and stopped him in his tracks.

Half-a-dozen oil lamps burned in niches around the animal's stall that was placed in the center of the floor. A silver saddle straddled one of the timber partitions.

"Miss Elliot's mare, McBride," Drago said. "You've never seen a horse like that."

"Saw plenty of horses like that in New York, hauling coal carts."

"You're pleased to joke," the dwarf said. "That there sorrel is a thoroughbred racehorse brought all the way from Kentucky. She's faster than the wind and cost more money than you'll see in a lifetime."

McBride moved to turn his head, but a yell from Drago stopped him. "Look straight ahead or I'll blow it clean off your shoulders."

McBride looked to his front and asked, "Why does Allison keep her horse down here and not in the barn?"

"You'd like to know, wouldn't you?" The dwarf's voice was venomous. "Well, maybe I'll tell you after I shoot you in the belly, but maybe I won't."

"You're a little piece of dirt, Drago," McBride said. "Did anyone ever tell you that?"

The little man sniggered. "You talk big McBride. Let's see how big you talk a few minutes from now. Move! Into the tunnel over yonder."

McBride crossed the open area and stepped into a narrower, lower cave that would allow the passage of a man on a horse with only a few inches to spare. Here the walls showed traces of being mined and the floor dropped at a sharper angle. After walking for several minutes McBride felt a cold blast of air and knew the tunnel must end on the other side of the hill, probably at its base.

Someone had used the natural cave to get deep inside the hill, then had blasted and dug the rest of the way.

And suddenly he knew why.

"That's far enough, McBride," Drago said. "I'll kill you here." The dwarf stepped close to McBride, revealing himself for the first time. He wore a black cloak, the hood pulled up over his head, and his face was in shadow. Shoving the muzzle of his gun into McBride's belly, he said, "Sit down and put your back against the wall. Place the lamp at your feet."

In the lamplight Drago read something in the tall man's eyes. "Do it or I'll kill you now," he said.

McBride thought about going for it, but the dwarf was ready and the muzzle of the Colt dug into him deeper. "All right," Drago said, "then I'll shoot you now."

"We can talk," McBride said, desperately playing for time. He moved away and sat, placing the lamp beside him.

Now he saw Drago's grin in the orange glow of the lamplight. The little man's teeth were wet, stranded with saliva. "I'm glad you decided to talk for a while," he said. "It's good for a man to talk before he dies."

The dwarf took a seat on a low rock shelf opposite McBride. His gun was up and ready. He was still grinning, enjoying this. "What do you want to talk about?" he asked. "I'd say there's about five minutes of oil left in the lamp. That's plenty of time for talk."

"Allison Elliot used this tunnel to leave Suicide without being seen," McBride said. "She rode that fast horse, killed any of the originals trying to leave and got back here to the cave before anyone noticed."

"Close, McBride. But you're wrong. I killed some of them myself. Take Manuel Cortez now—I killed him. I got gold from Allison for that killing even though it was real easy."

"That's what you used to buy the boots you're wearing, huh?"

"Thanks to you, I paid too much. That's why I'm going to shoot you in the belly and not in the head, merciful like."

McBride played for time. Keep the little man talking. "And John Wright and his wife? Did you kill them?"

"Nah, that was Allison."

"Years ago, the young man and wife who were killed with their children? What was their name—?"

Drago sighed, letting McBride know he was getting bored. "Peacock. Allison and me did that. She gunned the adults and I took care of them caterwauling kids."

"And John Whitehead? And today, Conrad Heber?"

"Enough talk of killing, McBride." The dwarf's voice brightened. "The mare you saw in the cave? That will be mine one day very soon."

"Why all the murders, Drago? What is the rule and why was it made?"

The little man pouted. "See, you're making me angry. I said no more talk of killing, but you did. Now I'll have to shoot you."

McBride fought back a rising panic. Keep him talking, keep him talking.

"I'm sorry. Tell me about you and Allison."

The dwarf smiled, his face wicked in the shifting yellow lamplight. "Allison, yes . . . Allison. She takes me to her bed, you know, when she feels like it. But she won't tell me where her gold is hidden. When this is all over and there's no more need for the rule, I plan on taking her away from here. She doesn't eat, says she's too fat, so she can't live much longer. When we're in bed I tell her she's too fat, and when she stops eating completely and dies I'll have all the gold." Drago giggled. "If I don't beat her to death first one fine night."

"What about Moses?"

"After I kill you, I'll kill him. The Apaches will get the blame." He paused. "And there is one other I have to kill."

"Who is that?"

The dwarf shook his head. "This grows tiresome. I told you, no more talk of killing. Now I'll shoot you in the belly and we'll hear how you scream, huh?"

Drago's gun came up, leveled.

McBride threw himself at Drago, knowing he was too slow, already a dead man.

But the dwarf didn't fire.

Something very fast, long and thick as a man's wrist, struck like a bullwhip from out of the darkness. The fangs of the rattlesnake hit Drago in the corner of his right eye. The little man dropped his gun and shrieked with fear and pain.

McBride saw the strike, and threw himself away, rolling on the floor of the tunnel.

The dwarf sprang, screaming, to his feet. But the snake hit again in a blur of speed. This time the bite was lower, thudding into Drago's neck. The dwarf's shrill screech echoed through the cave, bounding among the stone pillars. Startled bats fluttered on the roof and the frightened mare was whinnying.

Drago staggered back along the tunnel in the direction of the house. He stumbled a couple of yards, then fell flat on his face.

McBride picked up the oil lamp and watched the nine-foot-long diamondback slither swiftly for the end of the tunnel. The rattler had hoped to find a warm, dry place to hole up for a spell. Instead it had found Jim Drago.

When McBride used his boot to roll the dwarf on his back, the little man was still alive. His eyes were wild as he felt numbing death draw closer to him. "I should have killed you when I had the chance," he rasped hoarsely, all the evil in him corrupting his voice.

"We heard how you screamed, huh?" McBride said. There was no pity in him.

"You . . . go . . . to . . . hell. . . ."

"Save a place for me by the fire," McBride said. Without another glance he stepped around the little man and walked back into the cave.

Now he had to find Allison Elliot.

Chapter 34

After retrieving his revolver, John McBride left the barn and angled toward the back door of the house, sleet cartwheeling around him. There was no sound of gunfire from the hill. Both Apaches and white men were lying low, biding their time until the storm passed before again trying to kill each other.

The door was open and McBride stepped into a hollow silence. Only the moaning of the wind made a sound as it prowled restlessly around the eaves of the building and gusted sleet that frosted the glass of the open windows.

He was in the kitchen and quickly crossed the floor and went through another door that led to a hallway. Wary of Moses and his scattergun, McBride held his Smith & Wesson up and ready, finger on the trigger.

The hallway led to the main reception area of the house and the grand staircase. In a numbing cold, McBride warily mounted the stairs, each creak of the old timber threatening to expose him to whoever might be listening.

He reached the landing and on cat feet made his way to the hallway leading to the turret room.

"Can I be of assistance, Mr. McBride?"

McBride turned and saw Moses standing a few feet behind him. The man was unarmed and wore a black armband around the left sleeve of his jacket.

"Where is Miss Elliot?" McBride asked, aware that his heart was hammering in his chest.

Moses spoke in a half whisper. "There has been a death in this house."

"Allison?"

"No, Mr. McBride, not Miz Allison. Someone else, someone very near and dear to her."

For a moment McBride thought Moses must know about Drago, but that was impossible.

"Who is it?" he asked.

The old giant did not answer. He stepped around McBride, paying no attention to his gun, then bowed and waved a hand toward the end of the hallway. "Please follow me. The deceased is this way."

Like a man walking through a surreal dream, McBride followed Moses along the hallway. He was at the bottom of the steps to the turret room when he heard sobbing, punctuated by the wrenching wails of a woman pushed to the edge by grief.

"Miz Elliot is taking this very hard," Moses said, his dark eyes shadowed by his own sorrow. "I fear for her now that the master is gone."

McBride was puzzled. Who was the master? A man he knew or someone who had managed to remain hidden in the house?

Moses interrupted his thoughts. "You go on up,

Mr. McBride. I will wait here. If Miz Elliot needs me, she will call out."

McBride nodded. He holstered his gun and climbed the stairs. The door to the turret room was open and he stepped inside.

Once again the foul stench in the room was a living thing that sought to choke him. Stunned by what he saw, McBride fought back the urge to be sick.

Allison sat on the edge of a steel cot, holding the bloodstained head of a man to her breast. A heavy rifle bullet had blown away part of his skull, but the face, streaked with fingers of scarlet, was intact. It was the face of a man in his early sixties, and it had been a good, strong face at one time. The cheekbones were high and prominent, a great hawk's beak of a nose above a large dragoon mustache. As far as McBride could tell, the man's hair was white, thin, revealing much pale scalp.

The dead man's legs were bare, obscene things, black and grotesquely swollen, and they had rotted out from under him while he was still alive. Maggots arched and crawled over the man's legs, and fed higher, under his nightshirt.

McBride, fighting back nausea, looked away to the window.

An overturned wheelchair lay in the middle of the floor and alongside it a .50-caliber Sharps rifle and some empty shell casings. A large ship's telescope, made of brass and mounted on a steel tripod, stood close to the open window. McBride told himself that whoever the dead man was, he could have looked through that spyglass and seen forever.

Allison sensed the presence of someone in the room. She turned her tearstained face and saw McBride. Gently she laid the man's head on the cot, then jumped to her feet. "John!" She threw herself into McBride's arms and he smelled the stench of death on her.

"Allison," he said, "who is he?"

"My father. He was hit by a stray bullet, John." She moved her head rapidly from side to side, like a woman distracted by despair. "John, my father, my life, my love, is dead."

The woman clung desperately to McBride and he felt his skin crawl. He pushed her roughly away from him. Suddenly he was no longer what he seemed. The thin veneer of the western man dropped from him, dragging with it all he had become in the past months, gunfighter, lawman, businessman . . . dupe.

All at once he was again Detective Sergeant John McBride of the New York Police Bureau of Detectives. And he was dealing with a cold-blooded murderess.

Allison was aware of the transformation and it troubled her. She wiped tears from her eyes with the back of her hand, smearing black mascara across her cheekbones. "John," she whispered, "what is wrong?"

"Jim Drago is dead. He died in the tunnel where you keep your racehorse."

"Did you kill him?" Allison asked the question without a trace of emotion.

"No, he was killed by a rattlesnake. Poetic justice don't you think, Allison—one snake killing another."

"I can see it in your face, John. Your eyes are like stone. The dwarf told you everything, didn't he?"

"He told me about the people you've murdered, Allison, yes. And the children you've killed." Mc-Bride nodded toward the dead man. "And he did his share. He used his Sharps to kill John Whitehead and then Conrad Heber down there on the slope, didn't he?"

"And why not?" Allison said defiantly, her face twisted with rage. "They failed him, all of them, and they had to die. My father planned to build a city, a great city, but the people who came here were too small to share his vision." The woman took a step toward McBride, her eyes, shining, on his. "Imagine it, John, a city where all the ills of society, poverty, misery, crime, would be banished, a utopia where people could live in peace, prosperity and harmony. My father was a great man, and that was his great dream."

McBride smiled without humor. "And instead of all that, the rule made the people of utopia his prisoners and he encouraged you and Drago to spread terror and death among them. In the end your father didn't create a paradise. He created a hell on earth."

"No! No! That came later, after the shiftless trash failed him. Father saw his dream become a nightmare as businesses went under, settlers stopped coming and the railroad lost interest. At the end, in his despair, he shot himself."

Allison stepped to the cot. "Look at him, John. See for yourself what they did to him. The bullet did not kill him, and Moses and I nursed him back to at least a semblance of health. But he was paralyzed from the waist down and later his body began to rot. Can you wonder that he looked down at his decaying legs and wanted all of them dead?"

"He made the rule and you and Drago enforced it."

"Yes, we did. Father wanted no one to leave Suicide. He planned to keep them all right here where he could kill them one by one. Some tried to leave—"

"And you used the tunnel to go after them. Your father had the powerful telescope and told you where the fleeing people were headed."

"In the early years Father began work on the tunnel through the hill to encourage the railroad. And yes, John, later I used the tunnel for another, much more noble purpose."

"And you hid him there the day I searched the house?"

"He was there. Moses took him to the cave."

McBride looked at the woman. Despite the stink in the room, despite the stench of death about her, even with her hair undone and her face swollen from tears, she was still a beautiful, desirable woman.

"Allison," he said, steeling himself, "I wish I'd killed you the day you murdered John Wright and his wife. God knows, I tried hard enough. It's amazing, but even now, after all I know about you, how evil you are, I would still like to spare you the pain that's coming to you." McBride drew himself up to his full height, his face carved from granite. "Allison Elliot," he said, "it is my painful duty as marshal of this town to arrest you for the murders of—"

"No, John! Not so cold!"

The woman crossed the floor and threw herself at McBride. "John, you said you'd help me and now I need that help. We can leave here, begin a new life together, you and I."

"Did you say that same thing to Drago?"

"The dwarf amused me, that was all. John, from the first time I saw you, it was always you. I love you, John. I have a little money left. It won't take us far, but we can start all over again back east." Allison smiled. "You'd like that, wouldn't you, to go back east with me?"

McBride did not understand. "There are five men buried on the hill and another dead in the cave who thought you had a fortune in gold hidden in the house."

"They were wrong, weren't they?"

"Then why did you kill them?"

"Father killed them, right from this room. He was defending his home, John. You can't fault him for that." Allison's smile grew wider. "I'll go pack. Then we'll put Father in his wheelchair to defend his house and leave."

McBride shook his head, a sense of unreality fogging his thinking. "Allison, we're surrounded by Apaches. We may not even live out this day."

The woman laughed and waved a hand. "La-la-la, John. The Apaches won't trouble us. We'll walk through them hand-in-hand like Arthur with his Guinevere and they'll stand back and look at us with . . . with . . . awe. Besides, Father will be watching over us with his Sharps."

A sane man confronted with madness will often begin to doubt his own sanity. He'll grope through the dark caverns of his mind seeking the light, any light, to banish the frightening, deranged shadows that lurk and threaten.

It was McBride's police training that helped him take a step back from the brink.

"Allison, if I survive this day, I will arrest you for the murders of the Peacock family, the carpenter John Wright and his wife, and many others. In the meantime you are confined to this house until I can turn you over to the Texas Rangers or a United States marshal."

"You think I'll run, is that it? Run from a thing like you? You're just the same as all the rest, McBride—weak, shiftless and gutless." The woman's eyes were alive with hate. "You won't put my head in the noose, McBride."

"Allison, you need help," McBride said. "I promise, you won't hang."

"You're damn right I won't hang."

Allison brushed past McBride and stepped to the door. "Moses! Get up here!"

Slow, heavy footsteps sounded on the stairs. McBride drew his gun and waited.

When Moses appeared he was still unarmed. His huge hands dangled by his sides, the fingers clenching and unclenching.

"Moses, it's over," Allison said. "It's all over. You know what to do. I'll tell you when."

The man bowed slightly. "I'll make the necessary arrangements, Miz Elliot."

"Allison, don't try to leave this house," McBride warned. "I'll have a man watching the tunnel."

"Father and I won't leave. We like it here." She sat on the cot and lifted the dead man's head to her breast again. "Don't we, Father?"

"Mr. McBride, it's best you leave now," Moses said.

On the cot, Allison was softly crooning a love song. The front of her dress was black with blood.

McBride stepped to the door. "Take care of her, Moses," he said.

The giant nodded. "I'll make the necessary arrangements," he said again.

McBride, wondering at Moses' meaning, left the house the way he had entered.

The sleet had stopped and suddenly the hill racketed with gunfire.

Chapter 35

The Apaches were running.

As McBride slid down the hill to where McKay, Channing and the others were standing, at least two dozen mounted men were riding among the fleeing warriors, shooting them down. McBride recognized Angel Guerrero among them. The bandit seemed to have experienced a sudden change of heart about Indians, because he was yelling at his men to let none escape.

A tall man wearing a canvas slicker, mounted on a rangy buckskin, charged three Apaches who had made a stand at the base of the hill. He had let the reins trail and had a Colt in each hand. The revolvers bucked, hammering lead, and the Apaches went down. The man rode around the sprawled bodies, shooting into each one again and again, his lips peeled back in a ferocious grin.

The surviving Indians fled to the west where they'd left their horses, but riders went after them, killing without mercy.

McBride scrambled down the hill, bullets thudding around him, and ran for the El Coyote Azul, mud spurting from his hurtling boots. He dodged horses and roaring, shooting men and reached the entrance. When he pulled the curtain back and ran inside, all was quiet.

His heart thumping, McBride stepped toward the kitchen, fearing what he might find. Apaches treated captive women like they treated horses: Use them until they drop, then find others.

Gun in hand, McBride pulled back the curtain and walked inside.

The two fat ladies looked up at him and giggled. The table was spread with food and the stove fires blazed.

Relief flooded through McBride. He joyfully hugged each woman in turn, saying words they did not understand. He was aware of Bear stepping beside him.

"I thought they might be dead, or worse," he said to the old scout.

Bear said something to the women in Spanish and they giggled, and both poured out a torrent of words that lasted several minutes. When they were finally quiet, McBride gave Bear a puzzled look.

"Breaking it down, John, the Apaches didn't bother them none. They fed the young bucks, gave them mescal and spoke to them in Spanish. The Apaches told the ladies that once the blancos were dead, they'd come back for them and take them to their ranchería."

One of the women spoke again, looked at the other, and both smiled.

"She says men are men." Bear smiled. "White, Mexican or Apache, they all want the same thing."

McBride grinned. "Tell them I'm glad they survived."

"I think they already know that, John. They say you hug like a grizzly."

The shooting had stopped. McBride and Bear left the kitchen and stepped outside.

McKay, Kaleen and Levy were standing in the middle of the street, surrounded by mounted men. There was no sign of Channing.

The tall man in the canvas slicker turned his head when McBride and Bear appeared. He kneed his horse to the cantina door and drew rein. "My name is Ransom Rentzin," he said. "I'm looking for my brother Roddy, who might have passed this way." He waved a hand toward the three men. "Your friends here seem to have developed a sudden case of the forgetfuls. Maybe one of you saw him?"

McBride shook his head. "Could be he passed on through."

Rentzin was thinking, his cold blue eyes moving from McBride to Bear and back again. Finally he said, "You, in the plug hat, what do they call you?"

There was no backing away from it. "John McBride."

Rentzin didn't seem surprised. "Roddy came to see you, figured you were a named man and he could add your scalp to his collection." He moved his slicker away from his guns. "You sure you didn't see him?"

McBride opened his mouth to speak but a shout from down the street stopped him. He turned and saw a mounted man leading a paint horse: Roddy Rentzin's horse.

"Recognize this, Ransom?" the man asked. "Damn my eyes if'n this ain't Roddy's pony."

"That's Roddy's hoss all right," another man said. "I'd recognize that paint anywhere. He's right purty."

McKay was ashen. He rounded on Levy and yelled, "I told you to get rid of that horse."

Levy looked more miserable than scared. "I couldn't do it, Jed. Like the man said, that's a right purty pony."

Rentzin's smile was a mean, angry grimace under his sweeping mustache. He said to McBride, "Mister, looks like you've got some fast talking to do. Did you gun my brother?"

Before McBride could answer, Bear took a step forward. "No, he didn't. I did. Yeah, he was here, Rentzin, and like you and the rest of your clan he was no good."

The tall man was quiet, seemingly thinking this over. He shifted in the saddle and his eyes moved down the street to the creek where the cottonwoods tossed their branches in the wind. He turned his head to his men. "Hang him," he said.

Bear tried to draw, but Rentzin rode his horse right at him. Bear fell against the cantina wall, his gun coming up, but Rentzin crowded him close. Men jumped on the old man and a big towhead wrestled his gun away and slammed the barrel across his face.

As Bear dropped, McBride was already wading into Rentzin's men.

In a blind fury, his fist thudded into the chin of the man who had pistol-whipped Bear. As the towhead staggered back, McBride went after him. He threw a right to the man's belly; then as he doubled up, he brought up his knee into the man's face. The towhead let out a bubbling scream as his nose shattered, spraying blood and splintered bone. His head snapped back and McBride hit him again. He didn't see the man drop. Something hard crashed into the back of his skull and the sky fell on him.

The round, concerned face of one of the fat ladies swam into McBride's view as he woke. She was pressing something cold to the back of his neck, waving a bottle with a vile smell under his nose.

He pushed the smelling salts away, and slowly his eyes focused. Angel Guerrero was sitting opposite him at the kitchen table, grinning from ear to ear.

"Ah, McBride, my friend, you are alive," the bandit said. "This is good news for Guerrero."

"How long have I been unconscious?" McBride asked.

"Not long." Guerrero shrugged. "Maybe an hour. Maybe two."

"Bear!" McBride tried to struggle to his feet, but the room spun around him and he sank back into the chair, helped by the bandit's hand on his shoulder.

"Sit still," Guerrero said. "It is all over for your friend. There's nothing you can do for him now."

Anger flared in McBride, the fact of Bear's death a knife in his heart. "You hanged him, you son of a—"

"I had no hand in that! Rentzin and his brothers hanged the old man. I will shoot a man, yes, but hang him?" Guerrero opened his shirt collar. A livid white scar circled his brown throat. "I know what it's like to be hanged, McBride. I was lucky. The merciful angels broke the rope and saved me." He shook his head sadly. "There were no angels at the creek today, I think."

"Why are you here, Guerrero? I hardly think you're concerned about my welfare."

"I came to say good bye to an old friend." The bandit smiled. "Ransom Rentzin will kill you tomorrow and that will not be good for you."

McBride's smile was bitter. "My plan was that you and Rentzin would kill each other."

"And that was a good plan, McBride." Guerrero tapped his temple with a forefinger. "A very clever plan."

"Then what went wrong?"

The bandit shrugged. "When I saw how many men Rentzin had, I did not want to fight him so bad anymore, so first we had a parley. He told me I was his good friend and that we should join forces and take all the gold from the Elliot house. He said to me, 'I know there's a woman in the house with a buffalo gun, but she can't shoot all of us. Why, if we lose two or three or even a dozen, it only means more gold for you and me.' Like yours, McBride, it was a clever plan and I thought, well, why not?"

"Angel," McBride said, "you've sold your soul to the devil."

"Not so fast. After your friend was hanged, I thought about many things and asked the holy saints for help. They told me to ride away from this place and leave Miss Elliot alone. 'She has always been good to you, Angel,' they told me. 'She lets you keep the rents you collect and warns you when the law is near.'

"I heed the holy saints, so my men and I will not take part in the attack tomorrow."

"You could stop it," McBride said. He raised his head, winced against the pain and smiled at the fat lady who had placed a cup of coffee in front of him.

Guerrero's constant grin faded to a frown. "I could try, but I would lose all my compadres. I am a great bandit, this is true, but my men and I, except for Papan, are no match for Rentzin and his gunmen. This I know, McBride, though it pains Guerrero deeply to say it."

McBride tried his coffee. It was hot and sweet, the way he liked it, and it helped him feel a little better. "There is no gold in the Elliot house."

Guerrero's smile returned. "Ah, McBride, you are trying to protect your ladylove, I think. Everyone knows the house is stuffed to the rafters with gold."

"Any gold there was is long gone. Allison Elliot's father spent it all trying to turn this dung heap into a great city where he could play king of the castle. Well, it didn't work out that way."

The bandit rubbed his chin. "No gold, huh?

McBride, you would not lie to Guerrero about such a serious matter?''

"There is no gold and the woman up there in the house is my prisoner. She has murdered many people and I intend to bring her to justice."

The bandit looked shocked. "I have heard a rumor of such things, but never believed it."

"Believe it."

Angel Guerrero rose to his feet. "I have told Ransom Rentzin that I will not attack the house. He says he doesn't care, that he has men enough and it will mean all the more gold for him." He put his hand on McBride's shoulder, looking into his eyes. "I will attend your funeral tomorrow and then ride on." The bandit grinned. "If you are mistaken and there is gold, perhaps there is a place on the trail where I can wait in ambush and take it from him."

"Why does Rentzin want to kill me? I didn't shoot his brother."

"That is easy. You are the man who killed Hack Burns, so Rentzin will kill you. That is how reputations are made."

"Good. Give me a gun and six feet of ground and he can try for it."

Guerrero shook his head. "Alas, my friend, that is not how it will be. Rentzin is no fool. He knows you might outdraw and kill him. No, he will just shoot you and ride away from here."

"Murder me, in other words."

"Yes, hard words, but true."

Guerrero stepped to the door, then stopped. "Be of good cheer, McBride," he said. "Tomorrow I will say many prayers for you and the angels will carry you to heaven."

"Like they did Bear?"

"I did not say any prayers for Bear Miller." Guerrero shrugged. "He did not own a prosperous cantina in Suicide."

After the bandit left, McBride rose and walked to the front door, the two women anxiously fluttering around him. He stepped outside where a couple of Rentzin's men were standing.

"Back inside, McBride," one of the men snarled. "Ransom will deal with you real soon." The other man grinned. "He aims to hang you next to your friend."

"Good for him," McBride said.

"I wonder if you'll be as brave when ol' Ransom comes a-callin'. He was gonna hang you tomorrow, but changed his mind on account of how you broke his brother Reuben's nose. Right now good ol' Rube is sharpening his knife. He figures on turning you into a steer afore you get hung."

The gunman's grin grew wider. "McBride, best you try to make your peace with your Maker if'n you and him are on speaking terms."

Chapter 36

John McBride had hoped to prosper as owner of the El Coyote Azul, but now the cantina had become his prison. How soon would Rentzin and his men come for him?

He checked out every wall of the building and the roof. But the place had been built solid, with Apache attacks in mind. Watching his restless prowling, the two fat women looked at McBride with a mix of dread and apprehension. They could not have failed to hear Rentzin's men talking to him outside. They may not have understood the language, but they probably guessed at its drift.

Something bad, *muy malo*, was about to happen to their patron. That much they knew.

Down the street at the saloon the Rentzin gunmen were getting roaring drunk, working themselves up before the hanging. Somebody was playing "Barb'ry Ellen" on the piano and a few voices were raised in drunken song.

There was still an hour or two of daylight left, but

the afternoon was already darkening. Menacing black clouds hung low over the rooftops of the town and a cold wind whispered the promise of winter.

McBride, fearing for the two women, had sent them home after he came inside, though they had loudly and tearfully protested. He sat at a table in the gloom of the cantina, prepared to sell his life as dearly as he could, his only weapon the chair he sat on and the broken bottle that lay near his right hand.

He heard the wind and in his mind's eye saw Bear's body swinging down by the creek, the roped branch creaking, the rustling leaves of the cottonwoods the old scout's only requiem. Bear had not died clean, but if by some miracle McBride survived, he vowed to bury him decent.

The calico cat had been weaving around his feet and he gently picked up the little animal and carried it into the kitchen. When the fight started it could easily get hurt. He stepped back into the cantina, picked up the bottle and chair and crossed the floor. When they came for him he'd put his back to the wall and make his fight.

Outside a man said something—and a woman laughed. Another man muttered words and the woman laughed again, a high-pitched cackle, coarse and common. McBride heard a scuffle of feet and a man's voice, this time hoarse, thick with lust, demanding that the woman come to him.

The curtain parted and the woman stepped inside, her crimson lips parted in a smile. Joan Whitehead had undone the front of her dress, revealing the rounded tops of her breasts.

She pirouetted, laughing, her skirt flaring. McBride's two guards followed her inside, their eyes hot. "Me first, Jake," one said, his moist mouth open. "I'm the oldest."

"The hell with you." The younger man grinned. "I'm the fastest."

He died with those words on his lips.

The Deringer that suddenly leaped into the woman's hand roared and a small, red rose appeared between the young gunman's eyes. As his companion fell, the older man went for his Colt. He was still to clear leather when Joan Whitehead's second bullet hit him square in the chest.

"Get out, McBride!" she yelled. "Now!"

"What about you?"

"Leave me!"

Men were shouting down by the saloon. McBride stepped around the two bodies and ran into the ashy murk of the dying afternoon. He sprinted to the rear of the cantina, ran between scattered shacks and cabins, then into the grassy edge of the prairie. Bullets scarred the air around him and each breath tore out of his chest in an agonized, labored gasp. He glanced behind him and saw men shooting at him. He wasn't going to make it.

A bullet kicked up dirt at his feet as McBride angled toward a narrow arroyo, its base overgrown with brush and stands of prickly pear. A dull, gray haze on the horizon was all that was left of the sun as he plunged into the brush, trying to lose himself in shadow.

Whiskey saved him—the forty-rod Rentzin's men

had drunk in the saloon. The gunmen were in no condition to cross broken ground in growing darkness. It had shaped up to be fun to drag a cowering wretch out of the cantina and hang him. But chasing down a strong, dangerous man like McBride in a wilderness where a threat lurked in every shadow and bush was a different matter entirely.

McBride inched farther into the arroyo. He heard Ransom Rentzin curse his men, followed by a sharp crack and the cry of a woman in pain. Rentzin was taking his rage out on Joan Whitehead. A few moments passed; then a gun roared, the blast reverberating through the dreary chasms of the evening.

McBride clenched his fists, his jaw set as he was swept by a terrible, violent anger. That single shot meant Mrs. Whitehead was dead. But she would not go unavenged. As yet he didn't know how, but he was going to kill Ransom Rentzin . . . and he'd make sure the man knew he was dying and the reason for it.

Weather changes without warning in the Guadalupe Mountains country. Shortly after midnight the black storm clouds slid across the sky, unveiling scattered stars and a horned moon. Around McBride the coyotes sang their mournful sonata to the night and farther away an owl anxiously repeated its question to the darkness.

McBride left the arroyo and, wary of the moonlight, kept to the gloom of the prairie as he made his way past the rear of the town's buildings toward the creek. He had no plan in mind. Reduced to a primitive fight for survival, he thought only of finding safe haven well away from the prying eyes of Rentzin's gunmen—and of paying his last respects to a dead old man.

Because of the sleet and rain, the creek was running fast, busily bouncing over its rocky bottom. The moonlight had turned the leaves of the cottonwoods to the color of smoke and touched the water with rippling bands of silver.

As McBride approached, two unlikely Madonnas stood at the base of a tree, a body at their feet. The heads and shoulders of the fat ladies were covered with black lace mantillas, the mourning veils of Mexican women.

Without a word, McBride kneeled beside Bear. He removed the noose from the old man's neck, the end of the rope frayed from a knife cut, and took him in his arms. Gently, almost tenderly, he lifted Bear from the ground. The faces of the women were in shadow. They were silent, patient, unwilling to hurry either the living or the dead.

McBride nodded and the women turned and walked toward the settlement.

Their cabin lay at the edge of town, close to the creek. One of the women opened the door and McBride carried Bear's body inside. The table had been cleared except for a basin of water and a pile of clean white rags.

By gestures, the fat ladies indicated that McBride should lay the body on the table. He did and then stepped back. They moved beside Bear and began to remove his buckskins.

McBride did not care to wait. The last thing he wanted was to see the old scout naked, without dignity. The women would not mind his nakedness as they washed his body, but it was not a thing a man should see. He reached out, squeezed Bear's cold hand, then stepped to the door.

"*¡Espera!*"

One of the women held up her hand. She walked quickly to a dresser and returned with a short-barreled Colt that she held out to McBride. "*Esto es para usted,*" she whispered.

McBride took the gun. The woman gave him a fragile smile. "*Vaya con Dios, mi amigo.*"

McBride walked outside and the door closed behind him. One of the women was sobbing. Were the tears for Bear or for him? He did not know.

Chapter 37

John McBride spent the night by the creek. At first light he rose, arched a kink out of his back, then checked the Colt. All six chambers were loaded. He made his way back into town, staying well away from the street. The sky was ablaze with color, gold clouds slowly moving across a backdrop of pale scarlet ribboned with jade. The air was cool and smelled clean, like the newly washed hair of a beautiful woman, and the wind was light, blowing from the south.

McBride held the heavy Colt in his right hand, his thumb ready on the hammer spur. He stepped behind a tar-paper shack with a collapsed roof and looked around him. There was no sound and nothing moved.

He calculated that, not counting his brothers, Rentzin had at least ten men left, unless Reuben's broken nose would keep him out of a fight, and that he doubted. It was thirteen against one . . . and those were long odds to buck. The very thought of it set McBride's stomach to churning.

His eyes moved to the hill. There was no sign of life at the Elliot house, but he noticed that the turret room window was open. Did Allison somehow know that Rentzin planned to attack the place? In a town like Suicide, anything was possible.

Another shack stood behind the saloon, closer to the street. McBride was about to make his way there when he heard Rentzin speaking, his voice followed by the loud guffaws of his gunmen.

McBride strained to hear.

"Remember what I said, boys. I want that house torn apart, plank by plank to the foundations if need be, until we find the gold."

Another cheer went up from Rentzin's men. It seemed to McBride that they had assembled outside the saloon.

"And boys, if anybody gets in your way up there, man, woman or child, kill them."

"You can count on us to do that, boss!" a man yelled.

The others laughed and cheered.

"There's enough gold in the house to keep you men in whiskey and women for the rest of your lives," Rentzin hollered, a grin in his voice. "Now, let's go! The faster we get it done, the faster we all become rich men!"

McBride heard another resounding shout of approval, then the departing rumble of men in excited conversation.

He crossed a few yards of open ground and fetched up behind the saloon. He saw Rentzin and his gunmen already fanned out, climbing the hill.

McBride had left Allison with the Sharps. He glanced up at the turret window. Would she shoot? Then he realized she had nothing to defend. There was no gold.

McBride left the cover of the saloon and stepped out into the street. There was no sign of Guerrero and his bandits. McKay was standing outside his store with Nathan Levy and Clyde Kaleen, their eyes on the hill.

Levy saw McBride and called out, "Can you stop them, Marshal?"

McBride shook his head.

Levy opened his mouth to speak again, but McKay scowled him into silence.

Ransom Rentzin had reached the front door of the house. He drew his gun and urged his men to follow him inside. McBride saw that Reuben, a bandage over his nose, was with them.

The gunmen rushed into the house. A few moments of quiet followed; then came the sound of breaking glass and splintering furniture. A love seat crashed through an upstairs window, followed by a potted plant and then a chair.

Rentzin was making good on his promise to tear the house apart.

McBride walked toward the base of the hill. He was almost there when he looked up and saw Allison at the turret room window. For a single moment their eyes met; then Allison turned on her heel and walked into the room.

A second ticked past . . . then two. . . . McBride was at the base of the hill. Excited shouts came from inside the house, followed by the shattering noise of paneled walls being ripped apart. One by one the windows were being broken. . . .

An instant later the Elliot house exploded with a noise like thunder.

A brilliant mass of flame erupted on the hill. The walls of the house were blown apart and the entire roof, with its turret rooms, rose twenty feet into the air before crashing downward into a boiling cauldron of orange and scarlet fire. A thick column of black smoke rose into the sky as the building blazed. Inside, men screamed, but only for a few agonized moments. Then all fell silent, but for the crack and snap of burning beams and the sudden roar of a rising wind that fanned the fluttering flames into a glaring, crimson furnace.

McBride stood rooted to the spot, watching the inferno, the flames dancing in his eyes. This was what hell must be like, he thought, fire, screams, the blood-colored realm of the damned.

Now he remembered the kegs in Allison Elliot's basement. He'd been looking for a man, not barrels, and hadn't examined them. Allison, or maybe she and her father, had it all figured. If things went bad for them and they faced being brought to justice for the many murders they'd committed, they would not go meekly to the gallows. The house basement was crammed with gunpowder and when the time came they would use it to dictate the terms of their dying.

Moses had sacrificed his own life to set off the explosion, happy to see the woman he loved go out in the blaze of glory she so desired.

It was a tragedy. All that had been good about Allison, her beauty, intelligence and loyalty, had been sacrificed on the altar of hate. And in the end, because it is a madness of the heart, hatred always destroys the hater with the hated.

A sickness in him, McBride climbed the hill, aware of McKay, Levy and Kaleen trailing behind him, their eyes stunned and bewildered. Dave Channing emerged from the rocks. He held his smashed shoulder at an odd angle, but otherwise seemed unhurt.

Channing fell in step beside McBride and both men stopped at a safe distance from the burning house. The air was thick with smoke and the smell of scorched flesh, and the cartridges in the belts of the dead gunmen were exploding.

McBride said quietly to Channing, "It's over."

But it was not over, not right then.

Unbelievably, a man emerged from the smoke at the rear of the house, his clothing in tatters, his face streaked with soot and grime. He saw the two men and stopped. Ransom Rentzin had lost his gun in the blast, but, his clawed, scorched hands raised in front of him, he screamed and ran at McBride. "I'll kill you!" he shrieked, his eyes red, crazed with the lust to destroy.

Dave Channing drew and fired, very fast, very

smooth. Rentzin dropped, a hole in the middle of his forehead.

The gambler spun his Colt into the holster and smiled. "Now it's over," he said.

A week later John McBride sat alone in the El Coyote Azul, his head in his hands, lamenting his lack of customers. The fat ladies were in the kitchen, preparing lunch, but only for themselves.

The curtain across the front door parted and McBride looked up hopefully, but it was Angel Guerrero and Papan Morales who stepped inside.

A huge grin lit up Guerrero's swarthy face. "McBride, my friend, I am so happy you are still alive." He raised his eyes heavenward and made a quick cross on his chest. "When so many others are dead."

"The Elliot house blew up," McBride said.

Guerrero nodded. "That I heard. Now we will never know if Rentzin found the gold."

"He found only lead, right between the eyes. Dave Channing killed him."

"Ah, yes, Dave Channing. He is good with a gun, almost as good as my friend Papan." He turned his head. "Is that not so, Papan?"

"Almost," the man answered.

"Are you here to eat, Guerrero?" McBride asked, hope in his eyes. "Or perhaps to drink a glass or two of mescal?"

The bandit looked sad. "Alas, my friend, I cannot tarry long. I have urgent business with a stage line elsewhere." His face brightened. "You know,

McBride, my friend Papan still wants to kill you real bad. Is that not so, Papan?"

"That is so," the gunman said.

"And why?" Guerrero asked. "It is because you will not pay me my hundred dollars, McBride. And soon it will be two hundred and Papan will be twice as angry."

McBride looked up at Guerrero's grinning face and into Papan's cold eyes. He dropped his head into his hands again and groaned.

Another week passed before the sporting gent arrived. Baxter T. Quarrels drove into Suicide in a rented buggy and stopped at the El Coyote Azul for lunch. He ate a plate of frijoles and beef, then retreated into the relaxing comfort of mescal.

"Are you, my good man, the proprietor of this establishment?" he asked McBride as he brushed cigar ash from his fine broadcloth.

McBride allowed that he was and gave his name. It apparently meant nothing to Quarrels who said, "Please sit down, Mr. McBride. I have questions of a business nature to ask."

Vaguely interested and having nothing else to do, McBride took a chair opposite the man. Quarrels leaned forward conspiratorially, blue smoke spiraling from his cigar, and asked, "Are you a betting man, Mr. McBride?"

"Not that you'd notice."

"Ah, well I am. And I'm wagering that"—Quarrels looked over his shoulder and around the empty room—"a certain railroad"—here his voice dropped to a whisper—"shall we call it the Santa Fe?—plans on laying track between El Paso and Abilene as a boon to the cattle industry of southern New Mexico and northern Texas." Quarrels tapped the side of his nose with a stubby forefinger. "Don't ask me how I know, but I know." He winked. "I have contacts in high places."

McBride was puzzled. "And your question is?"

Quarrels put his mouth close to McBride's ear. "I believe the railroad will run right through this fair town, and a station and cattle pens will be built here. That's why I want to buy properties along the right of way." He leaned back in his chair. "Do you know of any such for sale at the right price?"

McBride rose to his feet. "Excuse me, Mr. Quarrels," he said. "I'll be right back."

He dashed into the kitchen and quickly put on his celluloid collar and his tie. Then he sat opposite Quarrels again.

"Why don't you buy this place?" he asked. "I've got two fat ladies in the kitchen and all you'd have to do is sit back and rake in the money. You will live a life of prosperity and ease."

Quarrels looked around the cantina and seemed impressed. "What kind of figure were you thinking of, Mr. McBride, huh?"

McBride said, "I have several young wards that I must send to finishing school back east and for that reason I'm letting the El Coyote Azul go dirt cheap."

"How much?"

"A thousand dollars. I assure you, the cantina is worth twice that amount."

Quarrels' face took on a calculating expression; then he said, thinking aloud, "A life of luxury and ease indeed." The man smiled. "Yes, you interest me, Mr. McBride. Tell me more."

And John McBride, very soon to be the ex-proprietor of the El Coyote Azul, did.

"A writer in the tradition of Louis L'Amour
and Zane Grey!"
—*Huntsville Times*

National Bestselling Author
RALPH COMPTON

**Available wherever books are sold or at
penguin.com**

No other series packs this much heat!

THE TRAILSMAN

**Available wherever books are sold or at
penguin.com**

Penguin Group (USA) Online

What will you be reading tomorrow?

Tom Clancy, Patricia Cornwell, W.E.B. Griffin,
Nora Roberts, William Gibson, Robin Cook,
Brian Jacques, Catherine Coulter, Stephen King,
Dean Koontz, Ken Follett, Clive Cussler,
Eric Jerome Dickey, John Sandford,
Terry McMillan, Sue Monk Kidd, Amy Tan,
John Berendt…

You'll find them all at
penguin.com

*Read excerpts and newsletters,
find tour schedules and reading group guides,
and enter contests.*

Subscribe to Penguin Group (USA) newsletters
and get an exclusive inside look
at exciting new titles and the authors you love
long before everyone else does.

PENGUIN GROUP (USA)
us.penguingroup.com